Novels by
John Dickson Carr
available in IPL Library of Crime Classics® editions:

Dr. Fell novels:
DEATH TURNS THE TABLES

HAG'S NOOK

THE SLEEPING SPHINX

TILL DEATH DO US PART

Non-series:
THE BURNING COURT

JOHN DICKSON CARR

THE BURNING COURT

INTERNATIONAL POLYGONICS, LTD.
NEW YORK CITY

THE BURNING COURT
Copyright © 1937 by John Dickson Carr. Copyright renew-
ed 1964 by John Dickson Carr.
Cover: Copyright © 1985 by International Polygonics, Ltd.

Library of Congress Card Catalog No. 85-81385
ISBN 0-930330-27-7

Printed by Guinn Printing, Inc., Hoboken, N.J.
Printed and manufactured in the United States of America
First IPL printing November 1985
10 9 8 7 6 5 4 3 2 1

CONTENTS

I

INDICTMENT

"*Here we supped very merry, and late to bed;
Sir William telling me that old Edgeborrow, his
predecessor, did die and walk in my chamber,
did make me somewhat afraid—but not so much
as, for mirth sake, I did seem.*"

—SAMUEL PEPYS, April 8th, 1661

I

"THERE was a man lived by a churchyard—" is an intriguing beginning for a story left unfinished. Edward Stevens also lived by a churchyard, in more senses than one: which is the soberest possible statement of the fact. There was a miniature of the sort next door, of course, and the reputation of Despard Park had always been unusual; but that was not the most important churchyard.

Edward Stevens, who was not much different from you or me, sat in a smoking-car of a train which would reach Broad Street station at 6:48. He was thirty-two years old, and he had a tolerably important position in the editorial department of the publishing house of Herald & Sons, Fourth Avenue. He rented an apartment in the East Seventies, and owned a cottage at Crispen outside Philadelphia, where he spent many week-ends because both he and his wife were fond of that countryside. He was going there to join Marie on this Friday evening (which was in the far-off days of spring, 1929); and in his briefcase was the manuscript of Gaudan Cross's new book of murder-trials. Such, baldly stated, are the facts. Stevens himself now admits that it is a relief to state facts, to deal with matters that can be tabulated or arranged.

It must be emphasized, too, that there was nothing unusual about the day or the evening. He was not stepping across a borderland, any more than you or I step across it; he was simply going home. And he was a robustly happy man with a profession, a wife, and an existence which suited him.

The train was on time at Broad Street. He stretched his legs round the station, and saw on one of the black number-boxes over the gates that he could get a train for Crispen in seven minutes: an express, first stop Ardmore. Crispen is some thirty-odd minutes out on the Main Line, the next stop after Haver-

3

ford. Nobody has ever yet discovered why there should be a stop or a separate division there at all, between Haverford and Bryn Mawr. There were only half a dozen houses, all set very far apart, on the way up the hill. But it was (in a way) a community of its own: it had a post-office, a druggist's, and a tea-room almost hidden in the noble copper beeches where King's Avenue curved up to Despard Park. It had even—though this was scarcely either customary or symbolical—an undertaker's shop.

This undertaker's had always surprised and puzzled Stevens. He wondered why it was there, and who patronized it. The name *J. Atkinson* was on the windows, but in letters as discreet as a visiting-card. He had never seen so much as a head or a movement beyond those windows, which displayed a couple of shapeless little marble blocks—presumably you stuck flowers in them—and black velvet curtains run waist-high on brassy rings. Of course, it was not to be presumed that an undertaker's any-where drove a roaring trade, or that a stream of eager customers would constantly animate its doors. But undertakers, by tradition, are merry men; and he had never seen J. Atkinson. It had even given him the vague germ of an idea for a detective-story. The plot (he thought) should concern a mass-murderer who was an undertaker, and was thus able to explain the presence of inconvenient bodies in his shop.

But, after all, J. Atkinson had probably been called in at the death of old Miles Despard so recently. . . .

If there were any reason why Crispen existed at all, that reason was Despard Park. Crispen had been named after one of the four commissioners who, in the year of grace 1681, had been sent out to prepare the site of a city in the newly ceded territory of Pennsylvania, just before Mr. Penn himself came to make peace with all men in the gracious woods between the Schuylkill and the Delaware. William Crispen, a kinsman of William Penn, had died on the voyage out. But a cousin named Despard (the name, according to Mark Despard, was originally French and had undergone some curious changes of spelling) had obtained a grant of land in the country, and there had been Despards at the Park ever since. Old Miles Despard—that stately reprobate, the head of the family—had died less than two weeks ago.

Waiting for his train, Stevens wondered idly whether Mark

Despard—the new head of the family—would drop in for a chat that night, as he usually did. Stevens's cottage was not far from the entrance-gates of the Park; they had struck up a friendship two years ago. But he hardly expected to see either Mark or Lucy, Mark's wife, tonight. True enough, old Miles's passing (he had died of gastro-enteritis, after reducing the lining of his stomach to a pulp with nearly forty years' high living) would be not much lamented: old Miles had lived so much abroad that the rest of the family scarcely knew him. But there would be a great deal of business on the skirts of death. Old Miles had never married; Mark, Edith, and Ogden Despard were the children of his younger brother. Each should inherit substantially, Stevens thought without great interest.

The entrance-gates to the station platform had rattled open now; Stevens swung aboard the Main Line train and pushed forward to the smoking-car. The spring night had turned from grey to black. But even in the gritty air of the shed, even in the thick air of the car with its pale dispirited roof lights, there was a smell of spring that would stir the blood in the countryside. (This led his thoughts to Marie, who would meet him at Crispen with the car.) The train, less than half full, had its usual somnolent air of people crackling fat newspapers and blowing smoke over their shoulders. Stevens settled down with his briefcase across his knees. With the idle curiosity of a contented man, he fell to turning over in his mind two rather puzzling happenings which had been occurring to him all day. It was characteristic of the man that he did not try to reason them out; he only tried to devise imaginative explanations which would fit them.

For instance? Well, for instance, he had in his briefcase the manuscript of Gaudan Cross's new book. He had been looking forward to reading it. Gaudan Cross (which, strangely enough, was the man's real name) was a discovery of Morley, the head of the editorial department. Cross appeared to be a recluse who devoted himself to retelling the histories of murder cases from real life. His great talent lay in a narrative vividness which was like that of an eye-witness; a sort of devilish reportorial ability in things he had not seen. It was often deceptive. An eminent judge had unwarily written that the man who gave such an account of Neill Cream as that in *Gentlemen of the Jury* had, beyond any doubt, been in the courtroom at the time. "Since

Cream was tried in 1892," commented the *New York Times,* "and Mr. Cross's age is given as forty, he must indeed have been a precocious infant." But it was no bad advertisement for the book.

However, Cross's popularity did not depend so much on his style as on his selection of materials. He took one or two celebrated cases for each book. But chiefly he devoted his research to unearthing picturesque crimes of which few people seemed to have heard at all: wonders in their own time, unquestionably, but appearing with a shock of novelty to modern readers. Despite photographs and documentary evidence, some of the accounts were so remarkable that one critic accused the whole thing of being an elaborate hoax. After another stir—again no bad advertisement—Cross was proved to have invented nothing. In this case, which was that of an atrocity at Brussels in the eighteenth century, the doubting critic received a furious letter from the Burgomaster of Brussels, who was very proud of the local monster. Thus Gaudan Cross, without being a national best seller or hit-of-the-year, was among the props of the Herald list.

That Friday afternoon Stevens had been called into the editorial head's office. Morley sat behind his desk in the quiet-carpeted room, blinking at a neat pile of sheets in a buff container.

"That's the new Cross," he said. "Will you take it home with you over the week-end? I'd like to have you talk about it at the May sales conference. You're particularly enthusiastic about that sort of thing."

"You've read it?"

"Yes," said Morley, and hesitated. "It's the best thing he's done, in a way," Morley added, hesitating again. "The title will have to be changed, of course. He's given it some thundering long and technical thing that the sales force will never stand for; but we can worry about that later. It's a gallery of women poisoners, and it's strong stuff."

"Good!" said Stevens, heartily.

Morley remained half abstracted, half puzzled, looking round the room. There was evidently something on his mind. He asked, "Ever meet Cross?"

"No. I think I've seen him in the office once or twice, that's all," Stevens answered, with a recollection of a broad back ducking round a corner or pushing through a door.

"Well . . . unusual sort of fellow. About his contracts, I mean. There's one clause he insists on having in every contract, and it's not what you could call a common clause. Otherwise he doesn't care; I don't believe he even bothers to read the contract through. The stipulation is that the back of the jacket on every one of his books must contain a large photograph of himself."

Stevens made a noise in his throat. The wall was lined with shelves of bright-jacketed books; he reached up and flipped down a copy of *Gentlemen of the Jury*.

"So that's the reason for it," he remarked. "I'd wondered about that, but nobody seemed inclined to mention it. No biographical details; just a large photograph with his name under it—and on a *first* book." He studied the picture. "Well, it's a strong face; an intellectual face; I should think a good face. But why is he so proud of it that he wants it plastered round ——?"

Morley shook his head, still immobile in the chair. "No. It isn't that. He's not the sort who would want any personal publicity of the kind; far from it. There's some other reason."

Again Morley looked at him curiously, but dismissed the matter by picking up something from his desk. "Never mind; take the manuscript along with you. Be very careful of it. He's got photographs attached. Oh—and you might come in and see me first thing Monday morning."

With that last casual word he had left it. Sitting now in a train that was rattling towards West Philadelphia, Stevens half-opened the catch of the briefcase to have a look at the manuscript. But he hesitated, his mind still full of idle puzzles.

If the business of Gaudan Cross had been neither important nor clear-cut, that of old Miles Despard was even less so. Stevens's thoughts went to Despard Park, to the old smoky stone among the beeches, and the gardens that would be stirring from sleep. He remembered old Miles, the previous summer, walking in the sunken garden behind the house. "Old" Miles had not been really old, as time went; he had been only fifty-six when they screwed down his coffin. But his punctilious bearing, his scrawny neck emerging from shiny white knives of collars, his curled grey moustache and air of far-off hilarity, had always seemed to put him in a different age. Stevens remembered him in the warm sun, formally raising his rakish hat. His eyes looked puffed and troubled.

Gastro-enteritis gives no easy passing; Miles Despard, returned to his home after wandering the earth, had found a slow and cruel death which he bore with a stoicism that had roused the blubbering admiration of the cook. Mrs. Henderson —cook, general housekeeper, and tyrant—said that sometimes he had screamed, but not often. They buried him in the crypt under the private chapel, where nine generations of Despards had been set away in tiers like outworn books, and the stone slab which sealed the crypt had been put back into place again. But one thing seemed to have impressed Mrs. Henderson very deeply. Before he died, Miles Despard had in his hands an ordinary piece of string, tied at equal spacings into nine small knots. They found it under his pillow afterwards.

"I thought it was so nice," Mrs. Henderson had confided to the Stevenses' cook. "I suppose he thought it was a rosary, or something like that. Of course the family aren't Catholics, but all the same I thought it was so nice."

One other thing had induced in Mrs. Henderson a kind of hysteria, so that nobody had been able to straighten out the matter even yet. It was Mark Despard, the nephew, who had mentioned the matter to Stevens, with annoyed amusement.

Stevens had seen Mark only once since Miles's death. The old man had died on the night of April 12th, a Wednesday: Stevens remembered the date particularly because he and Marie had spent that night at Crispen, and it was not usual for them to visit the cottage except at week-ends. They had driven back to New York next morning without hearing anything of the tragedy, and only learned of it through the newspapers. When they visited Crispen again on the week-end of the 15th, they had paid formal condolences at the house, but had not attended the funeral: Marie had an almost shuddering horror of death or the sights of death. And on the evening after the funeral Stevens had met Mark striding along in the gloom and emptiness of King's Avenue.

"Our Mrs. Henderson," Mark had said, abruptly, "has been seeing things."

It was a raw and windy twilight, with the buds barely

8

opening in the woodland through which King's Avenue curved up to Despard Park. Nevertheless, the great trees seemed to shake and move over Mark's head like shadows. Mark's hook-nosed face was pale if boisterous under the light of a street lamp; he leaned against the lamp-post with his hands in his pockets.

"Our Mrs. Henderson," he repeated, "has been seeing things. I'm not even quite certain what it was that she didn't see, because she's kept it to hints and prayers. But it would appear that on the night Uncle Miles died there was a woman in his room, talking to him."

"A woman?"

"No, not what you're thinking," said Mark, formally. "I mean merely that a woman—in what Mrs. Henderson describes as 'queer old-fashioned clothes'—was in his room, talking to him. Now that's possible, of course. On that night several of us, Lucy and Edith and myself as well, went to a masquerade ball at St. Davids. Lucy was dressed as Madame de Montespan, Louis XIV's favorite. Edith was somebody in bonnet and hoopskirts; Florence Nightingale, I believe. With my wife as a great courtesan and my sister as a great nurse, I was well protected.

"However," he added, scowling, "it's rather improbable. You didn't know Miles very well, did you? He was an amiable old devil. He kept by himself in his own room, and wouldn't let anybody go into it—you knew that—although he was always polite. He even had his meals sent up to him. When he was taken bad, of course, I had a trained nurse brought in. He kicked up a hell of a polite row about that. We put the nurse in the room next to his, and we had a lot of trouble preventing him from locking the communicating door so that *she* couldn't come in whenever she liked. . . . Consequently, Mrs. Henderson's vision of a woman in 'queer old-fashioned clothes,' though it's possible——"

Stevens could not understand what was bothering him.

"Well, I don't see anything particularly strange about it," he said. "Have you asked Lucy or Edith about it? And, anyway, if nobody was allowed in the room, how did Mrs. Henderson see the woman at all?"

"Mrs. Henderson claims to have seen her through a window, which Miles usually kept curtained, giving on an upper sun porch. No; I haven't mentioned it to Lucy or Edith." He hesitated, and then laughed boisterously. "For a very good reason. *That* doesn't bother me; I'm not trying to make any mystery of it. It's the other part of Mrs. Henderson's tale that puzzles me. According to her story, this woman in the old-fashioned clothes —now attend to me carefully—first had a little talk with Miles, and then turned round and went out of the room by a door which does not exist."

Stevens looked at him. Mark Despard's thin hook-nosed face wore a gravity which may or may not have been satirical.

"You don't say so," Stevens observed, with a noncommittal noise. "Ghosts?"

"I mean," said Mark, frowning over a careful definition of terms, "a door which has been bricked up and panelled over for two hundred years. Mysterious visitor simply opens it and walks out. Ghosts? No; I doubt it very much. We've managed to struggle along for a very long time without producing any ghosts. We've been too cursed respectable. You can't imagine a respectable ghost; it may be a credit to the family, but it's an insult to guests. More likely it's something wrong with Mrs. Henderson, if you ask me."

Abruptly he had strode off down the avenue.

That was a week ago; and Stevens, thinking over the interview in the train that was carrying him to Crispen now, touched the puzzle-bits without much attention. He was considering merely isolated instances—the talk with Morley at the office, the talk with Mark Despard in the road—and wondering not how they could be explained, but how they could be fitted together in the form of a story. Granted that they bore no relation to each other, any more than separate newspaper items. But here they were: a recluse of an author, Gaudan Cross, who had a passion for seeing his own photograph, not from motives of vanity; a recluse of a millionaire, Miles Despard, dying of stomach inflammation, and under his pillow a piece of string tied into nine knots; finally, a woman in old-fashioned clothes (date not specified) who was alleged to have walked out of a room through a door that had been bricked up for two hundred years. Now, how would a skilled story-teller tie together those unrelated facts or fancies into one pattern?

Stevens gave it up. But, still curious about Cross, he opened the briefcase and drew out the manuscript in its container. It was fairly bulky; it would run, he estimated, about a hundred thousand words; and, like all Cross's manuscripts, it was neat with an almost finicky preciseness. The chapters were punched together with brass fasteners; the prints, photographs, and drawings affixed with paper-clips. After running his eye down the table of contents, he glanced at the heading of the first chapter—but that was not what made his grip on the manuscript loosen, so that it almost slid off his knee.

Fastened to the page was an old but still very clear photograph of a woman. Under it in small neat letters had been printed:

Marie D'Aubray: Guillotined for Murder, 1861.

He was looking at a photograph of his own wife.

II

FOR a time he sat quiet, insistently examining the name, insistently examining the features. All the while that he went over and over them, he was hazily conscious that he still sat in the smoking-car of the 7:35 train for Crispen. But he still seemed to be in a great void.

Presently he looked up, settled the manuscript more firmly in his lap, and looked out of the window. His feeling (it was a commonplace one) was something like that of sitting up in a dentist's chair after an extraction: a little light-headed, conscious of a little quicker heartbeat; nothing more. He was not even conscious of being startled now. He saw that they were flashing through Overbrook, with a clackety-roar of rails, and a few street lamps shining on asphalt below.

There was no possibility of coincidence or mistake. The name was hers: Marie D'Aubray. The features were hers, even to an expression he knew. The woman in the picture, the woman who had gone to the guillotine seventy years ago, had been a relation of his wife's—say her great-grandmother, which would make the dates about right. But the throwback to her features was uncanny, when the great-grand-daughter even caught a shade of expression.

It did not matter a tinker's damn, of course. It would not have mattered if her fathers or mothers or uncles had themselves been tipped under that evil plank. And in this age seventy-year-old devilry has already a flavor of the historic: we are apt to take it with a sort of casual and indulgent approval, as unrelated to the business of ordinary life as a *papier-mâché* skull on a desk. Nevertheless, it was startling; because in the picture there was even indicated the very tiny mole just below the angle of the jaw, and the antique bracelet he had seen Marie wear a hundred times. Furthermore, it was not going to be very funny if his own publishing firm issued a book with his wife's photograph plastered opposite the title-page in a gallery of poisoners. Was that what Morley had meant, "You might come in and see me first thing Monday morning?"

No, it was of no consequence. All the same——

Turning back to study the picture again, he detached it from the page to get a better look. Now, why should he have a queer feeling when he touched it? Actually, though he could not have analyzed it, the realization that came over him in such a rush was the realization of how thoroughly and violently he remained in love with her. The photograph was of very thick cardboard, its grey stiplings touched in places with brown. On the back, with letters indented in the cardboard, was the photographer's name, "Perrichet et Fils, 12 rue Jean Goujean, Paris vii." Sprawled across this in curly handwriting, the ink now faded to brown, someone had written, "Ma très, très chère Marie; Louis Dinard, le 6ième janvier, 1858." Lover? Husband?

But what really came up as though in a wave from this picture, what grotesquely mingled the old-fashioned and the modern, was the woman's expression. It survived even the stilted photography. The picture was a large half-length, having for its background a landscape with trees—and doves. The woman stood unnaturally, as though she were about to wobble over to one side, and her left hand rested on the top of a little round table which was chastely draped with an antimacassar. Her high-necked dress was of some darkish taffeta material, which gleamed in bunches. And from this high collar the head was carried a little back.

Even though the dark-golden hair seemed somewhat differently arranged (there were a couple of curls which gave it a stiff archaic look), still it was Marie's. She faced the camera, but looked slightly past it. Her grey eyes, with the somewhat heavy lids, large pupils, and dead-black irises, wore what he had often called her "spiritual" expression. The lips were open

12

and faintly smiling. The eyes fixed on you before you noticed it, like a painter's trick. Framed in these surroundings of doves and trees and antimacassars, it had an almost unpleasantly sugary appearance. Yet to the senses it conveyed something altogether different. The thing was alive. It had become a sort of Monkey's Paw in Stevens's hand, and he found his wrist joggling.

His eyes went back to the words, "guillotined for murder." Women were very rarely guillotined for murder. If they were, it was because what they had done was such that no other course could be taken.

Stevens said to himself: This whole business is a joke or a hoax of some kind. Damn it, this *is* Marie. Somebody is putting something over on me.

He said this to himself, although he knew quite well it was not true. After all, these startling resemblances of descendants to their forebears did crop up sometimes; there was nothing strange in that; it was a fact. Her great-grandmother had been executed, but what of it?

After all, he knew very little about her, although they had been married for three years. He had not been particularly curious. He knew that she came from Canada, out of a moldering house rather like Despard Park. They had met in Paris and had been married in a fortnight. They had met (with a sort of accidental romance) in the courtyard of an old empty *hôtel* near the cabbage-stalls of the rue St. Antoine. What he could not remember was the name of the street, or why he had strayed there during some explorations through Old Paris. It was the rue ... the rue ... Hold on! He associated it somehow with a suggestion made by his friend Welden, who held a chair in English at the College, and was also a murder-trial-fancier. Over three years ago Welden had said:

"You'll be in Paris this summer? Then, if you're interested in scenes of violence, look up number blank in the rue Blank."

"What's there?"

"See," said Welden, "if anyone in the neighborhood can tell you. Or there's a puzzle; work it out."

He had never found out, and he had forgotten to ask Welden since; but he had met Marie there, apparently roving like himself. She said that she did not know what the place was. She said that she had seen doors half open into a curious Old

13

World court, and she had gone in. When he first saw her, she was sitting on the rim of a dead fountain in the centre of the court, where rank grass grew. Round her on three sides were the railings of the galleries, and the chipped stone faces carved on the walls. Though she did not look French, still he was surprised to hear her address him in vigorous and ordinary English, and to see how her rather "spiritual" good looks were made suddenly vigorous by her own smile. It was, in a way, an allure of sheer health.

But why hadn't she ever told him? Why the unnecessary secrecy? That house, probably, was where the Marie D'Aubray of 1858 had lived. Afterwards the family must have gone out to Canada; and now Marie, a descendant, was revisiting evil scenes with a natural curiosity about the elder Marie. Her life had been humdrum enough, to judge by the occasional letter she received from Cousin This or Aunt That. She sometimes supplied an anecdote of her family; but, to tell the truth, he had never very much thought about it. There were odd corners and unexpected ideas in her nature: why, for instance, could she never bear the sight of a funnel, an ordinary kitchen funnel? Then again——

This would not do. All the while he had been aware that the picture of Marie D'Aubray the First was looking up at him, with something like a jeer behind its ethereal smile. Why didn't he get down and read what this first Marie D'Aubray had done, and not be half afraid of an Easter-card angel whose head had dropped into the guillotine basket? Why put it off? He picked up the manuscript again, thrusting the photograph behind the first chapter. Cross's genius, he reflected, was assuredly not for titles. After giving the whole book some ponderous title, this writer had attempted to freshen it up with more sensational story-heads. Each was called "The Affair of the—Something"; and in this instance he had called it, "The Affair of the Non-dead Mistress," which gave a nasty jar.

It began abruptly, with one of Cross's hand-grenades flung into the camp of fiction:

"Arsenic has been called the fool's poison; never was anything less aptly named."

This is the pronouncement of Mr. Henry T. F. Rhodes, editor of *The Chemical Practitioner*, and Dr. Edmond Locard, director of the Police Laboratory at Lyons, agrees with him. Mr. Rhodes goes on:

"Arsenic is not the fool's poison, nor is it true that its popularity is due to the unimaginativeness of the criminal. The poisoner is seldom stupid or unimaginative. On the contrary, the evidence is all the other way. As a poison, arsenic is still used for the reason that it is still the safest poison to use.

"In the first place, a physician has the greatest difficulty in diagnosing arsenical poisoning unless he has some reason to suspect it. If carefully graduated doses are administered, the symptoms almost exactly resemble those of gastro-enteritis. . . ."

Stevens's eyes stopped there. The type grew to a meaningless blur, because his brain was suddenly full of other things. You couldn't help the thoughts that came into your mind. You might sneer at yourself; call yourself insane or plain disloyal; but who can keep out a random thought? Gastro-enteritis, of which Miles Despard had died two weeks ago. What he was thinking was a joke, a not-very-funny joke. . . .

"Evening, Stevens," said a voice just behind his shoulder, and he became aware that he had jumped a little.

He looked round. The train was slowing down for its first express stop at Ardmore. Dr. Welden of the College was standing in the aisle, his hand on the back of the seat, and looking down with an expression as near curiosity as his solid well-trained face would permit. The lean face had a high framework of bones, like an ascetic's; the jaws were sharp-angled; he wore a clipped moustache and a rimless pince-nez; he remained expressionless except for an occasional chuckle or roar when he told a story. At such times he would open his eyes wide, and point with the cigar he was usually smoking. Welden was a New Englander, a brilliant man at his job, and friendly behind his reserve. He was always soberly well dressed, and carried, like Stevens, a briefcase.

"I didn't know you were in the train," he observed. "Everyone keeping well? Mrs. Stevens?"

"Sit down," said the other, glad that he had pushed the photograph out of sight. Welden was getting out at the next stop, but he compromised by sitting down gingerly on the arm of the seat. "Oh — fine, thanks," added Stevens, somewhat vaguely. "And your family?"

"Pretty well. The girl's had a touch of flu; but we've all had it, in this weather," replied Welden, complacently. During this exchange of the usual Stevens was concentrated on wondering what Welden would have said if he had opened this manuscript and found a picture of his own wife.

"By the way," Stevens said, with some abruptness, "about your hobby of noted murders: did you ever hear of a poisoner named Marie D'Aubray?"

Welden took the cigar out of his mouth. "Marie D'Aubray? Marie D'Aubray? Ah! I see. That was her maiden name, of course." He turned round and began to grin, throwing into higher relief the bony framework of his face. "Now you mention it, I've always forgotten to ask you——"

"She was guillotined in 1861."

Welden stopped. "Then we can't be thinking of the same person." He seemed a little ruffled that the conversation had gone so suddenly from influenza to murder. "In 1861? Are you sure of that?"

"Well, it's in here. I only wondered, that's all. This is Gaudan Cross's new book. You remember there was a rumpus a couple of years ago, about whether or not he was inventing his facts. Just out of curiosity——"

"If Cross says it's so," declared Welden, looking out of the window as the train gathered speed again, "I should take his word for it; but it's a new one on me. The only 'Marie D'Aubray' I've ever heard of is much better known under her married name. In fact, she's a classic. You must have read the case somewhere. Don't you remember, I sent you to see her house in Paris?"

"Never mind. Go on."

Though he did not ask a question, Welden was puzzled. "She was the celebrated Marquise de Brinvilliers, a fleshly charmer who will probably remain the outstanding example of fascination allied to gentle murder. Read the report of her trial; it's sensational enough. In her age, the word 'Frenchman' was almost synonymous with the word 'poisoner'; there came to be so much of it that a special court had to be——" He stopped. "Look it up, and read about the teakwood box and the glass mask and the rest of it. Anyhow, she disposed of a pretty large number of people, including her own family, and used to get her hand in by practising on the patients in the hospital at the Hôtel Dieu. Arsenic, I believe it was. Her confession, read at the trial, would be a curious piece of hysteria for psychologists

16

to study nowadays: it contains, among other things, some remarkable sexual statements. So you are warned."

"Yes," said Stevens; "yes, I remember something about it. What were her dates?"

"She was beheaded and burnt in 1676." Welden got up, brushing ash off his coat, as the train slowed down again. "Here's my station. If you've got nothing better to do over the week-end, you might ring us up. My wife instructs me to tell you that she's got hold of that cake recipe Mrs. Stevens wanted. Good night."

His own station was only two minutes farther on. Automatically Stevens put the manuscript into its container, and then into the briefcase. This was all wrong, and nonsensical. This unnecessary confusion with the Marquise de Brinvilliers, he thought, only threw him off and had nothing to do with the case. He kept thinking of only one sentence: "If carefully graduated doses are administered, the symptoms almost exactly resemble those of gastro-enteritis."

A spectral voice bawled, "Cris-pen!" somewhere at the head of the train, and they pulled to a stop with a clanking sigh. When he got out on the platform he found that this nonsense was blown away by the high, cool night. He went down a flight of concrete steps, and out into the little street. It was rather dim there, for the druggist's was some way down; but he saw the lights of the familiar Chrysler roadster waiting by the curb.

Marie was inside, holding the door open for him. The moment he saw her, values shrank and altered; there had been some sort of infernal spell about that photograph, which distorted even ordinary flesh. And it was gone now; so much so that he merely put one foot on the running-board, looked at her, and was amused. She was wearing a brown skirt and a sweater, with a light coat thrown over her shoulders like a cloak. Through a shop window near by, a very faint glow fell on her dark-gold hair. She stared back at him, puzzled. Her voice, a contralto despite her apparent slenderness, made the world practical again.

"What on earth," she said, with a sort of annoyed amusement, "are you standing there grinning for? *Stop* it! Have you been having some dri—" She struggled, and then joined

17

in the inane mirth. "You ought to be ashamed of yourself. Here you are disgustingly drunk, and I've been dying for a cocktail, but I wouldn't have one until you got here, so that we could get disgustingly drunk together——"

"I am not drunk," he said, with dignity, "disgustingly or otherwise. It was only something I was thinking. You—here!"

He glanced past her shoulder to see the origin of the very faint glow which was touching her hair and which stood out with such pallor in the dark street. Then he stopped. It came from a shop window. He could see a few small and rather shapeless marble blocks, and black shapeless curtains hung waist-high on brass rings from an iron rail. The pallor appeared to issue from beyond these curtains; it emphasized the iron rather than the brass. Just beyond the curtains, in silhouette, a man was standing motionless. He appeared to be looking out into the street.

"Good Lord!" Stevens said. "It's J. Atkinson at last."

"I don't suppose you're really drunk," she observed, "but you seem to have got light-headed. Jump in! Ellen has got something special in the way of dinners." She glanced over her shoulder at the motionless figure in the window. "Atkinson? What about him?"

"Nothing at all. It's only that this is the first time I've ever seen hide or hair of anyone inside that place. I suppose," Stevens added, "he's waiting for somebody."

She turned the car round, with her own broad style of driving. They went down under the elms and copper beeches, across the Lancaster Highway, and beyond into the gloom where King's Avenue curved up the hill for half a mile to the gates of the Park. The thought occurred to Stevens that this ought to be Halloween instead of the end of April, for, as they moved away, he could have sworn he heard some one in the street calling his name. But the exhaust of the car was sputtering rather loudly, because Marie had begun to race the engine when they turned round, and he could not be sure. He stuck his head out to look behind, but he did not mention the matter to Marie—especially since the street was empty. She was so completely normal, so delightedly glad to see him, that his notions began to wake self-distrust. He wondered whether over-tiredness could produce such things as he appeared to be seeing and even hearing. Which was nonsense, for he was as strong as an ox, and, Marie sometimes complained, as dense-minded as one.

"It's nice, it's nice," she was saying. "Don't you feel the way it's in the air? There's a lovely show of crocuses by that big tree out by the fence. You remember? And I noticed some primroses this afternoon. Oh, it's *all* lovely!" She breathed deeply, and flexed her muscles, and threw back her head. Then she turned round, smiling. "Tired?"

"Not a bit."

"Sure?"

"No, I tell you!"

She looked puzzled. "Ted dear, you needn't snap my head off. You do need a cocktail. Ted—we're not going out tonight, are we?"

"I hope not. Why?"

Marie kept her eyes fixed intently on the road, frowning a little.

"Well, Mark Despard has been calling up all evening and asking to speak with you. He wants to see you. He says it's terribly important, but he wouldn't tell me what it was. Then he made some kind of slip, and I thought it must be about his uncle Miles. He sounded very queer."

She turned round on him that same "spiritual" look he knew so well, and which, with her eyes wide open in the flash of a street lamp—staring straight at him—gave to her face a complete sugary loveliness.

"Ted, whatever it is he wants, you won't pay any attention to it, will you?"

III

"**D**OES he?" said Stevens, mechanically. "You know I won't go out if I can help it. It depends on whether he's . . . really got something on his mind, or——"

He stopped, because he did not know what he meant himself. There were times when Marie's expression retreated from him; he touched fog. That look had doubtless been an illusion of light from the street lamp. For she dismissed the matter of Mark Despard from her mind, and went on talking about some slip-covers she was having made for the living-room furniture in the

19

New York apartment. After he had had a cocktail, he thought, he would bring the matter up, and make a joke of it; and then they could forget it.

He tried to remember whether she had read any of Cross's books. She might have seen the manuscripts, since she did a great deal of reading for him. Her own reading had apparently been surprisingly large, though sketchy: it was concerned mostly with details of places and people. He glanced at her, and saw that the sleeve of her coat had fallen back. On her left wrist she wore the bracelet—it was a wrought bracelet, having a clasp like a cat's head with a ruby in the mouth—which he had seen in that accursed photograph.

"By the way," he said, "did you ever meet up with any of Cross's work?"

"Cross? Who's that?"

"He writes those accounts of murder cases."

"Oh! That! No; but then I haven't got a morbid mind like some people." She seemed to grow serious. "You know, I've often thought that you—you and Mark Despard and Dr. Welden—being interested in those murders and ugly things—don't you think it's a little unhealthy?"

Stevens was flabbergasted. Even in what he called her Elsie-Dinsmore moods, he had never heard her talk quite like this; it struck a wrong note; it was all wrong. He looked at her again, and saw that the plump face was quite serious.

"It has been stated by a high authority," he said, "that, so long as the American people preserve their wholesome interest in murder and adultery, the country's safe. And if you should happen to feel morbid"—he tapped the briefcase—"here's Cross's new one. It's a book of women poisoners. I believe there's a 'Marie' in it, too."

"Oh? Have you read it?"

"Just glanced into it."

She showed not even any mild curiosity; she dismissed the matter with a frown of concentration as she maneuvered the car into the drive beside their house. He got out, feeling suddenly very hungry and very tired. The frame cottage, built after the New England fashion, and painted white with green shutters, was cheerful with lights through fresh curtains. There was a smell of new grass and lilac; a hill of trees tumbled away behind it, and up the hill, a hundred yards or so, the great wall of Des-

20

pard Park ran at the end of the avenue which had been named for King Charles the Second.

Inside the house, he would have liked to sit down in a chair and stay there. To the right of the hall was the living-room: with the sofa and deep chairs covered in some reddish-orange material, the fat-bowled lamps on the tables, the shelves of bright-jacketed books let into white panelling, the one good copy of the Rembrandt over the fireplace—even the cocktail-shaker, which has become a part of our lares and penates—in short, typical of a hundred thousand homes. Through the glass doors to the dining-room across the hall he could see fat Ellen creaking about, setting the table.

Marie, taking his hat and briefcase, shooed him upstairs to wash. Which was better. He came downstairs, whistling; but he stopped before he got to the lowest step. He could see his briefcase lying on the telephone table in the hall, the silvered catch gleaming; and the catch was unfastened.

The worst of this was feeling like a conspirator in your own house. He hated this fog; he liked to have things out in the open. Feeling as guilty as it was possible to feel, he went over to the telephone table and made a hurried examination of the manuscript inside.

The photograph of Marie D'Aubray was missing; and that was that.

Refusing to give himself time to think, he went hastily into the living-room. It occurred to him that the atmosphere had subtly altered. On the sofa, lounged back easily against it, Marie sat by the cocktail-table with an empty glass in her hand. Her face was flushed, and she pointed to another glass on the table.

"You've been an awfully long time," she said. "Drink that. You'll feel better."

While he drank, it occurred to him that she was watching him. The thought which flashed through his head was so ugly that, in irritation at it and defiance of it, he poured out another cocktail and drank again. Then he put down the glass with great care.

"By the way, Marie," he said, "there's a little mix-up here. Number 1 King's Avenue has suddenly become a house of mystery. I should not be surprised to see clutching hands coming through the curtains and bodies falling out of cupboards. Tell me, do you know of anybody, having the same name as yours,

21

who was in the habit of poisoning people with arsenic a dog's years ago?"

She stared at him, with a pucker of concentration. "Ted, what on earth are you talking about? You've seemed queer ever since you got home." She hesitated, and laughed. "Do you think I've poisoned your cocktail?"

"Oh, I wouldn't put it past you. But seriously, wild as it sounds, did you ever hear of anybody—it must have been nearly a hundred years ago—anybody who was your exact double to the life, and even wore a bracelet like that cat's-head one of yours?"

"Ted, what on earth *are* you talking about?"

He dropped his light tone. "Listen, Marie. Let's not make a mystery of it. The thing isn't important, and it's not worth it. The point is, somebody might think it was a good joke to have your photograph, in eighteen-fifties costume, put into a book as the authentic portrait of a woman who must have murdered half the neighborhood, to judge by what happened to her. But nobody's going to swallow it. Cross has been accused by hoaxes already; you remember that fuss Ladbourne kicked up in the *World?* This will seem too much of a hoax. Frankly, now: who was this Marie D'Aubray? Was she a relation of yours?"

Marie had got up. She did not seem angry, or startled; she looked at him with a sort of breathless half-bewilderment and solicitude. Then she stood back primly. He had never noticed before how oddly she could change color, as though with amusement, or the little wrinkle along the side of her neck.

"Ted," she said, "I'll try to be serious, because you seem to be. There is somebody named Marie D'Aubray (the name's pretty common, you know), who killed people umpty-umph years ago. And you think that I'm her, or she's me. And so you play the Grand Inquisitor. If I'm that Marie D'Aubray"— she stole a glance at herself, over her shoulder, at a wall mirror behind, and for a second he thought there must be something wrong with the mirror—"if I'm that Marie D'Aubray, *you* can testify that in the more important respects I've worn terribly well, haven't I?"

"I didn't say that. I asked whether you might be remotely descended from——"

"Remotely descended from! Give me a cigarette. Pour me out another cocktail. Bosh, darling. Get along with you."

Stevens drew a deep breath. He sat back and studied her.

"I've got to award you the prize," he admitted, "for your ability to put everybody else in the wrong. All right, my wench, I don't mind. Have it your own way. The only thing is, a respectable publishing-house can't lift photographs out of authors' manuscripts and keep 'em. . . . Look here now, Marie. Man to man, didn't you open my briefcase a few minutes ago?"

"No."

"You didn't open it and take out a photograph of Marie D'Aubray, who was guillotined for murder in 1861?"

Her own temper was beginning to flare. "I most certainly did not!" Then her voice broke. "Oh, Ted, what *is* all this nonsense?"

"Well, somebody took it, because it's not there. There's nobody else in the house except Ellen. Unless a sinister Chinaman sneaked in and stole it while I was upstairs washing, I don't see how it can have got away. Cross's address is on the title page of the manuscript. I've been wondering whether I ought to telephone him and ask him if he'd mind suppressing that picture; but we can't have the damned thing stolen——"

The stolid Ellen poked her head in at the door. "Dinner's ready, Miz Stevens," she said, with great cheerfulness. And at the same time, out in the hall, the knocker on the front door rapped sharply.

There is nothing very strange or startling about a rapping on the knocker; it may happen a dozen times a day; but for two or three seconds Stevens could not move. He sat on the sofa, looking out sideways through the arch into the hall, at the porcelain umbrella-stand in one corner. He heard Ellen mutter disgustedly, and then he heard Ellen's creaking shoes moving towards the front door, and the scrape of the lock.

"Mr. Stevens in?" asked Mark Despard's voice.

Stevens got up. Marie was standing there expressionless, and as he passed her Stevens (from a cloudy motive he could not analyze) lifted her hand and put it to his lips. Then he was out in the hall, greeting Mark with jovial heartiness, saying that they were about to sit down to dinner, and wouldn't Mark have a cocktail?

Mark Despard stood just inside the door, and there was another man—a stranger—behind him. The light of the bronze lantern in the hall shone on Mark's clean, hook-nosed face, sensitive despite the strong jaw and bony powerful figure; on the very quick, very light blue eyes which moved round the hall. He had wiry sandy eyebrows, meeting in the middle, and wiry sandy hair. Mark was a young lawyer, with an office in Chestnut Street he had inherited from his father, who had died only half a dozen years before. Mark's practice was small, because he was too much of a theorist: *he* said it was because he was cursed with the ability to see two sides to everything. While he moved round Despard Park, which was the thing he loved most, he liked to wear a sort of squire-cum-gamekeeper costume: shooting-coat and flannel shirt, corduroy breeches with laced boots. He stood looking round the hall, turning his hat round in spatulate fingers, a musician's fingers; his voice was polite, apologetic, and resolute.

"Sorry to break in like this," he said. "But you know I wouldn't do it if it weren't important, and I'm afraid it can't wait. Er——"

He turned round to the man behind him, who had stepped inside the door. This was a shorter, burlier man with an air as courteous though rather defensive. He had a blue-chinned, strong-featured face, a good face despite the fact that the strong features were being padded out with quiet, unobtrusive drinking; there was a V between his heavy brown eyes, but his mouth was pleasant. Even in the way he wore his heavy topcoat there was a curious air of distinction; you would remember him.

"This," went on Mark, "is a very old friend of mine, Doctor —Mr. Partington." He corrected himself quickly; Partington's expression did not change. "We'd like to have a word with you in private, Ted. It may be a rather long word, but I thought if you knew it was in a good cause you wouldn't mind postponing . . ."

"Hello, Mark!" said Marie from the archway, with her usual smile. "Back to your study, Ted; and all of you. There's plenty of time for dinner."

After the introductions Stevens led them rather hurriedly back to his own room, down a couple of steps at the end of the hall. It was a small room, and the three of them seemed to fill it. He turned on the hanging lamp over the typewriter-desk, which gave the place a cold, murky look. Mark shut the door carefully and stood against it.

24

"Ted," he said, "my uncle Miles was murdered."

Stevens had been expecting it. He was not nervous, but still he felt as though his insides were shaking. And it was the baldness of the words, the sudden stripping-off, which gave him a genuine start.

"My God! Mark . . . "

"He was poisoned with arsenic."

"Sit down," said Stevens, after a pause. He indicated two leather chairs in the cramped room among the books, and backed into his own at the desk. Sitting with his back to the desk, his arms stretched out along it, he looked at them. "Who did it?"

"I don't know, except that it was somebody at our house," answered Mark in the same heavy voice. He drew a deep breath. "Now that I've got that off my chest, I can tell you *why* I tell you."

He was sitting forward, his long arms hanging down between his knees, his light-blue eyes fixed on the hanging lamp.

"There's something I must do and that I want to do. To do it, I shall need three people besides myself; I've got two of them, and you're the only other person I can trust. But if you decide to help us, one thing you must promise. Whatever we discover in that old man's body, no word of it must ever reach the police."

Stevens looked down at the carpet to hide the uncertainties of his own thoughts. "You don't want the—whoever-it-is, punished?"

"Punished? Oh yes," said Mark, nodding with the air of a cool fanatic. "But you don't understand. We live in a queer civilization, Ted. If I have a rage, it is a rage for minding my own business and having other people mind theirs. If there is one thing I hate, it is the word publicity. I mean personal publicity. To our American mind it has become a god and a mania and a wielder of destinies. There probably never was a more damnable doctrine than, 'I don't care what you say about me; just mention my name'—because it really has come to mean that a man's achievements for good (or bad) are measured by the same thing that could be said about him in the telephone directory. It's not the newspapers' fault; they can't help it, any more than a mirror can help who insists on looking into it. And it's all fair enough if it's only for vanity. But this is different. Murder

25

or no murder, I'm not going to have our private affairs put up as a greasy heart-throb for readers to whom I wouldn't even bother to tell the time of day. That, you see, is how I feel. That's why no word of it must ever come out.

"Tonight, if you will help us, we are going to open the crypt, open my uncle's coffin, and open his body. We must have definite proof whether or not there is arsenic in it, though I'm quite certain already. Let me tell you as much as I know myself:

"I've known for well over a week that he must have been murdered. But I couldn't do anything. In order to make certain, the body would have to be opened and a post-mortem performed. The question was how to do that in secret. No doctor would—that is——"

Partington spoke pleasantly.

"What Mark means," he said, "is that no reputable doctor would perform such a post-mortem. So he had to send for me."

"I didn't mean that!"

"I know you didn't, old man." Partington looked at Stevens, and drummed on his hard hat. "You had better understand my position in this business. I am Mark's oldest friend, and ten years ago I was engaged to marry his sister Edith. I *was* a surgeon; ten years ago I had a very fair practice in New York. I performed an abortion; never mind why; I thought the reason was good; but there was some hysteria afterwards, and I was found out." He seemed to take pleasure in prodding himself with these details, though there was no bitterness in the way he smiled. "It must have been a dull season, for Mark's newspaper friends made the most of it. I was struck off the register, of course. That didn't matter greatly; I had saved my money. Also, Edith always believed that the woman on whom I had performed the abortion was . . . which is all ancient history," concluded Partington, staring across at the door, his forehead wrinkled, and rubbing his blue chin. His throat had grown dry with the uttering of even so few words. Stevens saw why, and he got up and took a bottle of whisky out of the cupboard. "Since then," Partington said, "I've been living in England and I've been very comfortable. But over a week ago Mark cabled me—he said he couldn't do anything until I got here—and I took the first boat. Now you know as much as I do."

Stevens set out glasses and a siphon of soda.

"Look here, Mark. I'll keep the secret, naturally," he said, with more fervency than the other could know. "But suppose you do find what you suspect; suppose you prove he was murdered? Then what are you going to do about it?"

Mark pressed his hands to his forehead. "God knows. That's what's been driving me half crazy. What can I do about it? What would you do about it? What would anybody do about it? Execute private vengeance? Commit another murder? No, thanks. I wasn't fond enough of Uncle Miles for that. But we've got to KNOW: you see that. We can't go on knowing there's a poisoner in the house. . . . And I hate the deliberate infliction of pain, Ted. Uncle Miles didn't snuff out quickly; it was a cruel death. Somebody must have enjoyed very much watching a man die." He struck the arm of the chair. "And another thing—straight— if you want to know it. Somebody had been systematically poisoning him for days, or even weeks. I don't know. It may be impossible to tell just when the arsenic began to be administered, because he really did have that stomach trouble that gives the same symptoms as arsenic poisoning. Before he was taken bad and we had to bring in a trained nurse, he always had his lunch and dinner sent up on a tray. He wouldn't even have Margaret" —Mark turned to Partington—"he wouldn't even have Margaret—that's the maid—take the tray into his room. He always made her put it down on a table outside the door, and he would take it in at his own leisure. Sometimes it stayed there for quite a while. Consequently, anybody in the house (or any outsider, for all I know) could have got amusement out of soaking the food with poison. *But*——"

"But," said Mark, his voice rising in spite of himself, "on the night he took his last full dose and died at three o'clock the next morning, it was a different matter. There we get into a realm of detective-story suspects. And I've got to thrash this thing out. I've got to get to the root of it somehow, if only to prove that the person who killed Uncle Miles wasn't my own wife."

Stevens, who was getting out a box of cigars, stopped with the box held in mid-air. Whoever had dealt the cards for this little game of devilment, there were some very odd hands turning up. Mark and Lucy: he thought of Lucy—trim, good-looking, efficient, with her black hair parted on one side, her faint trace of freckles round the nose, her laughing face; the kind of whom everyone speaks as "a good sort on a party"; and partner in another thoroughly happy marriage—he thought of Lucy, and found it nonsensical.

Mark jeered savagely.

"I see what you're thinking," he observed. "Crazy, isn't it? Absolute bosh and drivel, isn't it? Yes, I know that. I know it as well as I know I'm sitting in this chair; but that isn't the point. I know that the whole night during which Miles got his last heavy dose Lucy was with me at a masquerade ball at St. Davids; but still that isn't the point. It's the damned circumstantial evidence I've got to get round. You don't have to face a situation like that, Ted, and you can thank your lucky stars you don't. It's the damned circumstantial evidence you've got to get round, though you know there's nothing in it, because you hate secrets and funny business. I have got to find out who killed Uncle Miles, so that I can find out who was trying to put her in a bad position; and then, I warn you, there's going to be trouble. I don't suppose I can explain it to you so you'll understand. . . ."

"Think not?" remarked Stevens. "Well, never mind. You talk about circumstantial evidence. What circumstantial evidence?"

So far the bottle and the glasses had remained untouched on the table. Mark, drawing a breath as though he were inhaling smoke deeply, poured several fingers of whisky into a glass, held it up against the light, and then drained it neat.

He said: "Mrs. Henderson, the cook and prop of our household, saw the murder done. She saw the last dose administered. And, by what she says, the only person who could have given it was Lucy."

IV

PARTINGTON leaned forward. "You take it coolly, and that's a good sign," he asserted. "But it strikes me that there's a weak star witness."

His heavy eyes followed Mark while the latter drank. Stevens saw that Partington wanted liquor badly: but he would make no move to take it, and affected not to notice the glass in Mark's hand. Stevens mixed him a whisky-and-soda, which he took

28

casually, and with that curious stateliness which points out the quiet, unobtrusive, steady drinker. Partington went on:

"You mean Mrs. Henderson, the old woman who's been with you for so long? Isn't it possible that she was——?"

"Anything's a possibility," Mark told him, wearily, "in this mess. But I don't think she was either hysterical or lying. She's an inveterate gossip, of course; but did she ever strike you as being the hysterical sort? Furthermore, as you say, she and her husband have been with us since I was a kid; she nursed Ogden . . . you remember my brother Ogden, Part? He was a boy in grade school when you left. . . . And I know that Mrs. H. genuinely is fond of our family. She's fond of Lucy; I know that too. And, you see, she doesn't have any suspicion at all that Uncle Miles was really poisoned. She thinks he died of stomach trouble, and that what she saw was an ordinary unimportant incident. That's why I've had such a devil of a job keeping her quiet."

"Wait a minute," interposed Stevens. "Does this story of hers concern the mysterious woman in old-fashioned clothes, the one who walked through the door that didn't exist?"

"It does," admitted Mark, and stirred uneasily. "That's what's got me going. For there, right there, is the one part of the whole story which will not fit in anywhere. It won't make sense! I tested it out on you the other day, to see how you'd take it, and I had to make fun of the whole busi—Well, look! Judge for yourselves." His restless, spatulate fingers were busy again with cigarette-papers and a little bag of tobacco; Mark liked to roll his own cigarettes, and made almost a sleight-of-hand business out of it. "I'll tell you the whole thing from the start, because there are such queer places in it that I feel I'm making a map of hell, somehow. And I'd better begin with a little family history. By the way, Part, did you ever meet Uncle Miles in the old days?"

Partington reflected. "No. He was always off in Europe somewhere."

"Uncle Miles and my father were born within a year of each other: Uncle Miles in April, '73, and my father in March, '74. You'll see why I stress these details. My father married early, at twenty-one; Uncle Miles never married at all. I was born in '96, Edith in '98, and Ogden in '04. The money came

29

from land—the old Despards got a tolerable slice in Philadelphia, and a good deal of land hereabouts. Miles inherited most of it, but it never worried my father; he was a good up-and-at-'em kind, who had a flourishing law-practice. (Both my mother and my father died six years ago, of pneumonia; she insisted on nursing him, and she caught it.)"

"I remember them," put in Partington, briefly. He was sitting with his hand shading his eyes, and he did not seem to relish the memory.

"And I tell you this," growled Mark, "to show how commonplace the whole background is. No bad patches. No bad blood. No luridness. Miles was an old rounder, yes; but the kind of high-flown boozings and gallantries he used to carry on were done so much in the old style that they seem decorous in this day and age. I think I can say that he literally hadn't an enemy in the world. In fact, he'd lived so much abroad that he hardly knew anyone hereabouts. If some one poisoned him, it was for the pleasure of seeing a man die . . . or for his money, of course."

Mark faced them.

"If it was for his money, you can say that all of us are under suspicion, myself most of the whole crowd. Each of us inherits a heavy sum. We knew we were going to get it. As I told you, Miles and my father, being born so close to each other, were brought up almost like twins and were good friends; Miles never intended to marry, so long as my father produced heirs. There was never a question of anything else. And this, my lads, was the quiet domestic situation when someone began to feed him arsenic."

"I want to ask two questions," interposed Partington: still stolidly, but with more fluent ease. "First, where's your proof that he *was* being fed arsenic? Second, you've been dropping vague hints about your uncle's behavior being odd towards the end—shutting himself up in his room, and the rest of it. When did that behavior start?"

Again Mark hesitated, opening and shutting his hands.

"It's easy to give a wrong impression," he said, "and that's what I want to avoid. Don't get the idea that he'd turned wildly eccentric, or was a crank, or disrupted the household; he always prided himself on his old-school manners. I suppose it was the difference in him from the old days. We first noticed a trace of that difference not quite six years ago, when he returned from Paris after my parents died. He wasn't the genial uncle any longer; not that he'd become depressed, but simply that he seemed abstracted, or puzzled, and that something had got into his mind. He didn't shut himself up then, either. That began . . . h'm." Mark reflected. "By the way, Ted, how long have you been living here in this house?"

"About two years."

Mark nodded, amused by the coincidence. "Well, it was a couple of months after that. He didn't exactly shut himself up; he only had his lunch and dinner there, and spent the evening there. You know his routine. He would come downstairs to breakfast, and walk in the garden in good weather, and smoke a cigar. He spent some time in the picture-gallery, too. He was just—puzzled, you'd have said; wandering round in a fog. By noon he'd be back in his room for the rest of the day."

Partington scowled. "But what did he do there all that time? Reading? Studying?"

"No, I don't think so. You couldn't call him a man of books. There's a back-stairs rumor that he just sat in a basket-chair looking out of the window. There's also a rumor that he spent a lot of time changing his clothes, apparently for lack of something else to do. He had an enormous wardrobe; he was always very proud of his appearance, and the figure he cut.

"Six weeks ago he began to have these attacks—vomiting, cramps, the rest of it. And he wouldn't hear of having a doctor in. He said: 'Nonsense! I've had this before. A mustard plaster and a glass of champagne will put me right again.' Then he had such an acute one that we got Dr. Baker in a hurry. Baker shook his head—gastro-enteritis, all right. Too bad. We got a nurse in, and whether or not it had really been only stomach trouble before, it's a notable fact that from that time on he began to get well. At the end of the first week in April he was so much improved that nobody had any more anxiety. And so we come to the night of April 12th.

"There were eight people in the house: Lucy, Edith, Ogden, and myself; old Henderson—you remember, Part? he's a sort of groundkeeper-gardener-general-utility man—and Mrs. Henderson; Miss Corbett, the nurse, and Margaret, the maid. Lucy and Edith and I went to a masquerade ball, as I told you.

31

Moreover, the arrangements were such that nearly everybody was to be out of the house that night. Like this:

"Mrs. Henderson had been away for nearly a week. She was standing godmother to some relative's kid in Cleveland; she likes being a godmother. There was to have been a big family celebration there and she had a good stay of it. The 12th, a Wednesday, was Miss Corbett's regular evening off. Margaret had an unexpected date with a boy-friend about whom she raves, and didn't have much difficulty persuading Lucy to let her go out. Ogden was going into town—a party somewhere. That would leave only Henderson in the house with Uncle Miles.

"Edith, as usual, fretted about that. She has the usual idea that only a woman is any good when somebody's sick, so she was going to stay at home herself. But Miles wouldn't hear of it. Besides, Mrs. Henderson was due back home early that evening; she was to be on the train that comes into Crispen at 9:25. Then Edith got a new cause for worry. Henderson was going down with the Ford, to meet the old girl at the train, which would leave a full ten minutes while there would be nobody in the house. So Ogden said, 'Oh God,' and agreed to wait there until Mrs. H. turned up. Consequently, everything was settled smoothly.

"Margaret went out early; so did Miss Corbett, leaving instructions written for Mrs. H. in case she should need 'em. Lucy, Edith, Ogden, and I had a light dinner about eight o'clock. Miles had sent down word that he didn't want anything to eat, and wouldn't have anything; he was in one of his touchy moods. He consented, though, to have a glass of warm milk. After dinner, when we were all going upstairs to dress, Lucy carried it up on a tray. Here's one thing I have good cause to remember: Edith overtook her on the landing, and said, 'You don't even know where things are in your own house. That's the sour milk you've got.' But they both had a taste of it, and it was good."

Stevens, listening to Mark's deliberate voice, had no difficulty in calling up that scene at Despard Park, on the landing of the oak staircase under the big window. There was a big portrait on the wall, and underfoot an Indian rug as heavy as a bath mat, and in the embrasure of the window a telephone-table. Why, Stevens wondered, did his mind keep running on telephone-tables? He could imagine Lucy, very brisk and pleasant, with her black hair parted on one side, her suspicion of freckles; the "good sort on a party." He could imagine Edith, taller, brown-haired, still good-looking, but drying and growing faintly hollowed round the eyes; inclined to fussiness and to speak much of Good Taste. He could imagine them wrangling without rancor over a glass of milk (for there never was any friction in that family)—while satirical young Ogden stood in the background, his hands in his pockets. Ogden lacked Mark's tensity and seriousness. He was a good sort on a party, as well. . . .

But what obsessed Stevens's mind was the question: Am I certain where Marie and I were on that same night? He knew the answer, though he did not like to know it. They had been here, at the cottage in Crispen. It was not usual for them to come down from New York during the middle of the week. But he had to come down on business, to see the *Rittenhouse Magazine* people about serial rights. So he and Marie had spent the night here after driving from New York, and had gone back early in the morning: he had not learned of Miles's death until two days later. And they had spent a quite ordinary evening at home, having no company in, and going to bed fairly early. Yes, they had gone to bed early, with all serene.

He became aware that Mark was speaking again.

"So, I repeat, the milk was good," Mark continued, looking from one to the other of them. "Lucy carried it up, and knocked at Miles's door. She was going to set it down on the table there —I've told you that usually he didn't come to the door immediately—but this time he opened the door and took the tray himself. He was looking a whole lot better. He didn't have quite so much of that misty look, as though he were searching for something and didn't know quite what it was. (You never saw him, Part. Imagine a handsome oldish gent, going a little scrawny round the neck, with a grey moustache, and a high forehead.) That night he was even wearing a blue quilted dressing-gown of the old-fashioned sort, with a white collar and a scarf round his neck.

"Edith said: 'You're *sure* you'll be all right now? Remember, Miss Corbett is out, and nobody can hear your bell downstairs. If you want anything, you'll have to get it for yourself. Can you do it? Wouldn't it be better,' she said, 'if I left instructions

33

for Mrs. Henderson to come up and sit in the hall after she gets back?'

"Uncle Miles said: 'Until two or three o'clock in the morning, my dear? Nonsense! You go along, and I shall be perfectly comfortable. I've beaten it now.'

"Just then it happened that Joachim—Edith's cat—who had been stalking something imaginary in the hall, sidled round Miles's foot and into Miles's room. Miles liked Joachim. He said something about the cat being all the company he needed; he told us to have a good time, and closed the door. So we all went to dress."

Stevens threw in a question with apparent irrelevance. "I think you told me," he suggested, "that Lucy went to this party dressed as Madame de Montespan?"

"Yes. That is . . . officially she did," replied Mark, and seemed (for some reason) startled for the first time. He eyed Stevens. "Edith—I don't know what had got into her head—insisted it should be Madame de Montespan. Maybe she had an idea it would be more respectable." He grinned crookedly. "Actually, her dress (Lucy made it herself) was an exact copy of one in a full-length portrait in the gallery. It's a portrait of a lady contemporary with Montespan, anyhow: though who it may be is still dubious. Most of the face and part of the shoulder have been defaced with some sort of acid, apparently very many years ago. I remember my grandfather once told me somebody had tried to have it restored; but it was impossible to do it. Anyhow, it appears to be a genuine Kneller, which is why they keep it, though it looks like nothing on earth. It's supposed to be a picture of a certain Marquise de Brinvilliers. . . . What the devil's the matter with you, Ted?" he demanded, with a fretful jump, as though his nerves were wearing thin.

"I need food, I suppose," Stevens said, casually. "All right. Keep on going. You mean the seventeenth-century French poisoner? How do you happen to have a picture of her?"

Partington muttered to himself. He leaned out, with his usual laborious movements, and this time was not backward about pouring himself more whisky.

"If I remember," said Partington, looking up, "there's some traditional connection, isn't there? Or she was associated with some one in your family back in the very misty past?"

Mark was impatient. "Yes. Didn't I tell you our name's

been changed and Anglicized? It used to be spelled Desprez, and it was French. But never mind *madame la marquise*. I was only telling you that Lucy copied the costume in the picture, and made it herself in three days.

"We left the house about nine-thirty. Lucy was in her finery, Edith in her Florence Nightingale hoopskirts, and I in some contraption which the man at the costumer's in town confidently declared to be 'cavalier.' It was surprisingly comfortable, considering the look of it; and, anyway, who can resist wearing a sword when you get the chance? Down we went to the car, with Ogden standing on the porch under the roof light and making riotous comments. Just as we turned down the drive, we passed Henderson in the Ford, coming back from the station with Mrs. H.

"The dance wasn't a great success. For a masquerade, it was a tame and much-too-sober affair. I was frankly bored stiff, and spent most of the time sitting round, while Lucy did the dancing. We left at a little past two o'clock. It was a fine night, with a moon, and I felt cool and comfortable for the first time in hours. Edith had torn her lace trousers, or whatever they call those things under the hoopskirts, and she was inclined to be pettish; but Lucy sang all the way home. The house seemed to be all dark. When I ran the car in the garage, the Ford was there, but Ogden's Buick hadn't come in yet. I gave the key of the front door to Lucy, and she ran on ahead to open it, with Edith. I stood out in the drive and just breathed. That's my domain, and I like it.

"Then Edith called out from the porch. I went round, up the steps and into the hall. Lucy was standing with one hand on the light switch, half looking up at the ceiling, and she was frightened.

"She said to me: 'There was some sort of horrible noise. There was! I heard it just a second ago.'

"That hall is very old, and sometimes it gives you notions at night; but this was nothing of the sort. I went upstairs in a hurry; I wasn't encumbered with a sword then. The upstairs hall was dark, and there was something wrong in it. I don't mean *with* it or *about* it, but *in* it. Did you ever have the feeling —something has passed this way, trailing, and the something is bad? I don't suppose you have. . . .

"I was just going towards the light-switch when there was

35

a bumping sort of noise, a sound like that of a key turned in a lock, and the door of Uncle Miles's room bumped open about half-way. There was a dim light burning inside, and it half illuminated Miles and half silhouetted him. He was still on his feet, but he was bent far over forwards, with one hand pressed across his stomach, and the other hand holding to the door-post. I saw the big veins. He hung there wobbling, very nearly doubled, and then he managed to look up. His skin was like oiled paper across the bridge of the nose, his eyes seemed about twice as big as normal, and his forehead was wet. Every breath he drew seemed to shake clear down inside him: you could hear it. Then he looked up in a glazy sort of way. I suppose he saw me, but, when he spoke it didn't seem to be to anyone in particular.

"He was muttering: 'I can't stand it any longer. I can't stand the pain any longer. I tell you I can't stand it any longer.'

"And he was mumbling this in French.

"I ran over and caught him before he tumbled. I picked him up—for some reason he flapped and fought as much as he could with the cramp—and I carried him to the bed in his room. He seemed to be trying to look at me, and haul back to look, and . . . what's the word I want? . . . disentangle me in his mind, to straighten me out of the mist. First he said, like a very scared child, 'Not you too?' I tell you very simply it went through me hard. But evidently he came to himself, for his eyes cleared up a good deal, and he seemed to see my face in the dim reading-lamp over the bed; he stopped shrinking away like a child. It was a complete transformation I can't describe; but he spoke dazedly, in English. He said something about 'those tablets in the bathroom that would take the pain away,' and cried out to me to get them. He said he hadn't strength to get to the bathroom.

"They were the veronal tablets we had used when he had a bad attack before. Lucy and Edith were standing in the door, dead white. Lucy had heard what he said, and she ran off down the hall to get them. We all knew he was dying. Mind, there was no idea of poisoning then. It seemed like the old trouble; and when a man gets as far gone as that, you can't do anything; you can only give him his medicine and grit your teeth. I told Edith quietly to phone for Doctor Baker in a hurry and she was quiet and efficient. All I wondered was about that expression on his face—what he had seen, or thought he had seen, that was so horrible. Why the expression of a scared child jumping away from you?

"I said, maybe with some idea of distracting his mind (from that pain), 'How long have you been like this?'

" 'Three hours,' he answered, and did not open his eyes. He lay on his side, pulled up together. I could hardly hear him for the pillow.

" 'But why didn't you call out, or go to the door . . . ?'

" 'I didn't try,' he said to the pillow. 'I knew it had to be sooner or later; I thought it was better now than waiting for it; but I found I couldn't stand it.' Then he seemed to pull himself together. He looked up at me, as though he were looking up out of a hole. He was still a little scared, and his breathing was still shakily noisy. And he said, 'Look here, Mark, I'm dying.' He wouldn't listen to my platitudes. 'Don't talk; listen. Mark, I'm to be buried in a wooden coffin. Do you understand: a *wooden* coffin. I want you to swear you'll see to that.'

"He was too insistent; he wouldn't look anywhere except straight at me, even when Lucy brought in the tablet and a glass of water. He hung to my cloak, talking of a wooden coffin, over and over. He had a difficult time swallowing the pill, for he'd been vomiting a good deal; but I got it down him at last. Then he muttered something about being cold, and wanting a quilt, and closed his eyes. There was a folded quilt at the foot of the bed. Lucy, without saying anything, picked it up and tucked it around him.

"I got up and looked for something else to put over him. There's a big cupboard in the room, where he kept most of his fancy wardrobe, so I thought there might be a blanket on the top shelf. The door of the cupboard was a little ajar. There was no blanket, but there was something else.

"On the floor of the cupboard, just before a line of shoes neatly arranged in their trees, was the tray that had been brought up earlier that night. So was the glass, empty but for a blur of milk. So was a thing that had not been brought up: a fat silver cup, about four inches in diameter—curious embossed thing, of no special value so far as I know. It's been, downstairs on the sideboard for as long as I can remember. I don't know whether either of you has ever noticed it? Well, in the cup were the dregs of some sticky-looking substance. And

37

stretched out beside it was the body of Joachim, Edith's cat. I touched the cat, and found that it was dead.

"Then was when I knew."

V

FOR a minute or two Mark Despard remained quiet, regarding his clasped hands.

"I suppose," he reflected, "it's possible for suspicions to accumulate at the back of a man's mind, and pile up and up intangibly, without his ever being aware that they're there; then something crystallizes, or a door opens all of a sudden——

"Yes, I knew. I turned round to see whether Lucy had seen what I had seen. Evidently she hadn't. She was standing with her back nearly turned towards me, at the foot of the bed, her hand on the bed-rail; and I thought she looked pretty helpless in contrast to her usual briskness. There was only one light in the room, the dim one at the head of the bed, but it brought out her costume—a reddish-colored silk thing with blue and diamonds in it, and a wide skirt.

"While I was standing there everything came back to my mind in Uncle Miles's past symptoms. His trouble in eating; his catarrh of the nose and eyes—the reddish puffed way he looked at you—the husky voice; the rashes and thickening of the skin; even the way he walked, so that his legs seemed too rickety to support his body. Arsenic poisoning. You could hear Miles breathing heavily under the covers, and from out in the hall you could even hear Edith's low, savage voice sizzling at the telephone operator.

"I didn't say anything. But I closed the door of the cupboard; there was a key in the lock, so I locked the door and put the key in my pocket. Then I went out in the hall and down to the landing where Edith was telephoning. We'd *got* to get a doctor, that was all. The nurse wouldn't come back until next morning. I tried to think what in God's name you did in cases of arsenic poisoning, but I couldn't remember. Edith had just put down the phone; still calm, though her hands looked shaky; she couldn't get Doctor Baker at his house, and we knew nobody else within striking distance. But I knew there was a doctor at the residential hotel about a mile down the road, though I couldn't remember his name. I started to ring up the hotel, while Edith hurried up to Miles's room—she always has an idea she can do something in sickness, although she isn't sure what it is—but Lucy came out into the hall before I'd got the number.

" 'You'd better come up here,' she said. 'I think he's gone.'

"He had. No convulsions; his heart simply stopped, and he wasn't hurt any longer. While I was turning him over to make sure, my hand went under the pillow and I found the piece of string you've probably heard about. It was an ordinary piece of wrapping-string, about a foot long, and tied at equal intervals into nine knots. I didn't know what it means; I still don't."

"Go on!" Partington prompted, sharply, as he stopped. "What then?"

"Then? Nothing. We didn't rouse the rest of the house. It wasn't necessary: there were only a few more hours until morning. Lucy and Edith tried to go to bed, though they didn't sleep. I said I would stay up: a gesture of respect, or something. That was how I put it, though actually I wanted a chance to get that cup out of the room. Also, Ogden wasn't in yet. I said I had better stay up on guard, in case he came home with a few under his belt at the wrong time . . . you know.

"Lucy locked herself in our room. Edith cried a little. What we were all doing, in a stupefied sort of way, was blaming ourselves for negligence, but I knew it wasn't that. After they had gone I went back into Miles's room and put a sheet over his face. I took the silver cup and the glass out of the cupboard, and wrapped them both up in a handkerchief. Don't ask me about fingerprints! My only instinct . . . I suppose it's always like that with me . . . was to hide the evidence until I could decide what to do."

"Didn't you have any idea of revealing it?" asked Partington.

"If we could have reached a doctor in time to help Miles— yes, naturally. I'd have said, 'Never mind this gastritis business; he's been poisoned.' But we couldn't. And so—no." Mark seemed almost fanatical, and Stevens studied him as he held tight, stiffly, to the arms of the chair. "You ought to understand that, Part. You remember how I almost——"

"Steady," said Partington, and cut him off sharply. "Go on with the story."

"I took the cup and the glass downstairs, and locked them up in a drawer of my desk in the library. You understand, so far there wasn't an ounce of proof. And I had to dispose of the cat somehow, so I wrapped it up in my cavalier cloak and took it outside, by the side door, so as not to wake up the Hendersons at the back. There were some newly turned flower beds on the other side of the lawn, across the drive; and I knew that Henderson often kept a spade in the little closet as you go out the side door. I got the cat and buried it very far down. Edith doesn't know what happened to it yet; they all suppose it wandered away. By the time I was finishing my job, I saw the lights of Ogden's car coming up; for a second I thought he had seen me, but I got inside ahead.

"That was all, for the moment. The next day—after I'd heard Mrs. Henderson's story—I took the glass and the cup to town, to an analytical chemist I could trust absolutely, for a confidential report. It didn't take long. The glass was harmless. The cup contained the dregs of some concoction made of milk and port wine, with an egg beaten into it; and in the dregs were two grains of white arsenic."

"Two grains?" repeated Partington, turning his head.

"Yes. That's a lot, isn't it? I've been reading up——"

"For the dregs," said the other, grimly, "it's a devil of a lot. There's a case recorded of death ensuing from taking two grains. It's the lowest amount recorded, yes; but if there was so much in the remains of the cup the full drink must have been loaded with it."

"What's the ordinary fatal dose?"

Partington shook his head. "There's no 'ordinary' fatal dose. As I say, death has ensued from taking two grains. On the other hand, a victim has been known to swallow two hundred grains, the largest known dose, and recover afterwards. You've got a pretty broad range between. For instance, you've heard of the case of Madeleine Smith, the Glasgow beauty who was accused of poisoning her French lover in 1857? Yes. There were eighty-eight grains of arsenic in L'Angelier's stomach. Counsel at the trial, therefore, argued that the death must have been suicide, for no person could have swallowed such an enormous dose without noticing it at the time. Undoubtedly it had an effect on the verdict—the Scotch verdict of 'Not proven,' which they say is the equivalent of 'Not guilty, but don't do it again.'—Still, six years after that business a woman named Hewitt was tried at Chester for the murder of her mother. The old lady had died without suspicion; the doctor said death was due to gastro-enteritis; and it wasn't until the body was dug up that they discovered a hundred and fifty-four grains of arsenic in the stomach alone."

Partington's tongue was loosened; he even seemed to be enjoying himself; though the judicial expression remained on his blue-jowled face.

"Then again," he went on, waggling an empty glass, "there was the case of Marie D'Aubray at Versailles, in the early 'sixties. A bad business. Very little motive to *her* various bumpings-off, it would seem . . . just the pleasure of watching them die. . . . One of the victims got as little as ten grains of arsenic, another as much as a hundred. She wasn't as lucky as Madeleine Smith. She got the guillotine."

By this time Stevens had risen and was sitting on the edge of his desk. He tried to nod casually and understandingly, but he was looking across at the white-painted door to the hall. For some moments he had been noticing something about that door. The light in the hall was brighter than the one in here. As an ordinary thing, you could see a glow shining through the large keyhole; but no chink was visible now, for someone must be listening outside the door.

"However," said Partington, "that's not the most important thing: I'll do the post-mortem. The important thing is when the poison was administered. If you've got all your times straight, it was damned rapid. Say a very large dose is given. Ordinarily the acute symptoms will come on anywhere from minutes to an hour afterwards—depending whether it was in solid or liquid form—and death will ensue from six to twenty-four hours afterwards, or even longer. It's been known to hold off for several days. So you can see how quickly your uncle went. You left him at half-past nine, in at least tolerably good health. You returned and found him on his last legs at half-past two, and he died not long afterwards. Is that right?"

"Yes."

Partington brooded. "Well, it's entirely on the cards, of course. It's even probable. He was already eaten up with the organic disease; he was being slowly poisoned on top of it (if you're right); so he'd be finished off quickly with a heavy dose. If we knew just when he took the last one——"

"I can tell you exactly when it was," snapped Mark. "It was at a quarter past eleven."

"Yes," put in Stevens, "and that's this mysterious story Mrs. Henderson told, isn't it? That's what we want to know, and you keep putting it off. What the devil was the story? Why don't you like to talk about it?"

He was afraid he had shown more excitement, more of a trace of nerves, than he ought to have allowed, but Mark did not notice it. Mark had the air of one coming to a decision.

"For the moment," he said, "I'm not going to tell it."

"Not going to tell it?"

"Because you'd think I was crazy, or Mrs. H. was," the other answered, as though he were groping in his mind. He raised his hand. "Wait! Wait a minute, now! I've been over this whole thing a hundred times. I can't sleep for thinking of it. But when I tell somebody for the first time, when I put out each fact as plain as beef . . . why, I see that the other part of the story would be plain incredible. You might even think I was leading you on a wild-goose chase over opening the crypt. And Uncle Miles's death has got to be settled. Will you give me a couple of hours' leeway? That's all I want, until we can settle the first part of it."

Partington stirred. "You've changed, Mark. By George! I don't understand you! Here: what's so incredible about this story? What you've told us already isn't anything very wild; bad, if you like, or devilish, or——but not out of the way. It's plain murder. What's so incredible about the rest of it?"

"That a long-dead woman," said Mark, calmly, "might still be alive."

"What damned nonsense . . . !"

"No, I'm absolutely sane," Mark told him, nodding calmly. "Feel my pulse; give me a crack across the knee and watch my leg jump. I don't believe it, naturally—any more than I believe Lucy had anything to do with it. There are two theories, both impossible. I only tell you it's a stray idea that's got stuck in the back of my mind, so I want to drag it out and laugh at it. But, if I told you now, God knows what you'd get to thinking. . . . *Will* you help me open that crypt first?"

"Yes," said Stevens.

"What about you, Part?"

"I haven't come three thousand miles to back out now," the doctor grunted. "But understand: you're not going to keep up this mumbo-jumbo once I've done the business. By George! you're not! I wonder how Edith—" There was a flash of anger in his stolid brown eyes, but he became affable as Mark filled his glass for the third time. "How do we open this crypt?"

Mark was brisk again. "Good! Good! It's not a hard job, but it'll require plenty of time and muscle and elbow grease. It'll need four men—the fourth is Henderson, who can be trusted and who's right in his element at this sort of work. He's the only one in the house now. Besides, his and Mrs. H.'s living-quarters are right beside the path going to the crypt: we couldn't disturb a stone without his knowing it afterwards by one look. ... All the rest of 'em I've got rid of on one pretext or another; you couldn't as much as shuffle a couple of stones—let alone what we've got to do—without everybody at the back of the house hearing it. As for the work . . ."

Stevens thought of the scene. At the rear of the long, low grey house there ran out a broad and straight path laid out in crazy-paving with concrete between the stones. On either side was a sunken garden. Beyond the gardens the path was lined with elm trees, and it terminated, some sixty yards from the house, in a small private chapel which had been shut up for more than a century and a half. Not far in front of the chapel, and to the left of the path as you walked down it, was a small house where the Despards had once "kept" a clergyman. The Hendersons lived there now. Stevens had heard that the entrance to the crypt (of which no sign was visible) was somewhere under the crazy-paving before the chapel door. Mark explained it now.

"About seven square feet of paving will have to come up," he said. "And, since we have to work in a hurry, there'll be a lot of breaking. We'll get a dozen steel wedges—long ones —into the concrete between the stones, and drive them in as far as they'll go, and then knock them to one side. That'll lift and split most of the joinings. Then we crack it all over with a sledge-hammer, and we can take it up in pieces. Under that there's gravel and soil; six inches or so. Under *that* there's a flat stone that covers the hole down into the place. The stone's six feet by four, and, I warn you, it weighs between fifteen and eighteen hundred pounds. The heaviest job will be to get bars under it and lever it up on its end. Then we go down the stairs. I know it sounds like a lot of work . . ."

"It's a lot of work, all right," grunted Partington, and slapped his knees. "Let's get down to it, then. And look here: you don't want anybody to know about this, do you? After we make all that mess, do you think we can get it back afterwards so that nobody will know it's been disturbed?"

"Not altogether, no. Anybody with an eye for it, like Henderson or myself, would see it. But I doubt whether anybody else would. There was a slight tear-up at the edges last time it was opened, for Miles's funeral; and most crazy-paving looks alike." Mark had become restless again. He got to his feet, brushing the matter away, and took out his watch. "That's settled, then. It's half-past nine now; let's get started as soon as we can. There'll be nobody up there to disturb us. We'll go on up ahead, Ted; you get something to eat and follow us as soon as you can. Better wear old cl—" He stopped, in an alarm that was growing out of his uneasy nerves. "Good God! I forgot! What about Marie? What excuse are you going to make to her? You won't tell her, will you?"

"No," Stevens said, with his eye on the door; "no, I won't tell her. Leave it to me."

He could see that they were both surprised at his tone, but both appeared to have concerns of their own and they believed him. With the smoke-filled air of the room and his own lack of food, he found when he got up that he was a little light-headed. And it made him remember something else about the night of Wednesday, April 12th, which he and Marie had spent at this cottage, and on which he had gone to bed so early. He had gone to bed at ten-thirty because he had felt unaccountably drowsy, and had nearly banged his head forward against the manuscript on the desk. Marie said it was a taste of the open air, after New York.

He accompanied Mark and Partington out into the hall. Marie was not in sight. Shouldering ahead, Mark appeared in a hurry to get out of the house. Partington hesitated near the front door, looked round politely with his hat against his chest, and murmured something about Mrs. Stevens before his footsteps creaked after the other's down the brick path. Standing in the open door, breathing the night, Stevens saw the lights of Mark's car go on; he heard the jerk and throb of the engine, and the trees rustling at gossip. Well? He turned back, closing the door with care, and looked at the brown porcelain umbrella-stand. Marie was in the kitchen: he could hear her moving about, half humming, half singing, *"Il pleut, il pleut, bergère—"* that china-shepherdess song she liked so much. He went out through the dining-room, and pushed open the swing-door to the kitchen.

Ellen, evidently, had gone. Marie, wearing a house apron, stood at the kitchen cabinet, cutting cold-chicken sandwiches, spreading them with lettuce, tomato, and mayonnaise, and ranging them in neat piles on a plate. When she saw him she pushed back a strand of the dark-yellow hair with the hand that held the bread-knife. The heavy-lidded grey eyes looked at him gravely, yet with an expression which suggested a smile. What went through his head was Thackeray's jingle in burlesque of Goethe:

> Charlotte, like a well-conducted maiden,
> Went on cutting bread and butter.

The kitchen was white-tiled, and there was a humming noise from the electric refrigerator. This whole business was nonsensical.

"Marie—" he said.

"I know," she declared, cheerfully. "You've got to go. You eat these, darling." She tapped the sandwiches with the bread-knife. "They'll stay by you."

"How do you know I've got to go?"

"I listened, of course. You were all so horribly mysterious. What did you expect me to do?" There was a very faint look of tensity about her face. "It's spoiled our evening, but I know you've got to go, or you'd never get it off your mind. Darling, I did a good thing tonight to warn you—about being morbid. I expected this."

"Expected?"

"Well, maybe not exactly that. But they're talking about it in what few houses Crispen has. I got here this morning, and I've heard a hint of it. I mean that there's something wrong at the Park; *something;* nobody seems to know what. Nobody

45

knows how the rumor got started. If you try to trace it back, you can't find it. Even if you try to remember who told it to you, you can't. Be careful. Won't you be careful?"

Yet there was an air of change about the kitchen; all things had changed. Even when he looked at the brown porcelain umbrella-stand in the hall, it had an appearance of being painted in new colors. Putting down the knife with a small rattle on the enamelled shelf of the cabinet, she came up to him and took him by the arms.

"Listen, Ted. I love you. You know I love you, don't you?"

He did know it, in his bones and soul.

"And as," he said, "for what I was thinking——"

"Listen again, Ted. That will last as long as I know you, or you know me. What you may have got into your head I don't know. Sometime I may tell you about a house at a place called Guibourg, and my aunt Adrienne, and you'll understand. But it isn't the kind of thing you ought to be thinking about. Don't grin in that superior way. I am older than you, much, much older; and if you saw my face shrivel up and blacken right at this minute——"

"Stop that! You're hysterical!"

The knife had fallen out of her hand and her mouth was pulled open. She picked up the knife.

"I'm crazy," she said. "Now I'll tell you something. You're going to open a grave tonight, and my guess . . . it's only a guess . . . is that you'll find nothing."

"Yes. I don't think we'll find anything, either."

"You don't understand. You wouldn't understand. But please, please, don't tamper with this too far. If I asked you for my sake not to, would you? I want you to think. And that's as much as I can tell you now. Think what I've said; don't try to understand it; but just trust me. Now eat up a few of these sandwiches, and take a glass of milk. Then go up and change your clothes. That old sweater of yours will do you, and there's a pair of old tennis-flannels in the cupboard of the spare room; I forgot to get them cleaned last year."

Charlotte, like a well-conducted hausfrau, went on cutting bread and butter.

46

II

EVIDENCE

"Fly open, lock, to the dead man's knock,
Fly bolt, and bar, and band! ——"
                    —R. H. Barham, *Ingoldsby Legends*

VI

STEVENS walked up King's Avenue the short distance to the gates of the Park. There was no moon, but a crowding of stars. As usual, the iron-grilled gates—with each entrance pillar topped by an unimpressive stone cannon-ball—stood wide open. He shut them, and dropped the bar. The gravel drive went slightly uphill; it was a long distance to the house, and seemed longer by reason of the drive's windings among shrewd landscaping. Henderson required two assistants to keep these grounds in order. With all their riding round on motor mowing-machines, somebody's head was always to be seen up over the top of an ornamental hedge, or seeming, in ghostly fashion to stick out of a tree: to the accompaniment of a snip-snip-pause-snip-snip of shears. It made a drowsy sound in summer, when you might lounge in a deck-chair at the crest of the lawns, and look down over a blaze of flower-beds under the sun.

As he went up the drive, Stevens kept himself thinking of this. He refused to think of anything else. *Non cognito, ergo sum.*

The house was long and low, built of stone in the form of the head of a letter T with its short wings towards the road. There was nothing at all distinguished about the house, except that it had grown old well. It did not butt against the years, or show its bones and wait for death; but it had become a part of the soil. Its curved roof-tiles had become an unobtrusive reddish brown; its thin chimneys seemed proper, though no smoke went up from them. The windows were small, in casement fashion after the French style of the late seventeenth century. Some one in the nineteenth century had added a low front porch, but even this had ceased to obtrude itself, and had almost taken root. The porch light was burning. Stevens went up and hammered the knocker.

Otherwise the house seemed to be dark. After a few minutes Mark opened the door. He led the way through the familiar hall, which smelt of age and Bibles and furniture-polish, out through the house into the kitchen. Modern implements looked small in that kitchen, and it had the appearance of a workroom as well. Partington, more bulky than ever in ancient sheathing of Harris tweeds, remained stolidly by the gas-range and smoked a cigarette. At his feet lay a black bag and a large leather-covered box. Ranged against the table were the hammers, the shovels, the picks, the steel wedges, and two flat steel bars about eight feet long, of which Henderson was taking stock now. Henderson was a smallish but very wiry old man in corduroys, with a long nose, blue eyes encircled in wrinkles like walnuts, and a bald head brushed over with such indeterminate wisps of grey hair that they seemed like an illusion of hair. There was an air of uneasiness in the kitchen, a conspiratorial air which drew everyone together, and Henderson was the most uneasy. When Mark and Stevens came in, he jumped up, scratching the back of his neck.

"It's all right," Mark said, testily. "We're not going to commit any crime. Got all your doings, Part? You, Ted, you can make yourself useful. Fill these up." From under the sink he brought out two lanterns and a big tin of kerosene. "I've got a flashlight for the crypt, but these will be the only things to use while we dig. Yes, I hope it's all right. You know, we're going to make a hell of a lot of racket with those hammers. . . ." He hesitated. "You don't suppose——?"

Henderson spoke aggrievedly, in a heavy bass voice. He still scratched the back of his neck, and squared round. "Well, Mr. Mark, don't *you* get to being nervous now. I don't like this thing, and your pap wouldn't 'a' liked it; but if you say it's all right, I'll do it. If you want me to, I can muffle up them hammers a little, so they'll make less noise. Do you remember, I did it once when Miss Edith was sick and we were changing the wall in the garden? But I don't think anybody'll hear, down as far as the road; no, it's not likely anybody'll hear, down as far as the road; and all I'm afraid of is that maybe your wife or your sister or my wife will come back here, or Mr. Ogden. I can tell you, and you know yourself, Mr. Ogden he's a pretty curious young fellow, and if he takes it into his head . . ."

"Ogden's in New York," Mark said, shortly. "The rest of them are in good hands, and they won't be back until next week. Ready?"

Stevens had found a tin funnel in the kitchen cupboard, and had filled both lanterns. Laden with their gear, they went out the back door. Mark and Henderson walked ahead with the lanterns swinging. That homely, honest, look-out-for-the-railway-crossing light gave a better look to their body-snatchers' implements. All the same, the Park did not like it. Ahead the broad path stretched in patchwork paving, first with the sunken gardens on either side, then the tall lines of elms, and, far at the end, the chapel dark under starlight. Presently they passed the small house occupied by the Hendersons, and some twenty feet farther on—no great distance in front of the chapel door—Mark and Henderson set down the lanterns. The latter dug the heel of his boot into mud and drew out on the stones the area they were to attack, before he put each into position.

"Now just you be careful you don't kill each other with them picks," he said, rather malevolently. "That's all I ask of you, just you be careful. Make a hole with the pick for the wedge to go in, and then use your hammers. All I have to say is——"

"Right," said Partington cheerfully . "Let's go."

The picks came down with a crash, and Henderson wailed.

It took two hours. At a quarter to twelve by his wrist watch, Stevens found himself sitting back flat in the wet grass beside the path, taking big breaths. His whole body was clammy with sweat in the cool wind, his heart was bumping, and he felt as though he had been through the wringer. Sedentary life, eh? That was it. But, with the possible exception of Mark, he was the strongest of the three, and he felt that the whole weight of that stone had been on him.

Taking up the paving had not been over-difficult, though it seemed to rouse such a hellish din that he felt it must be audible for half a mile, and once Mark had made a trip to the front of the house to find out whether it was as bad as it sounded. Nor was the removing of the gravel and soil too difficult; but Henderson, a martinet, insisted on having it in neat piles afterwards, and it had taken some time. Afterwards the levering up of a stone slab weighing nearly half a ton was the hardest; once Partington had slipped, the stone had wavered, and for a second Stevens thought the whole thing was coming over on them. Now the stone stood upright on its side, like the lifted lid of a chest, held there by its own weight. The entrance to the crypt had the appearance of the inside of a chest, being a stone-walled oblong with a flight of stone steps going down ten feet.

"Done it," said Partington, still cheerfully, although he was panting and coughing. "Any more impediments? If not, I'll go back to the house and wash my hands for what's got to be done."

"*And* to get yourself a drink," breathed Mark, looking after him. "Well, I don't blame you." He turned back again, holding up the lantern, and grinning at Henderson like a wolf. "Do you want to go down first, H., my lad?"

"No, I don't," snapped the other, "and you know I don't. I've never been down in that place, not when your father nor your mother nor your uncle was buried, and I wouldn't go down now if it wasn't for helping you lift the coffin—"

"You needn't worry about that," Mark told him, holding the lantern higher, "if you don't want to go down. It's a wooden coffin, not very heavy, and two men could handle it easily."

"Oh, I'm going down, all right; you can bet your last dollar on that; I'm going *down*," declared Henderson, with belligerent emphasis which was a trifle scared just the same. "You talking about poisons, like books! Poisons! Your pap'ud poison you if he was here! I never heard such foolishness in my life. I know, I know, I oughtn't to sass you back. I'm only old Joe Henderson, that whacked you good and hard many's the time when you was a kid. . . ." He stopped and spat. Now appeared the real reason behind this querulousness, for he said, quietly: "Honest to God, now, are you sure you haven't heard anybody around here watching us? I been feeling like that ever since we came out here."

His eyes flashed over his shoulder. Stevens got up, opening and shutting stiff hands, and came over to join them by the mouth of the crypt. Mark moved the lantern round; wind stirred in the elms; nothing more.

"Come on," Mark said, abruptly. "Part'll catch up with us. Leave the lanterns here. They use up air; and there's no ventilation down there; and we want all the ventilation we can get. Smell it? I've got a flashlight.`. . ."

52

"Your hand's shaking, Mr. Mark," said Henderson.

"And you lie," said Mark. "Follow on."

The enclosure of the little staircase, although damp, was completely free from marshiness. Its close air pressed the lungs with almost a feeling of warmth. At the foot of the stairs was a rounded archway, with a rotted wooden door hanging from its frame, opening into the crypt; and a heavier air stirred at their coming. The beam of Mark's flashlight moved inside. That crypt had been opened only ten days ago: which, Stevens thought, made it easier to go into now. Its damp closeness was still thick with an overpowering odor of flowers.

Mark's light showed a mausoleum oblong in shape, some twenty-five feet long by fifteen feet wide, and built throughout of massive granite blocks. In the centre an octagonal granite pillar supported the groined roof. On two sides the crypt was a catacomb. In the one long wall facing them as they entered, and in the short wall to the right, niches had been made in regular tiers to contain the dead. The exposed coffins were set into the wall endways, evidently from some one's business-like wish to save space even in the grave; and the niches were barely larger than the coffins. Near the top, where the old Despards lay, most of the niches were ornamented with marble facings, scrollwork, a contorted angel or two, even a Latin eulogy; but lower down they became more severe. Some tiers were filled, some almost empty; and eight coffins could be laid along one tier.

At the other end of the crypt, towards their left, the light picked out a tall marble plaque on the wall, inscribed with the names of those who had been buried here. Over it drooped a marble angel, with head hidden. On either side of the plaque stood a great marble urn, out of which a mass of dead flowers still drooped; and there were the remains of more flowers on the floor.[1] Stevens observed that on the plaque the first name was *Paul Desprez, 1650-1706.* The name turned into 'Despard' just past the middle of the eighteenth century; and it might be guessed that the family, having sided with the British during the French and Indian War, found it convenient to Anglicize their name. The last on the roll, boldly cut with a shock of

[1] The astute reader will have noticed that the principal features of this crypt are taken from a real mausoleum at Dunecht, near Aberdeen, described by Mr. William Roughead in his admirable account, "The Dunecht Mystery," from *What Is Your Verdict?*

obtruding the present, was *Miles Bannister Despard, 1873-1929.*

Mark's light moved away, and over to find Miles's coffin. It was in the wall directly opposite them, and in the lowest tier, which was only a few feet from the floor. It was the last in its tier. All the niches to the left were occupied, and there were several vacant places to the right. It stood out not only because it was new and gleaming, where all the others were crusted with dust or rust or corruption, but because it was the only coffin in its tier made of wood.

They stood for a moment in silence, and Stevens heard Henderson breathing behind his shoulder. Mark turned and handed Henderson the light.

"Keep this on it," he said. His voice came back in such echoes that he jumped; it was as though the voice itself raised dust. "Come on, Ted; take one side and I'll take the other. I could lift it down by myself, but we have to go easy."

As they moved forward, they all started again to hear footsteps coming down the stairs behind, and they whirled round. The lantern was burning on the path up at the top of the crypt; Partington, with his bag and box and two ordinary Mason jars perched on top. On either side of the coffin, Stevens and Mark Despard slid their hands into the niche and pulled. . . .

"It's damned light," Stevens found himself saying.

Mark said nothing, but he looked more startled than he had been that night. The coffin was made of polished oak scrolled at the edges, and of no great size; Miles had been five feet six. On the top was a silver name-plate, with Miles's name and the dates. With a very small heave they hoisted it out and put it on the floor.

"It's too damned light, I tell you," Stevens found himself saying. "Here, you won't need that screwdriver; this thing opens with two long bolts and clasps down through the centre of the edges. Catch hold."

They heard the clink as Partington put down his Mason jars, together with a sheet in which he was apparently going to do some wrapping-up. Mark and Stevens tugged at the bolts until the coffin-lid began to lift. . . .

The coffin was empty.

The coffin, bedded with white satin, gleamed under the shaking light in Henderson's hand; but it was empty. There was not even a pinch of dust.

Nobody said anything, though each could hear the others breathe. Mark sat back on his haunches so abruptly that he nearly fell over backwards. Then, with a common impulse, both he and Stevens turned down the lid of the coffin to look at the silver name-plate again.

"Mother of Go—" said Henderson, and stopped.

"You—you don't suppose we've got the wrong coffin, do you?" asked Mark, rather wildly.

"I'll swear on a stack of Bibles we haven't," Henderson declared. His hand was trembling so much that Mark took the light from him. "I saw him put into that. Look, there's the nick in it they made when they bumped it coming downstairs. Besides, what other coffin? All the others—" He pointed to the tiers of steel ones.

"Yes," said Mark, "that's his coffin all right. But where is he? Where's he got to?"

They looked at one another in the gloom, and into Stevens's mind had come unnatural notions which were as stifling as the air of the crypt. Partington alone seemed to remain quiet, steady with either common sense or whisky; even a trifle impatient. "Buck up," he said to Mark, sharply, and put his hand on the other's shoulder. "Here! all of you! Don't get any fool ideas about this. The body's gone; well, what of it? You see what it means, don't you? It only means that somebody's got here ahead of us and stolen the body out of there —for whatever reason."

"How?" asked Henderson, in a blank, querulous tone.

Partington looked at him.

"I said, How?" repeated Henderson, his voice rising doggedly. He backed away, his hands feeling behind him, as the full presentiment of what had happened soaked like water into every corner of his heavy mind. Mark put the light in his face, and the old man cursed and brushed the face with a corduroy sleeve as though to wipe something off. "How did somebody get in and out? That's what I want to know, Doctor Partington. I said a minute ago I'd swear on a stack of Bibles that was Mr. Miles's coffin, and I saw him put into it and carried down here. And I'll tell you something else, Doctor Partington: nobody *could*'ve got in and out of this place! Look at it. It took four of us, working two hours and making a racket fit to wake the dead, just to open the entrance. Do you think somebody could get in here—opening it up with me and Mrs. Henderson sleeping twenty feet away from it, with the windows up, and not hearing one single sound; and me a light sleeper, too?—and not only that, but of them putting all the things right back again, mixin' their own concrete right there and setting the pavement down again? Do you think that? Yes, sir, and I'll tell you something more. I laid that pavement myself, a week ago; I know how I laid it; and it's exactly as I put it down myself. I'll take my oath before God that nobody has touched that pavement, or monkeyed with it in any way, since then!"

Partington regarded him without anger. "I'm not questioning your word, my friend. But don't make too much of it, that's all. If the body-snatchers didn't get through that way, they got through some other way."

Mark spoke with slow reasonableness. "Granite walls. Granite roof. Granite floor." He stamped on it. "There's no other way in; it's all granite blocks set together. Were you thinking of a secret passage, or something like that? We'll look, but I'm dead sure there isn't one."

"May I ask," said Partington, "just what you think did happen here? Do you think your Uncle Miles got up out of his coffin and left the crypt?"

"Or do you think," said Henderson, with peevish timidity, "that somebody might have taken his body and put it in one of the other coffins?"

"I should think it highly unlikely," said Partington; "because in that case your problem is just as bad. How did somebody get in here to do it, and then get out again?" He reflected. "Unless, of course, the body was somehow stolen between the time the coffin was put in that niche and the time the crypt was sealed up?"

Mark shook his head. "That's decidedly out. The actual burial service—that 'dust-to-dust' business—was read in here by the minister, with a whole crowd of people in the place. Afterwards we all went up the steps."

"Who was the last person out of the crypt?"

"*I* was," said Mark sardonically. "I had to blow out the candles they were using, and gather up the iron standing-brackets the candles were in. But, since the whole process took the remarkable space of one minute, and since the saintly

56

pastor of St. Peter's Church was waiting for me on the steps, I can assure you the dominie and I have no guilty secrets."

"I didn't mean that; I meant after you all left the crypt."

"As soon as we were all out, Henderson and his assistants went to work and sealed it up. Of course, you can say that *they* had a guilty hand in it, but it happens that a number of people hung around, watching it being done."

"Well, if that's out, it's out," grunted Partington, and lifted one shoulder. "But don't worry yourself about somebody playing crazy pranks, Mark. That body was stolen out of here, and has been destroyed since or hidden somewhere, for a damned good reason. Don't you see what it was? It was to forestall just what we were going to do tonight. To my mind there's no doubt your uncle was poisoned. And right now, unless the body is found, the murderer is in an impregnable position. Your doctor certified that Miles died of natural causes. Now the body disappears. You're the lawyer and ought to know; but it strikes me that this is our old friend the *corpus delicti* again. Without the body, what proof have you that he didn't die from natural causes? Strong contributory evidence, yes; but is it strong enough? You find two grains of arsenic in a milk-and-egg-and-port mixture, and the cup containing it was in his room. All right, what of it? Did anybody see him drink it? Can it be proved that he did drink it, or had anything to do with it? Wouldn't he have mentioned it himself, if he had thought there was anything wrong? On the contrary, the only thing he was known to have taken into his own hands was a glass of milk you later proved to be harmless."

"You ought to 'a' been a lawyer yourself," said Henderson, with no pleasant inflection.

Partington wheeled. "I'm telling you this to show you why the poisoner somehow got that body out of here. We've got to find out how it was done. Meanwhile, we have only an empty coffin ——"

"Not completely empty," said Stevens.

During this time he had remained staring into it with such intensity that he barely saw it at all. Now something that had been hidden by the color of the satin lining became plain to him. It lay along one side, about where the right hand of the dead man would have rested. He bent down, picked it up,

57

and held it before them. It was a piece of ordinary wrapping-string, about a foot long, and tied at equal intervals into nine knots.

VII

AN HOUR later, when they stumbled up the steps into fresh air, they had satisfied themselves of two things:

1. There was no secret entrance, or any other way of getting in or out of the crypt.

2. The body was not still in the crypt, hidden in one of the other coffins. All the lower tiers of coffins they hauled out far enough for examination, and thoroughly examined each. Though it was impossible to open all of them, the state of undisturbed dust, rust, and tight-sealed lids showed that not one of them had been touched since it was put in there. Partington gave it up, going back to the house after another peg of whisky. But in an access of zeal Henderson and Stevens fetched ladders so that they could climb up and disturb the old Despards in their higher tiers: Mark uneasily refused to lend a hand at this breaking of bones. But here, where all things had a tendency to break under the touch, it was even more clear that the body had not been hidden. Finally, Mark even threw the flowers out of the urns and they tilted the urns over—without result. By this time they all knew the body was not in the crypt, for there was nowhere else it could have been. They were in a box of granite blocks. And the second of two possibilities was ruled out as soon as the first. Thus even in the unlikely event of some visitor creeping in here by nobody knew what way, removing the body from its coffin, hanging to the rows of coffins like a bat—an idea gruesome enough for Fuseli or Goya—while for some unaccountable reason he tried to put the body in another place, still there was no place for it to have been put.

Just before one o'clock, when all this was finished, all four had as much of the place as their noses and lungs would stand. When they came stumbling up, Henderson went into the trees beyond the path, and Stevens heard violent retching noises from his direction. They went into Henderson's little stone house, into a small living-room, and turned on the lights;

presently Henderson followed them, wiping his forehead, and quietly began brewing strong coffee. Then they sat round the table in the little gimcrack room, four grimy resurrectionists over their coffee, and did not speak. A clock on the mantelpiece, among framed photographs, said that it was ten minutes to one.

"Cheer up," said Partington at length, though his own geniality was beginning to wear off, and his eyes looked heavy. He lit a cigarette with great deliberation. "We've got a problem, gentlemen; a good, round, interesting problem; and I suggest we try to solve it before Mark here begins brooding again. . . ."

"Why the devil do you keep harping on *my* brooding?" demanded Mark, snappishly. "It's all you seem to talk about. I don't know whether you want to advance solutions; you only want to convince us that we ought to doubt the evidence of our own eyes." He looked up from his cup. "What do you think, Ted?"

"I wouldn't like to tell you what I think," Stevens answered, truthfully. He was remembering those cryptic remarks Marie had made: "You're going to open a grave tonight, and my guess is that you'll find nothing." He knew that he must make himself as inconspicuous as possible, and keep a stiff face before the others, while he lived with several unpleasant possibilities. The best thing to do would be to keep Partington at his mundane theorizing. Stevens's head felt queer, and the hot coffee burnt his throat. He tried to lean back easily: discovering a bulge in his side-pocket. Bulge? It was the tin funnel with which he had filled the lanterns; he remembered now that, just as he had finished filling the second lantern, they had begun to load him with a couple of picks and a sledge-hammer, and he had automatically thrust the funnel into his pocket. He touched it incuriously, before he remembered the strange and unaccountable quirk in Marie's nature. She could never endure the sight of so ordinary an object as a tin funnel. Why, in the name of reason? He had heard of an antipathy to cats, or to certain flowers and jewels; but this . . . this was as meaningless as though some one were to shrink back at the sight of a coal-scuttle, or refuse to stay in the same room with a billiard-table.

At the same time he said, "Any theories, Doctor?"

"Not doctor, if you don't mind," said Partington, and examined his cigarette. "But it strikes me that this is our old friend the locked room again, only in a much more difficult form. We've not only got to explain how a murderer got in and out of a locked room without disturbing anything: because it wasn't only a locked room. It was worse. It was a crypt built of granite, without even the advantage of a window; and closed up not by a door, but by a stone slab weighing nearly half a ton, six inches of soil and gravel, and a concrete-sealed pavement which one witness is willing to swear has not been disturbed."

"That's what I said," declared Henderson, "and that's what I meant."

"Very well. I say that we've not only got to explain how the murderer got in and out, but *how the corpse did as well*. Very pretty. . . . . Now, we've learned nearly all the tricks and dodges in this day and age," said Partington, smiling round with broad scepticism. "We can at least pare it down by determining the only ways it could have been approached. There are four possibilities, and only four, to draw on. Two of these possibilities we can discard; subject, of course, to the examination of an architect. We can pretty well decide that there is no secret passage, and that the body is not now in the crypt. Agreed?"

"Agreed," said Mark.

"That leaves us with two more. First: that, in spite of what Mr. Henderson says to the best of his own knowledge, and in spite of the fact that he and his wife slept within twenty feet of that pavement, somebody did manage to get in during the night, and replaced the whole thing undetectably."

Henderson was so contemptuous of this that he did not even reply. He had withdrawn to a tall creaky rocking-chair with a wicker back, where he sat with his arms tight folded, rocking with such an even and determined vigor that the chair was moving away.

"Well—I don't credit that much, myself," Partington admitted. "And so we're reduced to the last and only certainty—that the body was never put into the crypt at all."

"Ah," said Mark, drumming on the table. Then he added, "And yet I don't believe that, either."

"Nor me," said Henderson. "Mr. Partington: I don't like to keep on butting in, and seem to nag and raise hell with everything you say; but, I'm telling you that's the worst idea you've had yet. It isn't as if it was only me that said so. But, if you say he wasn't put straight down in that place, you've got to accuse the undertaker and both his assistants; and honest, Mr. Partington, you know *that* ain't likely, is it? Here's how it was. Miss Edith told me to stand by the undertakers while they were doing the business, and not leave Mr. Miles's body any time, case I was wanted for something. And I did.

"You see, nowadays they don't put the body in the coffin and put the coffin in the parlor for people to go past and look at—the way they used to. They keep the body, embalmed, right on the bed until it's time to bury it; then they put it in the coffin and close it up, and the pall-bearers take it downstairs. See? That's what they done with Mr. Miles. Now, I was right in the room with 'em while they were putting it in the coffin. . . . I hadn't left it much, anyway, by my orders; the Mrs. and I sat up all night with it, the night before the funeral. . . . Well, they put it in and screwed down the lid, and right away in came the pall-bearers, and *they* took over. They took it downstairs, with me following; and," said Henderson with energy, seeking the acme of respectability, "there was judges and lawyers and doctors among the pall-bearers, and I hope you don't think *they'd* do any funny business?

"Well, sir, they carried it right downstairs, and out the back, and out that path, and down to this place, and right down into—there." He pointed. "The rest of us that didn't go down into the place, we stood around at the top, listening to the preacher. Then the rest of 'em came up out of that place, and it was over. Right away Barry and McKelsie, my men, with young Tom Robinson helpin' 'em, they started in to seal it up again; and as soon as I'd gone in and changed my clothes, I came out and directed it. And there you are."

His rocking-chair gave a last emphatic squeak, moving in the direction of an ancient radio with a potted plant on top, and rocked more slowly.

"But, damn it," cried Partington, "it's got to be one thing or the other! You don't believe in ghosts, do you?"

The creak slowed away to silence. "So help me Harry," declared Henderson, slowly, "I believe I do."

"Nonsense!"

Henderson frowned at the table, still hugging his arms.

61

"Now, mind you," he said, "I don't care much whether there's ghosts or not. I'm not afraid of 'em, if that's what you mean, not if one was to walk in the room this minute. I'm not superstitious; and being superstitious is being afraid of ghosts." He considered. "You know, I always remember what old Mr. Ballinger says to me, forty years ago, out in the part of Pennsylvania where I come from. Mr. Ballinger, he was ninety years old if he was a day; and he always wore an elegant plug hat; but there he was every day, out weeding his garden or working round the house like anybody else; and once it gave everybody a fit when we saw him right out on the roof of his house, sixty feet and more up on a sloped roof, fixing the tiles, in his shirt-sleeves and his plug hat—at ninety. Well, sir, there was an old graveyard next to his place, that wasn't used any longer and that nobody paid any attention to. And when Mr. Ballinger wanted new paving for a part of his cellar, he just hops through the fence and takes some old gravestones. Yes, sir, that's what he did.

"Well, I remember I was coming past his back yard, where he was digging, and I said: 'Mr. Ballinger, ain't you afraid something might happen to you, for taking them gravestones?' So Mr. Ballinger he leans on his spade, and he spits about a pint of tobacco juice over one shoulder, and he says: 'Joe,' he says, 'Joe, I ain't a-skeered of any dead people, and don't you be a-skeered of any dead people, either. It's these *livin'* sons-of-bitches you want to watch out for.' Yes, sir, that's just what he said, and I never forgot it. 'It's these *livin'* sons-of-bitches you want to watch out for,' he said. Yes, sir. If they're dead, they can't hurt you. Leastways, they can't hurt me; that's the way I figure it out. And as for whether there is or there isn't any, I was hearin' just the other night, on the radio, what Shakespeare said ——"

Mark did not shut him off, but was looking at him curiously. Henderson, with a blank and profound expression on his face, was looking steadily at the edge of the table, and rocking in a slow pontifical manner. Whether he believed more in danger from the dead or the living, it was plain that he had got a bad fright just the same.

"I want to ask you something," said Mark, quickly. "Did Mrs. Henderson tell you the same story she told me?"

"About the woman in Mr. Miles's room the night he died?"

asked the other, not taking his eyes from the edge of the table.

"Yes."

Henderson seemed to reflect. "Yes, she did," he admitted.

"I told you a while ago," Mark went on, turning to the other two, "that I wouldn't begin with that story, or you might not believe me. But I can tell you now, now that I don't know what to believe, myself.

"The important thing about the first part of it was (as I think I told you) that Mrs. Henderson had been away for a week, and didn't get back home that night until we had already left for the masquerade. Consequently, she didn't know what sort of costume either Lucy or Edith was wearing. . . . Wait a minute!" He looked at Henderson. "Unless you told her. Did you tell her, when she got back?"

"Me? No," growled the other. "I didn't even know what they were wearing, myself. I knew they was working on fancy-dress costumes. But fancy dress is fancy dress, and it all looks alike to me. No, I didn't say anything."

Mark nodded.

"So this is the story she told me. That night, the Wednesday night, she got back from the station about twenty-five minutes to ten. First of all she took a trip through the house, just to see that everything was in place. Everything was. She knocked at Miles's door, and, though he didn't open it, he answered her through it. Like Edith, she was worried. Clear out there at the back of the house—where we are now—nobody would be able to hear him unless he opened a window and shouted. Like Edith, she wanted to come and sit in the hall, or at least downstairs. Miles wouldn't hear of it; apparently he was annoyed. He said something like 'What the devil do you think I am, a helpless invalid? I keep telling everybody I'm quite all right. Go back to your own place.' Which surprised her, because he was usually punctiliously polite to a point of the comic. She said: 'Well, anyway, I'll come back again at eleven o'clock and see how you are.'

"Now, she was coming back at eleven o'clock, in any case, and there hangs the story.

"For a good year, ever since it's been on the air, there's a certain radio-program which she's listened to every Wednesday evening at eleven o'clock precisely. It's called, I believe," said Mark, with sardonic and full-blown hatred rather than amusement, " 'the Ingelford Soothing Hour of Sweet Music,' being in fact half an hour, being anything but soothing, and advertising some sort of soothing syrup——"

Henderson blinked, looking genuinely shocked. "It's nice music," he said, with warmth. "It's mighty nice music, and don't you forget it. Sort of restful." He appealed to the others. "What he means is, I've got a radio down here, and it's a good one. But it's been on the blink for a couple of weeks, and the Mrs. asked whether she could listen in to the Ingelford Soothing Hour on the radio up at the house."

"That's it," said Mark. "And I think we'd better emphasize the Ingelford Soothing Hour, just to show there was no idea of —well, of the dark world, of anything wrong. Do you see? Suppose the powers of hell really could lay hold, suppose they could run on our smooth rails and get into our steam-heated lives past such a shower of banalities as Ingelford's Soothing Hour . . . then I tell you the powers of hell must be strong and terrible. We huddle together in cities, we make bonfires of a million lights, we can get a voice from across the ocean to sing to us so that we needn't feel lonely; it's a sort of charmed circle, with no heaths to walk at night in the wind. But suppose you, Ted, in your apartment in New York; or you, Part, in your flat in London; or John Smith in his house anywhere in the world—suppose you went home at night, and opened the ordinary door, and heard another kind of voice. Suppose you didn't want to look behind the umbrella-stand, or go down to attend to the furnace at night, because you might see something climbing up?"

"That," said Partington, very distinctly, "is what I meant by brooding."

"Ye-es, I imagine it is," agreed Mark, nodding and grinning. He drew a deep breath. "All right. I'll go back to the story. Here's Mrs. H. hurrying up to the house, to be in time for her radio-program at eleven o'clock. I ought to explain that the radio is in a sun porch on the second floor. I won't go into much detail, because I'm going to take you over the ground. I'll just say that at one end of the sun porch there's a French door opening on Miles's room. We always asked him why he didn't use it as a private sun porch of his own—we never used it a great deal, ourselves—but he never liked it, for some reason. As a rule he kept a thick curtain across the glass door. It's an ordinary sort of porch, a whole lot more modern and modern-furnished than the rest of the house—wicker furniture, bright covers, plants, and the rest of it.

"So she went upstairs. She was afraid she was going to be late for the beginning of the program, so she didn't loiter outside Miles's door in the outer hall; she just knocked, and said, 'All right?' and when he answered, 'Yes, yes, everything's fine,' she went on round the turn of the passage into the sun porch. Miles, I should mention, never objected to the radio being used; very often, again for some reason peculiar to himself, he said he liked it; so she had no scruples about that. She turned on the bridge lamp by the radio—which is at the end farthest away from Miles's glass door—and sat down. And, in the few seconds' interval while the set was warming up, she heard a woman's voice speaking behind Miles's glass door.

"Now, she was startled a good deal. She knew Miles's usual dislike of having anybody in his room when he could avoid it; and, furthermore, she knew everybody in the house was out . . . or was supposed to be out. The first thought that came into her head (she told me next morning) was a strong suspicion of Margaret, the maid. She knew Miles's reputation as an old rip. Margaret's a good-looking girl; and Mrs. Joe swears she's often thought Miles was casting an eye in her direction; and Margaret was sometimes allowed in the room when nobody else was. (That's excluding the nurse, but then Miss Corbett wasn't what you'd call a good-looker or inclined towards dalliance.) So there sat Mrs. Joe while the radio began to tinkle, glaring at it and putting together in a rush every suspicious circumstance: Miles's anxiety to be left alone that night, his bad temper when somebody knocked at the door, and she—didn't like it."

Mark hesitated, and glanced shrewdly at Henderson before he spoke the last three words. Henderson was fidgeting.

"So she got up, as quietly as she could, and went over to the glass door. There was a faint sound as though the voice were still speaking, but the radio was on now, and she couldn't make out anything at all. And then she saw a vantage-point. A heavy brown-velvet curtain was drawn close over the door, but it had been pulled a little crookedly when it was closed. At the extreme left of the door, rather high up, there was a chink where the curtain made a bulge; and another at the right of

65

the door, lower down. By straining, you could see through either of them with one eye. She looked first through the left-hand one, and then moved across and peeped through the other. There was no light in the sun porch except that bridge lamp at the other end, so there wasn't much chance of her being seen from the other side. . . . Well, what she saw put her moral scruples at rest and convinced her that nothing of sexual luridness was going on. She had expected to find an appropriate through-the-keyhole drama, on patterned lines of wifely horror; maybe it was a let-down, but somehow the lines had got all crooked. . . .

"Through the chink to the left, she could see nothing except the wall directly opposite her across the room, rather high up. In that wall (which is the rear wall of the house) there are two windows. Between the windows stands a very high-backed curious Carolean chair; and on the wall, which is panelled in walnut, hangs a small Greuze head of which Uncle Miles was fond. She could see the chair and had a good view of the painting; but no human beings. Then she looked through the chink at the right.

"This time she saw Miles and some one else. There was the bed, its head against the wall on her right-hand, its side facing her. The only light in the room was that same dim shaded light over the head of the bed. Miles was sitting up in bed, in his dressing-gown, with an open book face downwards on his lap; and he was looking straight towards the glass door in the direction of Mrs. Joe—but not at her.

"Facing him, her back to the glass door, stood a small woman. Remember that the light was dim, and she was in silhouette against it. She did not move; she was a kind of cloud; but it seemed a trifle strange that she did not move at all. Still, Mrs. Joe was close enough to make out every detail of her costume. And she describes it simply as 'just exactly like that one in the gallery . . . you know.' She explained which one she meant, that picture supposed to be the Marquise de Brinvilliers, but yet she would not mention it directly by name; just as you"— he looked at Henderson—"will never say, 'the crypt,' but only 'that place.'

"Now, what puzzled me for a second was why she should have thought there was *anything* queer about it, anything at all. She knew that both Lucy and Edith had gone to a masquerade that night, even though she didn't know what costumes they wore: the natural thing would be to think immediately it was one of them. And, she admitted to me, she did think it presently, and realized what it must have been. What I want to emphasize is that it didn't strike her as at all weird, but only with some momentary idea that 'it looked awful funny, somehow.' And when I tried to discover what this funniness consisted in, she thought it might partly have been Miles's expression. And that expression, distinct where he sat back by the dim light, was fear."

There was a pause, and through the open windows they could hear the vast rustle of the trees.

"But, my God! man," said Stevens, keeping his voice down as well as he could, "what about the woman? What else about her? Couldn't Mrs. Henderson see anything else about her? For instance—was she blonde or brunette?"

"That's it, you see. She couldn't even tell that," Mark replied in an even voice. He clasped his hands in front of him. "It appears that she had on her head some kind of thing made of a gauze material . . . not to cover her face, but to go over her hair and hang down the back a little way . . . not very big. It went down as far as the back of the square-cut dress, which was medium low. And again (mind you, I'm only quoting Mrs. H.'s own hazy ideas) there seemed 'something awful funny' about that. It didn't seem like any right kind of head covering; more like a misplaced scarf. All these, I should judge from the narrative, were quick ideas: for it also struck her that there was something also funny about the woman's neck. I had to drag it out of the witness, and it wasn't till several days afterwards that she came round and hinted at it.

"The idea was that the woman's neck might not have been completely fastened on."

VIII

STEVENS was conscious of all things sharply: of the dingy-papered room and the once-fine leather furniture with brown seams, which he supposed had formerly been used at the house; of the many domestic photographs; of their coffee-cups, and the pile of gardening catalogues on the table; above all, of Mark's clean hook-nosed face and light-blue eyes, with the sandy brows meeting in the middle, at the head of it. The lace curtains blew a little at the windows. It was fine weather.

He was also conscious that Henderson's face had gone a muddy color, and that Henderson's rocking-chair was nearly over against the radio.

"Greatgoddelmighty," said Henderson, not above a whisper. "She didn't tell me that."

"No, you can bet she didn't," said Partington, viciously. "Mark," he went on, "for your own good, I ought to hit you in the jaw. For your own good, to stop this poisonous rubbish——"

"Look out for squalls if you do," Mark said, mildly. He did not now seem under so great a nervous strain; he was calm and puzzled and a little tired. "It may be rubbish, Part. As a matter of fact, I think it is, myself. I'm only telling you what was told and suggested to me, and trying to make it as un-emotional as a case-history: if I can. Because, whatever it is, I've got to find a way out of it. . . . Shall I keep on going? Or, if you prefer, shall I get it all out of my system?"

"Yes. Yes, I suppose you'd better," Partington told him. He sat down again. "And you're right about one thing. If you had told us this story early in the evening, it's a question whether you'd have got help."

"I know that.—Again, to soften this business a little, we must all understand that it didn't hit Mrs. Henderson, or me, with such a complete shock as my telling it may do. I mean that it wasn't so bald as that. Things grow. Now you can say, if you want to, that I'm spinning a yarn because Lucy herself wore a dress like that; and if the police ever took this thing up they would have only one idea. Yes, you can say it, but I don't think you'll believe it.

"As I say, Mrs. Henderson saw the woman there: an ordinary figure, whom she thought to be Lucy or Edith. She didn't think much more than that, except about the funniness. So she walked away, and went back to her chair by the radio to listen to the Soothing Hour. After all, she couldn't admit she'd been peeping through a curtain, by rapping on the glass and singing out, 'Is that you, Mrs. Despard?' Still, I gather that she wasn't alto-gether soothed. So when the quarter-hour interval came, for the advertising, and somebody began extolling the benefits of

Ingelford's Soothing Syrup, she went back to the glass door again, and looked through the right-hand chink.

"The woman in the Marquise de Brinvilliers dress had moved, yes. But she seemed to have moved only six inches forward, towards the bed, and she was motionless again. It was as though she were making a slow progress; and the watcher had not *seen* her move. Also, she was turned just a trifle more to the right, so that her right hand could be seen. This hand held a silver cup, presumably the one I later found in the cupboard, and held it still. Mrs. Joe thought that there was no longer an expression of fear on Miles's face, which reassured her: she says there was no expression at all.

"At this minute, such is nature, Mrs. Joe thought she was going to cough, and couldn't stop herself. She felt the cough coming up in her throat; and, when she felt she couldn't keep it down, she ran away from the door, over to the middle of the sun porch, and let it out with as little noise as she could. But, when she got back to her vantage-point again, the woman had gone.

"Miles was still sitting up in bed, his head back against the headboard. In his left hand he held the silver cup, but his right arm was shading his face with the elbow across his eyes. And the woman had gone.

"The watcher began to get panicky. She tried to see more of the room, but the chink was too small; so on a chance she flew over to the chink on the left-hand side of the door. . . .

"Now, in the opposite wall containing the two windows, the one I've described to you, there was (once upon a time) a door. This door was bricked-up and panelled-over more than two hundred years ago; but you can still see the outline of the door-posts in the wall. The door was just between the two windows, and used to lead to a part of the house which was —destroyed"—Mark hesitated again—"at the same time the door was bricked up. To throw a crumb to sanity, I'll say that there *may* be a secret door there today, though what its use would be I can't say; but I've never been able to find such a thing, and to the best of my knowledge it's just a bricked-up door.

"Mrs. Henderson wanted to emphasize that there was no possibility of mistake or deception or trickery about what she saw; she saw the Greuze head on the wall, hung in the middle

69

of where the door used to be; she saw all things between, and the top of the high-backed chair as well. She even noted Miles's clothing neatly hung up across the top of the chair. . . . But that door in the wall was opening, and the woman in the Marquise de Brinvilliers dress was going out by it.

"The door moved outwards; the Greuze head moved with it; and the door touched the back of the chair while the woman slipped through. Hitherto it had been the immobility of the woman which was somewhat terrifying. But now that she did move—or glided, rather—the movement was equally bad. Mrs. Henderson was scared half to death, and I don't know that I blame her. I tried to ask her something about the door; did it have a knob, for instance? Which would have been the important thing if it were an honest secret door with a concealed spring somewhere. But she couldn't remember. Still, she never saw the woman's face; and the door closed. A second later it was exactly the solid wall she had known. It *changed back again:* that's the only way she could express it.

"She went over to the radio and for the first time she shut off the Ingelford Soothing Hour before its end. Then she sat down and tried to think. Finally she went up boldly to the glass door, and rapped on it, and said, 'I've heard enough of the radio for tonight. Is there anything you'd like?' And Miles sang out in a quiet voice, not angry in the least, 'Nothing at all, thanks. Go down and get some sleep; you must be tired.' So she took her nerve in both hands, and said: 'Who was that in there with you? I thought I heard voices.' He laughed and said: 'You must be dreaming; there's nobody in here. Run along!' But she thought that his voice was shaky.

"And she was, frankly, afraid to stay in the house any longer. So she ran down here. Now I've told you how we found Miles dying, later, at two-thirty, and the cup I found—all of it. Mrs. H. came to me next morning, still frightened, and told me the story secretly. When she learned the sort of dress Lucy had been wearing that night, she didn't know what to think. Also, remember, she still doesn't know Miles was poisoned. Now, with the body having vanished out of the coffin, there's something more to show that neither of us is insane. As I say, there may be a secret door in that wall. But, unless it leads to a secret passage or something going down between the walls, where does the door lead to? That's the back wall of the house, with the windows in it. Finally, I'm certain at least that there's no secret passage in the crypt. There's your problem, Part, and I've tried to make it as little sensational as I can. Does it mean anything to you?"

Again there was a pause.

"That's the story she told me, all right," volunteered Henderson, rocking glumly. "And, my Lord, the trouble I had with her when we had to sit up all night with Mr. Miles's body before the funeral! She got me almost seeing things myself."

"Ted," Mark spoke out, abruptly, "what's keeping you so quiet all evening? What's the matter with you, anyhow? You're sitting over there like a stuffed horse; and everybody's had a try at suggesting something except you. What do you think?"

Stevens pulled himself together. He thought he had better show signs of interest; yes, and go over theories, if only because there was a piece of information he must have without appearing to get it. He dived after his tobacco-pouch, and polished his pipe against his wrist.

"You asked for it," he said, "so let's try. Let's take what Partington would call the only possible alternatives. Can you stand having a case made out against Lucy, as the police might do it? You understand I don't any more believe Lucy would do such a thing than I believe that—that Marie would, for instance." He chuckled, and Mark nodded as though the comparison took a weight off his mind.

"Oh, I can stand it. Fire away."

"First, then, there's the theory that Lucy gave him arsenic in that silver cup: and afterwards left the room by a secret door, or by some mechanism we can't at the moment understand. Second, there's the theory that somebody was impersonating Lucy, wearing a similar dress because she knew what Lucy wore that night; that the open chinks in the curtain were left not accidentally, but deliberately; that Mrs. Henderson was intended by the murderer to look through and see the figure of a woman with her back turned, so that afterwards she could swear it was Lucy——"

"Ah!" said Mark. "Good!"

"Third and last, there's the theory that this business actually is . . . we won't say supernatural, because people fight shy of the word . . . but un-dead and un-human and on the other side of a threshold."

71

Partington let his hand fall with a smack on the table. "You, too?"

"No, not necessarily. I'm like Mark: I believe we ought to consider every theory even if we only demolish it. That's to say, don't throw out plain evidence just because its conclusion suggests something we can't believe. So long as it remains plain evidence, that can be seen and touched and handled, treat it exactly as you would treat any other sort of evidence. Suppose Mrs. Henderson said she saw Lucy (or Edith, or any woman we know) giving Miles a poisoned cup. Then suppose she said the cup was given him by a woman dead for over two hundred years. Well, treat the actual evidence with no more or less disbelief, and do Lucy at least the justice to admit the two theories are equally incredible. If you're talking of pure actual *evidence*, there's more evidence to show this thing was supernatural than it was natural."

Partington regarded him with sceptical pleasantry. "The academic sophistry, eh? I feel I ought to put my feet up on the table and call for beer. Go ahead."

"Take the first theory," Stevens went on. He bit the stem of his pipe; he knew that, in this rush to get things off his chest, he would have to control himself sharply so as not to say too much. But the deluge had to come out, and it steadied his voice. "Lucy is guilty, then. The objection is that she has a sound alibi. Now, she was with you all evening, wasn't she?"

"Yes, practically. Or with others who could swear to her identity," said Mark, with emphasis. "That is, she couldn't have gone away without my knowing it."

"Well, were you masked?"

"Yes. That was a part of the idea; we were supposed to keep all the others guessing as to who we w—" Mark stopped suddenly, and his pale-blue eyes grew fixed.

"When did you take off the masks?"

"The usual time; midnight."

"And the poison was administered, if it was administered at all," said Stevens, drawing lines in the air with his pipe-stem, "at fifteen minutes after eleven. And a person could go from here to St. Davids in much less than three quarters of an hour, in time for the unmasking. So the policeman in a detective story says to himself, 'What if the woman her husband saw, and the guests at the party saw, wasn't Lucy Despard at all; and two women in Brinvilliers dresses switched identities before the unmasking?"

Mark sat motionless. "You asked me whether I could take it, and I'm taking it. God damn it, man, do you think I wouldn't know my own wife, in whatever kind of masquerade? Do you think others wouldn't know her? They were only domino-masks; they don't fool friends to any extent. Do you think . . ."

"Certainly I don't think it," Stevens returned, testily and truthfully. "Nor will anybody else. That's your trump card; you could bring a dozen witnesses to show it, whereas . . . But I was only piling up the thing, and giving it its worst look, to show you that there's nothing in it at its worst; and that if you only examine it without the goblins you'll see there's nothing in it. Don't go down so easily under a poser. There are harder posers in this world. Besides—" He stopped with a new idea turning in his mind. If it were possible to handle it properly, it might throw dust and blame nobody: which was what he wished. "Besides, among the alternatives I've suggested there's another which doesn't seem to have occurred to us. What if there was no murder? What if the woman, supernatural or natural, had nothing whatever to do with the business, and Miles died just as the doctor said he did?"

Partington rubbed his chin. Something seemed to be bothering him as he studied Stevens covertly; he shifted and frowned, half-amused as though at something too foolish to bring up.

"I'd like to see it turn out that way," Partington said. "So would all of us, I think; it would be the easiest way. But— what about the body disappearing from the crypt? You can make a small bet that that's too solid to be supernatural. Besides, you would never get the police to believe that the business of the woman with a cupful of arsenic was (a) a harmless ghost-story, or (b) a harmless prank of dressing-up."

"The police aren't going to have the chance," snapped Mark. "Let's go on with your alternatives, Ted. Second, some one impersonating Lucy."

"You answer it. Who could do that?"

"Anybody. Provided," Mark insisted, tapping the table, "provided you can imagine it in connection with any of our ordinary, harmless, good-natured group—why, anybody. But that's what I can't swallow. Lucy in the rôle isn't much more crazy a conception than Edith. Or Margaret, the maid. Or—"

He reflected. "Here's one thing I've always wondered, when I've read accounts of murder cases; especially about the sober, quiet, respectable little fellow who goes around for twenty years tipping his hat and paying his insurance, and then all of a sudden, without changing, he kills somebody and cuts the body up into pieces to hide it. I don't ask what made him do it—but I'd like to know what his family and his friends think about him. Do they see any change, or blink in the eye; is he changed for them? He doesn't wear his hat any differently; he still likes mock-turtle soup. Isn't he still just John K. Johnson, and nothing else?"

"You've answered your own question," said Partington, grimly, "about the impossibility of thinking of any of your own crowd as a murderer."

"Yes, but try to be human! For instance, do you think that *Edith* could be a murderer?"

Partington shrugged. "She might be. If she were, I'd cover her up, which is more than— But Edith's out of my life now; she's been out of it for ten years; and I can take an impersonal view. I'm trying to look at it scientifically. You and Lucy, or Edith and I, or Stevens and——"

"Marie," supplied Mark.

Stevens was conscious of an uneasiness when he met Partington's gaze, although it was free and ordinary, as of a man taking casual examples.

"Yes, I thought I'd heard the name," said the doctor, lightly. "What I was trying to say was, any of us, scientifically considered, might commit murder. It's a plain fact."

"You could believe that," muttered Mark, slowly, as though he were turning over a problem apart from the present, "and yet you couldn't believe anything supernatural exists. To me it's the first alternative that's a staggerer. As for the supernatural, I frankly don't know and I'm frankly inclined to doubt. But, funny thing, to me it's more credible than seeing one of us as a murderer."

"Look here, let's take the third alternative for just a second," insisted Stevens, "even if we don't believe it. Let's assume that there's something of the non-dead about it, and apply the same rules of evidence we did to the other two. . . ."

"Why," asked Mark, "do you say the 'non-dead'?"

Stevens stared at him, and met Mark's bright and steady

eyes of interest. He was not conscious of having made any slip of speech; yet the word slipped out naturally where it was not one he might naturally have chosen. His mind groped back: Cross's manuscript. The story he had been reading there, attached to the photograph, had been called *The Affair of the Non-Dead Mistress*. Was that why it had stuck in his mind?

"I asked," said Mark, "because I've found only one other person who used the term. Funny. Most people say ghosts, or some synonym. Then there's another class, the vampires, that in mythological lore are called the un-dead. But the 'non-dead'! Yes, funny. I've come across only one other person who used that term."

"Who?"

"Uncle Miles, oddly enough. It cropped up in a conversation I had with Welden a couple of years ago—you know Welden, at the College?—yes. We were sitting out in the garden one Saturday morning, and the talk had gone from gardens to galleons to ghosts, in the way it does. So far as I can remember, Welden was enumerating the various forms and types of things that go bump in the night. Up strolled Miles, looking more far-away than ever, and listened for a couple of minutes without saying anything. Then he said . . . it's a long time ago, and I only remember because it sounded odd coming from Miles, who never read a book in his life . . . he said something like: 'There's one separate type you've forgotten, sir. That's the non-dead.' I said: 'What do you mean, the non-dead, except in the sense that everything alive is non-dead? Welden's alive, and I'm alive; but I don't think I'm non-dead.' Miles looked at me in a vague sort of way and said, *'How do you know?'* Then he wandered away. Welden evidently thought he was a little bughouse, and changed the subject. I forgot all about it. But I remembered —non-dead! What does it mean? Where did you get hold of it?"

"Oh, I came across it in a book somewhere," growled Stevens, dismissing the subject. "We don't want to get mixed up in a choice of words. Ghosts, if you like the term better. You said the house never had a reputation for having a ghost in it?"

"Never.—Of course, I myself might have my own views of things that have happened here in the past; but, as Part will tell you, that's because I'm a wild-eyed cuss who could see murder in green-apple colic."

"Then what the devil," demanded Stevens, "is your link with anything wild-eyed out of the past: your link with the Marquise de Brinvilliers, for one thing? You told me tonight the family was closely associated with her. You talk about a portrait, with the face gone from acid, that's supposed to be her. Edith doesn't seem to like the picture, and prefers to call it 'Madame de Montespan' when Lucy copies the costume for a masquerade; and Mrs. Henderson doesn't even like to say its name. What's the connection between a murderess in the seventeenth century and the Despards in the twentieth? . . . Was a 'Desprez' one of her victims, by any chance?"

"No," said Mark. "Something more respectable and law-abiding than that. A Desprez caught her."

"Caught her?"

"Yes. Madame de Brinvilliers had fled from Paris and the law, which was howling after her. She had taken refuge in a convent at Liège; and, so long as she stayed inside the convent, they could not take her. But clever Desprez, as a representative of the French government, found a way around that. He was a handsome dog, and Marie de Brinvilliers (as you may have read) could never resist a strutting sword and periwig. Desprez went into the convent piously disguised as a priest; he met the lady, set her a-burning for him, and then suggested that they should go outside for a little walk by the river. She went eagerly, but it was a different sort of assignation from what she had expected. Desprez whistled, and the guard closed in. Within a few hours she was on the way to Paris in a closed coach, amid an escort of cavalry. She was beheaded and burnt in 1676." Mark paused, and began to roll a cigarette. "He was a virtuous soul who had made a thrifty and well-deserved capture of a murderess who deserved to die. He was also, to my way of thinking, a black-souled Judas just the same. . . . He was the honored Desprez who, five years later, came to America with Crispen and laid the first timbers of the Park. He died in 1706, and the crypt was built for him to rest his bones."

In the same stolid voice Stevens asked, "How did he die?"

"Of natural causes, so far as is known. The only curious thing is that a woman, who could never afterwards be identified, appears to have visited him in his room before he died. It roused no suspicion and was probably a coincidence."

Partington was amused. "Now you're going to tell us, are

76

you, that the room he occupied was the same as your uncle Miles's room now?"

"No," answered Mark gravely. "But the set of rooms he occupied then adjoined what is now Uncle Miles's room. Access to the old Desprez's rooms was gained through a door which was bricked-up and panelled-over when that wing of the house was burnt down about 1707."

. . . There was a sharp knock at the door of the little living-room. The door opened, and Lucy Despard walked in.

That knock had brought Henderson's rocking-chair skittering against the radio again. That knock had brought them all to their feet, for they had heard no footsteps. Lucy Despard was pale, and she seemed to have dressed hurriedly for travel.

"So they've opened the crypt," she said. "So they've opened the crypt."

Mark fumbled before he found his voice. He moved forward, making soothing gestures in the air. "It's quite all right, Lucy," he told her. "It's quite all right. *We've* opened the crypt. Just a little——"

"Mark, you know it isn't all right. Please tell me. What's going on? Where are the police?"

Her husband stopped, and so, in one way, did the others; everything appeared to stop except the bustling little clock on the mantelpiece. After a moment during which Stevens felt his wits thicken, Mark said:

"Police? What police? What are you talking about?"

"We came as soon as we could," Lucy said, rather piteously. "There was a late train from New York, and we managed to get a late train out here. Edith will be down in a second. Mark, what's the matter? Look here."

She opened her handbag, took out a telegram, and handed it to him. He read it twice before he read it aloud to the others.

Mrs. Mark Despard,
　c/o Mrs. E. R. Leverton,
　　31 East 64th St.,
　　　New York.
DISCOVERY RELATING CIRCUMSTANCES MILES DESPARD'S DEATH. SUGGEST YOU RETURN HOME IMMEDIATELY.

Brennan, Philadelphia Police Dept.

IX

STEVENS never forgot Lucy Despard standing just inside the open door, her hand on the knob, with the great elms behind her, and the lanterns still burning on the path. Lucy's calm, alert, good-humored face had a strength about it: it was the alertness you first noticed in the light-brown, shining eyes, with very dark lashes, which were her best feature. She was small, and rather sturdy, but with an unconscious grace; nor was she exactly a beauty, except in the attractiveness and vigor of her expression. Now she was so pale that a few freckles stood out. She wore a plain tailored suit which contrived to suggest fashion without your knowing why; there was a touch of color only in her plain close-fitting hat, and the black hair was worn low over her ears.

Thus she stood while Mark read the telegram again.

"This is a hoax of some kind," said Stevens. "That telegram's a fake. No police officer would send a nice courteous message like that, inviting you to come home like a family lawyer. He'd phone New York and have them see you.—Mark, there's something damned fishy about this."

"You're telling me," said Mark, explosively. He took a few steps up and down the room. "Yes; whoever sent that telegram, it wasn't a cop. Let's see. Handed in at a Western Union office in Market Street at 7:35. That doesn't tell us much. . . ."

"But what *is* wrong?" cried Lucy. "The crypt's open. Aren't they here? Aren't—" She looked over Mark's shoulder, and stopped. "Tom Partington!" she said, blankly.

"Hello, Lucy," said Partington, with ease. He moved forward from the mantelpiece, and she mechanically gave him her hand. "It's been a long time, hasn't it?"

"It has, Tom. But what on earth are you doing here? I thought you were in England. You haven't changed much. Yes, you have—a little."

Partington made the customary remarks. It appeared that Lucy and Mark had not been married at the time he went away. "Only a flying visit," he explained. "I got in this afternoon. I thought, after ten years, you wouldn't mind putting me up for a couple of days. . . ."

78

"No, of course not! We're——" Again mechanically, Lucy glanced over her shoulder as though wondering how to deal with something. They all heard the footsteps now, and Edith came in.

Edith had more of a glitter about her, although at the same time she carried herself more consciously. It was not that she had grown stiff or at all fussy when only a year or more into her thirties; it was only that you were never quite so certain of her, or the movements of her mind, as you were with Lucy; and Stevens did not like to think what she might be in twenty years' time. She was taller than Lucy, and more slender in a thin-boned fashion. She had the family carriage, the family looks—the brown hair, the blue eyes, the air of brushing things aside as Mark did—and she was very good-looking, though inclined to become a trifle hollow round the eyes. It was noticeable that Henderson, as soon as she came in, backed away and began to assume a guilty look. Yet Stevens had often had a curious impression that she somehow concealed more weakness than her decisive actions would indicate. She wore a fur coat, and no hat; she was dressed (how could you describe it?) fluently. And when she saw Partington she stopped, but her expression did not change.

"Edith," said Lucy, hurriedly opening and shutting the catch of her handbag, "they *say* there's nothing wrong. They say that telegram's a fake and there are no police here at all."

But Edith was looking at Partington, and she smiled at him.

"This time," she announced, in a pleasant voice, "I can honestly say that one of my premonitions has come true. You do bring trouble with you, don't you?"

And she extended her left hand. Then she looked round the group.

"You've all been entrusted with the secret," she said. "Well, Mark, what is it? Lucy and I have been horribly worried, and we may as well know."

"It's a joke, I tell you. That telegram——"

"Mark," she said, "was Uncle Miles poisoned?"

A pause. "Poisoned? Good God, no! What put that idea into your head?" Mark looked at her face, which was more composed than Lucy's, but she was under no less a strain. And then Mark's nimble brain hit on a fairly shrewd lie, to be used on the spur of the moment. He put his arm round Lucy, patting

79

her on the back, and then turned again to Edith with a deprecating air. "You'll know it sooner or later, so you might as well
know now. It's no real trouble, no foolish business like murder. . . . Where did you get the idea, I wonder? . . . and
nothing to concern the police. But it's not pleasant. Somebody
has a taste for sending fake telegrams—and letters. I got a
letter, too—anonymous. It said that Uncle Miles's body had
been stolen out of the crypt." Evidently aware that this lie
sounded thin, he went on hurriedly: "I mightn't have paid
much attention to it if Henderson hadn't noticed a few queer
things. We decided to open the crypt and see. And I'm sorry
to tell you, Edith, it's true. The body's gone."

If anything, Edith seemed more nervous than before. She
did not appear to doubt him, but it was clear that the news
gave no reassurance.

"Gone?" she repeated. "But how could it—why—I mean
. . . ?"

Partington interposed smoothly, taking up the cue.

"Yes, it's a bad business," he said, "but it's not new, though
I don't believe the racket has been tried in America for over
fifty years. Did you ever hear, Edith, of the Stewart case in
1878? The body of the millionaire was stolen out of his tomb
and held for ransom. The same thing happened at Dunecht;
they burgled a crypt there, very much like this one. It's something our modern racketeers don't seem to have thought of."

"But that's horrible!" cried Lucy. "Kidnapping a dead body
—for ransom?"

"Mrs. Stewart offered twenty-five thousand dollars to get
it back." Partington was speaking easily, fixing their minds,
turning them away as though he led them by the hand. "In the
Dunecht case, they caught one of the gang and found the body.
The trial was peculiar because there were no precedents in
law. Every case of body-snatching recorded up to that time had
been for the purpose of selling the body to a medical school;
but this was different. I believe the man got five years. . . . In
this case, I suppose they've got it into their heads that you are
a family who want to keep the old crusted vault intact, and that
you'll pay through the nose to get your uncle's body back again."

Lucy drew a deep breath, disengaged Mark's arm, and leaned
on the table.

"Well, at least it's better than—you know—the other thing.

Yes, and I'll admit it: it's a relief. Edith, you had me horribly scared." She laughed at herself, for her evident feeling of relief had her almost on the point of tears. "Of course we'll have to tell the police now, but——"

"We'll do nothing of the kind. Do you think," said Mark, "that I want poor old Miles's body knocked around now like a dead fox with a pack of hounds on it? Yah! Not likely. If body-snatchers have taken it, as Part says, then I'm willing to pay to avoid a rumpus. Now cheer up, both of you."

"I might as well tell you," said Edith, very gently, "that I don't believe one word of it."

Was there such a thing, Stevens wondered, as a handsome hag? The term was over-strong to a ludicrous extent, for hag would be the last word you might apply to Edith; but it conveyed the idea of a handsome woman whose doubts shadowed her face in that fashion.

"You don't?" said Mark. "You don't still have those hallucinations about poison, do you?"

"Please come up to the house," Edith urged. She looked at Henderson. "Joe, it's very cold up there. Will you make up a fire in the furnace?"

"Yes'm. Right away," said Henderson, meekly.

"It's getting late," began Stevens, "and if you'll excuse me——"

Edith turned quickly. "No! You must come along, Ted; you *must*. We must thrash it out, all of us; Mark, make him come along. Don't you see there's something wicked, really wicked in this? Whoever sent that telegram is playing with us and laughing at us; it's no gangsters who want to steal a body for money. Why should anyone send a telegram like that? I've had a feeling something like this was going to happen, ever since—" She stopped, and looked out again to where the two lanterns were burning, and shivered.

It was a quiet group which went up the path. Partington tried to talk to Edith; but, although there was no outward constraint between them, there was a wall between, nevertheless. Lucy alone seemed inclined to treat the matter as no very deadly thing; as unpleasant and even terrible, but as nothing that need throw the world out of focus. "Whoever sent that telegram is playing with us and laughing at us"—these were the words of which Stevens kept thinking.

They went into the house, and through the big hall to the library at the front. It was the wrong sort of room to have chosen for such a conference; it put the past, and the odors of the past, too much in the midst of them. The library was very long and broad, but not very high, with a raftered ceiling. The walls had been plastered over and calcimined a dull green, to freshen it up with modernness; but the original room broke out in odd nooks and corners, including the fireplace. Edith sat down in an over-stuffed chair by a bright lamp, with the shuttered windows for a background. To the rarefied modern taste which sees beauty in the present style of decoration, it would also have seemed cluttered with odds and ends gathered by Miles or Mark from travels in far places: but the gusty seventeenth-century, with its fondness for toys and gauds, would have felt at home in it.

"Listen, Edith," urged Lucy, "must you bring all this up? I don't like the way you're going on; I didn't like what you were saying, coming out in the train. Can't we just forget it, and——"

"Well, we can't," said Edith, shortly. "You know as well as I do the rumor is all over the place that there's something wrong here."

Mark whistled. "Rumor?"

"And if you ask me who started it," said Edith, "I should say it was Margaret . . . oh, unintentionally, I admit. Something just—slipped. She may have heard the nurse talking to me, or the nurse to the doctor. Don't look so surprised, Mark. Did you know that that nurse was suspicious of us all the time she was here, and that's why she kept her room locked up whenever she wasn't in it?"

Mark whistled again. He glanced uneasily at Partington and Stevens. "Deeps," he said, "within deeps. Or wheels, or—Everybody seems to be keeping back something. Suspicious of us? Why?"

"Because," answered Edith, "some one stole something out of her room."

"I wish you wouldn't keep dribbling out bits of information." Mark spoke rather irritably, after a silence. "You always used to speak out hot and strong. Stole what? When? Why?"

"It was the week-end before Uncle Miles died—the Saturday. I think it was the 8th." She looked at Stevens. "You remember, Ted? You and Marie were up here to play bridge; only

Mark broke up the whole affair, and for some reason it degenerated into telling ghost stories?"

"I remember," said Lucy. She was trying to disguise her uneasiness with a pleased expression. "Mark had taken one too many highballs, that was the reason. But why do you say 'degenerated' into telling ghost stories? It was good fun."

Edith went on: "The next morning Miss Corbett came to me and said she seemed to have mislaid something. I thought she talked a little snappishly, and asked what it was. She became more definite. She asked me whether anyone had accidentally taken something from her room; something the doctor had ordered for Miles in such-and-such an event (she didn't specify what). She described it as a small square bottle. Finally, she added that it could be of no use to anybody, that it was a deadly poison if given in quantity, and that if somebody had taken it in mistake for smelling-salts—which she thought wasn't very likely—it would be a kindness to return it. Just like that. I don't think she was suspicious, exactly. She thought somebody had been monkeying about."

Mark almost slipped. Stevens saw that it was on the tip of his tongue to say, "But they wouldn't keep arsenic for a medicinal purpose"; he opened his mouth, but shut it in time. Mark looked at Partington in a puzzled way, and then back to Lucy. "Did *you* hear anything of this, Lucy?"

"No." She was troubled. "But that's not surprising, is it? I mean, they naturally go to Edith rather than me; anybody would. If I were somebody else, I shouldn't go to me—if you understand."

Mark stared round.

"But damn it all, somebody must have—" He stopped. "What did you say to Miss Corbett, Edith? What did you do?"

"I said I'd make enquiries."

"And did you?"

"No." The weakness, the doubt, the indecision, came back to Edith's practical face; she would run up to the breach, clanging arms, but she always hesitated there. "I suppose I was . . . afraid. Oh, I know it sounds silly, but I was. I don't mean I didn't say anything; I threw out enquiries, in a casual way, as though I were talking about a bottle of Uncle Miles's medicine; and nobody connected the two. I didn't mention poison. I *couldn't*."

"This is a devil of a mess," said Mark, "but it couldn't have been ar . . . h'm. Here, Part, this is a job for you. What sort of stuff could it have been?"

Partington frowned. "Depends on the doctor's ideas as to possible developments in the case; I haven't heard his own complete diagnosis. But it might have been several things. Just a minute! Tell me, Edith, did the nurse report this to the doctor?"

"Doctor Baker? Yes, of course. So, naturally, I didn't think——"

"And Doctor Baker had no hesitation about saying your uncle died of gastro-enteritis? He had no suspicion, in other words?"

"None at all!"

"Then," said Partington, curtly, "stop worrying. You can take it from me that it couldn't have been any medical preparation which could possibly have caused the same symptoms as your uncle died with—like antimony, for instance. Isn't that obvious? Otherwise both the doctor and the nurse would have been on to it immediately. . . . No; probably it was a sedative, or else a heart-stimulant like digitalin or strychnine. Those things can be deadly, as you know; but all of them are what are called neurotic poisons; and—again take it from me—not one of them could have caused the symptoms with which your uncle died. Far from it! So what are you worrying about?"

"I know," murmured Edith, miserably, and scratched her nails up and down the arm of the chair. "I know that, I told myself that all the time, and I knew it couldn't be. Nobody would do a thing like that!" She smiled, or tried to. "But with Miss Corbett locking her door every time she went out of her room afterwards, and even locking it on the night Miles died, after the little bottle had been returned . . ."

"Returned?" said Mark, quickly. "Yes; that's what I was going to ask you. What happened to the bottle? Baker didn't just let it float round the house, and laugh ha-ha, did he? You say it was returned?"

"Yes. Evidently on the Sunday night. It was gone only twenty-four hours, you see, so there wasn't time for a real fuss or hue-and-cry. Yes, it was the Sunday night; I remember because Marie had just been up to say hello and good-bye, that she and Ted were driving to New York next morning. I went

84

out of my room about nine o'clock, and met Miss Corbett in the upstairs hall. She said: 'Thank some one for me; the bottle has been returned. Some one put it on the table outside Mr. Despard's, meaning Miles's, door.' I said, 'Is everything all right?' She said, 'Yes, everything seems all right.'"

"Then I see it," declared Mark. "It means that Miles himself stole them."

"Miles himself?" repeated Edith, blankly.

"Exactly," said Mark, afire with a new idea. "Now tell me, Part, could that bottle have contained *morphia* tablets?"

"Yes, certainly. You say he had been in considerable pain, and wasn't sleeping well."

"And you remember," cried Mark, turning on the others and pointing his finger, "that Uncle Miles was always wanting more morphia than the doctor would give him, when he had the pains? Right! Now suppose Miles stole the bottle out of the nurse's room, lifted a few tablets—and returned it? Here, wait a minute! On the night he died he called out for somebody to go down to the bathroom and get the 'tablets that would ease pain,' didn't he? Suppose those were the stolen morphia tablets, which he put into the medicine-chest in the bathroom so the nurse wouldn't find them in his own room?"

"No, that won't work," said Lucy. "There were no morphia tablets there. Those were only the ordinary veronal tablets we keep there all the time."

"All right; but does the other part of it sound reasonable?"

"Yes, it's entirely possible," agreed Partington.

"What is the matter with all of you?" asked Edith. She spoke in a calm tone; but then, unexpectedly, her voice went up almost to a scream. "Don't you see what is happening? The first thing you tell me is that Uncle Miles's body has been stolen. Stolen!—taken out of that vault and maybe chopped up or heaven knows what; and that's the least, the easiest thing, that could have happened. Yet you all take it very calmly, and try to hoodwink me with gentle talk. Oh yes, you do. I know it. Even you do, Lucy. I won't stand it. I want to know what's going on, because I know it's something horrible. I've been through too much in the last two weeks. Tom Partington, why do *you* want to come back and torture me? All we need now is Ogden making jokes, and it would be complete, wouldn't it? I tell you I won't stand it."

Her hands were shaking, and so was her neck: it was the handsome hag come back again, fluttering on the edge of tears in the big chair. Lucy was regarding her with steadily shining brown eyes: Stevens noted the steady shining of that look, as of a sympathy too great to be expressed. Mark lumbered over and put his hand on her shoulder.

"You'll be all right, old girl," he said, gently. "You need one of those veronal tablets yourself; and a lot of sleep; that's all. Why not go upstairs with Lucy, and she'll give you one. You trust to us—whatever has happened, we'll handle it. You know that, don't you?"

"Yes, I know it," Edith replied, after a silence. "It was silly of me to fly up like that; but, really, I feel better for it. You can't help the thoughts that come sometimes." (An echo of Mark himself.) "I know I shouldn't lay any foolish claim to being psychic, although a gipsy woman once told me I was; but, Lucy, I knew it was unlucky of you to make a copy of that dress in the picture, and wear it. It's always been considered unlucky. I know we're supposed to have outgrown all that, and yet I shouldn't like to go through the world balancing common sense like a pail of water on my head, and not dare to bend my back or turn my head in case the pail should spill. Still, it's a plain scientific fact, isn't it, that the changes of the moon have a direct bearing on certain types of human brain?"

"For the moon is the mother of lunatics," said Partington, dreamily, "and has given to them her name.—Some say so."

"You always were a materialistic soul, Tom. Still, there's truth in it. And is there anything queerer or more outlandish in the supernatural,"—at this point Stevens saw the expressions on his companions' faces change; he had no doubt his own did as well—"than," said Edith, "that somebody's mind should be affected from umpty-million miles away by a—well, a——"

"A piece of green cheese," said Partington. "I suppose not, but why this mysticism?"

"Because I hope you'll laugh me out of it. I want," said Edith, grimly, "to see a piece of green cheese. Remember, Lucy, there was a full moon on the night Uncle Miles died; and how we admired it; and you and Mark sang coming home? When a person begins to think about the non-dead . . ."

Mark spoke as quickly and heartily as though he had never

heard the term; but his voice was, if anything, a trifle too loud. "The what? Here, where did you pick up that rubbish?"

"Oh, I read it in a book somewhere. . . . I'll not go upstairs, but I will go out and find something to eat. Come on, Lucy. I'm tired; I'm dreadfully tired. Will you make some sandwiches?"

Lucy bounced up briskly, and winked at Mark over her shoulder. When they had gone, Mark prowled twice round the room with moody absorption before he stopped by the fireplace and began to roll a cigarette. Somewhere in the room a concealed radiator began to rattle and whack as Henderson in the cellar got up steam.

"We're all keeping something back from one another," Mark said, and flicked a match across the stone. "You notice that Miles's body disappearing didn't seem to startle them—or at least Edith—overly. They didn't want details. They didn't want to peep. They didn't want to . . . Oh, damn it, what's in Edith's mind? The same thing that's occurred to us? Or is it only night-time and the jimjams? I wish I knew."

"*I* can tell you," growled Partington.

"And she read it in a book, too. The non-dead. She read it in a book, the same as you did." He looked at Stevens. "I suppose it was the same book?"

"It couldn't very well be. This one is still in manuscript. It's Cross's new one—Gaudan Cross. You've read some of his stuff, haven't you?"

Mark stopped. The match was still burning in his hand as he stared at the other; he held it levelly, and, as though at some instinct beyond sight, just before it burnt his fingers he twitched it out. But he continued to look at Stevens with eyes wide open.

"Spell that name," he requested. Then he said: "It can't be. You're right, Part; I am getting the jimjams, and very shortly my imagination will put me in a state where I need a sedative myself. The proof of it is that I've seen that name dozens of times, and yet it never occurred to me (in my right senses) to see any resemblance before. Gaudan Cross . . . Gaudin St. Croix. Ho-ho-ho! Give me a kick, somebody."

"Well, what about it?"

"Don't you see?" demanded Mark, with a sort of ghoulish eagerness and mirth. "When you get into such a business as this, all you've got to do is let your imagination run and it'll see anything you like. Here's Gaudan Cross, probably a harmless old son of a what not, who writes pretty good stuff; and yet by looking at that name you can construct a whole cycle of the non-dead, and a return for ever of the slayers and the slain. . . . Gaudan Cross. Gaudin St. Croix, in case it interests you, was the celebrated lover of Marie D'Aubray, Marquise de Brinvilliers, who first instructed her in all the arts of poison. He died before her; in his laboratory over his own poison-kettle; otherwise he'd have been broken to death on the wheel, or sent to the stake by the tribunal they established to deal with poisoning cases—a tribunal called The Burning Court. It was through St. Croix's death that they discovered evidence, in a certain teakwood box, which led Madame to be suspected. She had grown tired of him, and had grown to hate him; but that's neither here nor there. St. Croix died somehow. . . . Dumas says he was trying to manufacture a poison gas when his glass mask slipped and he fell forward dead of its fumes with his head in his own cauldron . . . and the hunt was up for Madame la Marquise."

"I've had about enough of this for one night," said Stevens, curtly. "If you don't mind, I'll get along home now, and we can wall up that tomb in the morning."

Partington looked at him. "It's a fine night," Partington said. "I'll walk down as far as the gate with you."

X

THEY walked down the drive, under great trees and past places of shrubbery. For a time both Partington and Stevens were silent. Mark had gone out for a last conference with Henderson, and to put the tarpaulin used for the tennis court over the entrance to the crypt. Stevens wondered what (if anything) was on Partington's mind; so he opened the attack.

"Any ideas about the theft and return of the bottle," he asked, "beyond what you told the women?"

"Eh?" Partington roused out of his abstraction. He had been looking up at the starlight, shuffling his feet on the gravel as though to pick up the way. Now he considered. "Well, as

I told you, I like to get things down on regular charts. We know that a small bottle, containing something which in a large dose would be a deadly poison, was stolen and afterwards returned. That's all we know, and all we're likely to know until we see that nurse. We don't even know whether it was in liquid or solid form, which is the most important point.

"But there are two possibilities as to what the stuff might have been. First, it might have been a heart-stimulant like strychnine or digitalin. If that's so—well, frankly, it's very bad. It might mean that the poisoner (if there is a poisoner) hasn't finished his work."

Stevens nodded.

"Yes," he said, "I'd thought of that, too."

"But I can tell you," said Partington, dryly, "that it isn't a very likely possibility. If anything like that had been stolen, the doctor would have had the house pulled apart until that sort of stuff was found or accounted for. Neither he nor the nurse seems to have been unduly disturbed. Irritated, rather; do you follow me? Similarly, what was stolen couldn't have been an irritant poison like antimony, for instance, or you can bet your last dollar they'd never have given a death-certificate testifying that Miles died of natural causes.

"No. Our second possibility is much more likely. Our second possibility is Mark's theory that a few morphia tablets were stolen."

"By Miles?"

Partington scowled. This point seemed to bother him more than any other.

"Yes, it's quite possible. And it's the easiest way out. We're all looking for easy ways, aren't we?" The pouched eyes turned round in the starlight, curiously. "But there are a few points against tacking it on Miles. There's the return of the bottle. Now, we know that Miles's room was next to the nurse's. We know that, after the bottle was stolen, the nurse kept her door locked—that is, the door to the hall. But there was another door, communicating directly with Miles's room, and presumably she didn't keep *that* locked as well against her patient. So, if Miles stole the bottle and wanted to return it, why didn't he walk through the communicating door and put it in her room? Why did he put it down on a table outside the door?"

"That's easy to answer. Because the nurse would know right away who had done it. He would be the only one with access to her room."

Partington stopped in the drive, and swore faintly.

"I'm getting soft-headed in my old age," he said. "That's plain, certainly. Also—look here, I was wondering whether the nurse might not have locked the communicating door to Miles's room as well as the door to the hall. She may have suspected Miles as well."

"Yes, but even so, what are you driving at?"

"The motive," Partington insisted, doggedly. He made a slight movement of his hands in the air, as of an intelligent man who finds difficulty in articulation. "The reason why morphia was stolen. Either Miles stole it, or somebody else did. Now, if Miles stole it, the motive is understandable. But suppose someone else stole it? What could it have been used for?

"It couldn't have been for another murder. A few tablets were stolen—two or three, perhaps. Not many more, or the doctor would have made a fuss about it. As a rule, morphia is given in quarter-grain tablets. It would take two or three grains to put a man in danger; four grains to make certain of the business. So it couldn't have been for murder. Next, disregard the idea that anybody in the house is a drug-user. If that had been the case, you can be pretty certain the whole bottle would have been taken and never returned. Next, was somebody merely aching for a good night's sleep? It's possible; but in that case why use such strong stuff, that'll blot you straight out and isn't necessary unless you're suffering? Why not take ordinary veronal tablets, such as were admittedly in the bathroom? In either case, why be so damned secretive as to STEAL the morphia?—So, if none of these things sounds reasonable, for what purpose did the thief want it?"

"Well?"

"Well, suppose you had a night's work to do," pursued the other, with toiling lucidity, "and there was somebody who might hear you or see you at it? If you dosed that person with a quarter-grain of morphia, the coast would be clear, wouldn't it?"

Again he stopped and turned around, with a lowering frown under the starlight. His eyes fixed on Stevens, and the latter braced himself for what he thought was coming. As though in a picture he saw, in that moment, the night when Miles had been poisoned: the night when he and Marie were at the cottage less than a quarter of a mile away; the night when he himself had tumbled over with unaccountable drowsiness before ten-thirty.

Then Partington spoke unexpectedly.

"You see, I was thinking of our biggest problem—the opening of the crypt and the vanishing of the body. But if both Mr. and Mrs. Henderson had been dosed with morphia, would they have heard body-snatchers at work? Would they?"

"By God, that's true!" Stevens exploded, with a violence of relief. He hesitated, nevertheless. "That is——"

"You mean that others in the big house might have heard the racket? And also that Henderson swears the entrance to the crypt hasn't been disturbed? All right; admit he's honest. But that's not the only consideration. It's true *we* made a lot of noise and a lot of mess. But remember what we did. We broke the paving-stones with wedges and hammers. Now remember how those stones are laid down. They're rather thin pieces of crazy-paving, set together with mortar in the crevices like the pieces of a jigsaw puzzle put together with glue. There's no concrete, adhesive concrete, under them, only soil and gravel. Why couldn't a whole piece of the paving have been cut out in one long block—and simply lifted up? It would require a little breaking of the mortar, but only one thin short line at either end. It could be tilted up on its side in one piece, and set down again like the stone slab under it. And Henderson, seeing an apparently whole pavement under him, could reasonably say what he did. You might make a mess taking out the soil and gravel. But remember that there were still traces of a mess from the opening of the crypt a week before."

Stevens wanted to believe it as much as Partington evidently did. If any doubts stirred at the back of his mind, they were not ones at which he could coherently think. He was occupied with another sort of problem, a more personal one. He and Partington had now come to the gates of the park. They stopped to look down into the breezy dimness of King's Avenue, where street lamps were far between, and the tarred surface of the road glistened in a black river underneath. Partington, who had lost some of his earlier diffidence, now went back to it. He added, more mildly:

"Sorry to talk so much. The point is, we've got to believe something. Edith's told you that I'm a materialist. I don't see any reason for being so scornful about that. I admit it. Edith told me a lot of things in the old days. She always believed that I performed the abortion on that girl because the business was my doing, and all because the kid worked in my office. Who was the materialist then, I ask you?"

That last drink, snatched before he left the house, had almost unlocked his tongue. A note of intensity would come up; and then, with equal suddenness, he would check himself in that way he had evidently learned so well.

"Yes, it's true. A primrose by the river's brim, a yellow primrose was to him: or to me at least: and not whatever it was the sage wanted me to see in it. It's not a symbol of nature, or a mystic bud flowering into an excuse for bad verse. There are a lot of things more beautiful to look at—a running horse, for instance, or the skyline of New York. Your damned primrose is simply a tolerably pretty flower that might make an ornament in a bowl on the table. Don't you agree?"

"Yes, I suppose I do."

"And, consequently, all this talk about ghosts and non-deads and—" He stopped, with a lumbering smile, faintly short of breath. "I WILL shut up, in spite of myself," he added. "You can depend on it, I've hit on the right explanation of the crypt. Unless, of course, there was some hocus-pocus on the part of the undertaker."

"The undertaker," repeated Stevens. "Do you mean J. Atkinson?"

He saw the doctor's eyebrows raise. "Old Jonah? Yes. I suppose you know him; he's quite a character. He must have buried several generations of Despards, and he's a very old man now. That's why our friend Henderson was so petulantly certain the undertaker couldn't have gone in for any hocus-pocus: because it was Atkinson. Mark pointed out his place again to me as we were coming through tonight. Mark says old Jonah's son has taken over the active work now, and is putting some ginger into the business. Old Jonah was a great favorite of Mark's father; Mark's father, with some sort of private joke, used to ask him whether he was still in his 'blameless tea-shop,' or his 'corner'; I don't know what he meant. Possibly— Oh, good-night."

Stevens, convinced that the man had passed that hazy line of tipsiness which separates sense from wandering, had bidden him good-night and set off briskly down the avenue. The briskness was a pose. He wanted to be alone. He did not slow down his quick walk until he heard Partington's own footsteps crunch away to silence up the drive.

Then he wanted to do something as a physical outlet for bewilderment: shake his fist, or hit something, or merely clench his teeth in hopeless perplexity. The whole thing was too intangible. If he could (as Partington wished to do) resolve these doubts into ruled lines, if he could have some cool-witted person stand in front of him and ask clear questions, he might understand better. He tried to ask himself the questions. Do you believe that there is something wrong with Marie? But how do you mean, wrong? In what particular way? And there was where the mind drew back, almost physically, as though from a fire; where the mind shut itself up. He could not answer the questions because he could not voice them. They were too fantastic. After all, through what odd crack in his brain had this idea been able to penetrate? Was there any actual evidence for it? It all centred round a photograph, not six square inches of cardboard; a similarity in names, a devilish similarity of feature—yes, and the fact that the photograph was missing. That was all.

He stood now before his own white cottage, staring at it. The light over the front door had been put out. There was no light anywhere in the house, except a red, shifting gleam through the window of the living-room. Evidently Marie had kindled a fire in the fireplace, which was curious, because she had a dread of fire. It gave him a vague sense of alarm.

The front door had been left on the latch. He opened it, and went into the dark hallway only faintly illumined by flickers from the living-room on the right. Nor was there any sound except the almost indistinguishable drawing and sizzling of the fire; green wood must have been used.

He called, "Marie!"

Still there was no sound. In the same sort of uneasiness he went into the living-room. Beyond any doubt the fire had been built of green wood; it was a large one, almost smothered in oily yellowish smoke through which little spiteful curls of flame wormed through. He heard its oozing hiss and pop. A little of the smoke spilled out over the hood of the stone fireplace. It was odd, he thought, how those split gleams distorted the familiar room, but there was light enough to see by the chimneypiece a tabouret bearing a plate of sandwiches, a thermos-bottle, and a cup.

"Marie!"

When he went out into the hall again, his footsteps seemed to fall so heavily on the floor that even the hardwood creaked. He brushed against the telephone table, and put his hand automatically on the briefcase still lying there. This time he could feel that the briefcase was open, the manuscript lying left askew inside, as though it had been taken out hurriedly and replaced.

"Marie!"

Even the treads of the stairs creaked noisily under him as he went up. A bedside lamp was burning in their room at the back of the house; but the room was empty and the lace coverlet of the bed undisturbed. On the mantelpiece a busy little clock animated the quiet: it was five minutes past three. Then he saw the envelope, propped up on the bureau.

DEAR TED [said the note]: I've got to go away for tonight. Our peace of mind depends on it. I'll be back tomorrow, and please don't worry, only it's horribly difficult to explain. Whatever you think, *it's not what you're thinking.* I love you.

MARIE

P.S.—I must take the car. Have left food for you, and coffee in a thermos-bottle, in living-room. Ellen will be in tomorrow morning to get your breakfast.

He folded up the note and put it back on the bureau. Finding that he was suddenly very tired, he sat down on the bed and saw the room as a blank neatness in front of him. Then he got up and went downstairs again, turning on lights as he passed. When he examined the briefcase in the hall again, he found what he expected to find. In Cross's book there had been twelve chapters. Now there were eleven. That dealing with Marie D'Aubray, guillotined for murder in 1861, was gone.

III

ARGUMENT

"Lawrence was up in the bedroom one day, and picked up a little mask covered with black velvet, and put it on for fun and went to look at himself in the glass. He hadn't time for a proper look, for old Baxter shouted out to him from the bed: 'Put it down, you fool! Do you want to look through a dedd man's eyes?'"

—M. R. JAMES, *A View from a Hill*

XI

AT SEVEN-THIRTY next morning, refreshed by a shower and clean clothes, Stevens was coming downstairs again when the front-door knocker rapped hesitantly.

He stood holding to the banisters, feeling suddenly tongue-tied and averse to answering. If it were Marie, he did not know what to say to her, despite the speeches he had rehearsed throughout the night. The downstairs lights were still on; the living-room was full of stale smoke. He had not gone to bed that night, for the reason that he could not sleep. His head ached a little, and his wits were none of the best: to thrash endlessly through the same thoughts all night is not a good preparation for a meeting, since you never say what you have so carefully planned to say. Even the hallway looked unfamiliar. Dawn had come up strangled in a cold white mist which pressed with a dead stare against the windows. The only heartening thing was a faint hiss and bubble from the dining-room, where he had connected the coffee-percolator.

He went downstairs, into the dining-room, and carefully disconnected the plug of the percolator. That early morning aroma of coffee was good. Then he answered the door.

"I beg your pardon," said an unfamiliar voice, and his heart sank again. "I wondered——"

He was looking down at a sturdy woman in a long blue coat. Though her manner was hesitant, a smoldering anger underlay it. She seemed vaguely familiar. Her face, under a small blue hat pulled down in waves as though by violence, was not good-looking; but it was attractive and intelligent. Sandy eyelashes hardly flickered over her alert brown eyes. She looked (as she was) direct, brisk, and capable.

"I don't know whether you remember me, Mr. Stevens," she went on, "but I've seen you at the Despards' several times.

I noticed that your lights were on, and so—I'm Myra Corbett. I nursed Mr. Miles Despard."

"Oh, Lord, yes; certainly! Come in."

"You see," she said, giving another twitch to her hat and glancing in the direction of the Park, "something seems to have gone wrong. Last night some one sent me a message to come here immediately——"

Again she hesitated. Another of those damned telegrams, Stevens knew.

"—but I was out on a case and I didn't get it until an hour or so ago, when I got home. Then, for various reasons"—the anger deepened—"I thought I ought to come as soon as possible. But when I went up there I couldn't make anybody hear. I hammered and hammered on the door, but nobody answered it. I can't imagine what's wrong. So, when I saw your light, I wondered if you would mind my sitting down and waiting a little while."

"Not in the least. Please come in."

He stood back, glancing down the road. In the gauzy white mist a car was chugging up the hill, its lights full on. The car swerved, rather erratically, slowed down, and then drew up at the curb.

"Heigh-ho, heigh-ho!" bellowed a voice. It was Ogden Despard, beyond a doubt.

A car door slammed and Ogden's rather tall figure moved up the walk out of the mist. He wore a light camel's hair topcoat, under which showed the legs of dress-trousers. Ogden was one of the throwbacks which occur in most families: he resembled nobody in it. He was dark, sleek, and somewhat hollow-cheeked, with a blue chin. Though he needed a shave this morning, his black hair was carefully brushed and shining like a helmet; the face, with lines drawn slantwise under the eyes, was so sallow that you could see every pore. His heavy-lidded dark eyes moved from the nurse to Stevens in amusement. Though he was only twenty-five (and often acted younger) he looked older than Mark.

"Good morning," he said, shoving his hands into his pockets. "The reveller returns. Hello! what's this? An assignation?"

Ogden usually made remarks like this. He was not exactly unpleasant; but it is true that you seldom felt comfortable with him. Stevens, who was in no mood to meet him this morning, led Miss Corbett into the hall, and Ogden sauntered after them, closing the door.

"The place is in a mess, I'm afraid," Stevens said to the nurse. "I've been working most of the night. But I've got some coffee boiling. Would you like a cup?"

"I would, very much," answered Miss Corbett, and suddenly shivered.

"Coffee!" said Ogden, with a contemptuous "puh!" "That's no way to greet a man on the morning after a party. But if you've got such a thing as a drink on the premises——?"

"There's whisky back in my den," said Stevens. "Help yourself."

He saw the nurse and Ogden eyeing each other curiously; but neither spoke, and a curious air of tension had begun to grow. With a stolid face Miss Corbett went into the living-room. Stevens got the percolator from the dining-room, went out into the kitchen, and began rummaging after cups. In the midst of it Ogden pushed through the swing door, carrying several fingers of whisky in a glass; he was humming to himself, but keeping a wary eye out. While he opened the door of the refrigerator in search of ginger ale, he spoke conversationally.

"So our Myra," he observed, "also got a telegram from the police department, requesting her presence here. The same as I did."

Stevens said nothing.

"I got mine last night," Ogden pursued, "but I was on a good round of parties, and I really couldn't let it interrupt my drinking. Still, I'm glad the cops have got on the trail. It'll establish what everybody knows." He took out the tray of ice-cubes, batted it in the edge of the sink, and dropped one cube into the glass as carefully as though he were sighting a plumb-line. "By the way, I see you spent the night helping Mark open the crypt."

"What makes you think that?"

"I'm not dumb."

"No. Not in any sense."

Ogden put down the glass. His sallow face looked somehow crooked and out of line. "What do you mean," he said quietly, "by that crack?"

"Look here," said Stevens, turning round. "In my present mood I would take great pleasure in pasting you straight

99

through that china-closet. Or anybody else who gave me the excuse. But, for the sake of keeping both our heads, try not to start a row at seven-thirty in the morning. Hand me the cream out of the refrigerator, will you?"

Ogden laughed. "Sorry. But I don't see why *you* should be on edge.—It's my detective instincts. There are a couple of Mark's self-rolled cigarettes in your den, where I got the whisky. There's also a little drawing of the paving over the crypt, evidently done by Mark. Oh yes; I notice everything. It helps. I knew Mark was considering doing something like that; it was why he wanted us all away from the house last night." His long face grew sharp and malicious. "What did the police say when they got there and found you boys having so much fun taking up the pavement?"

"The police didn't arrive."

"What?"

"What's more, it seems pretty evident that those telegrams didn't come from the police."

Ogden, chewing at his lower lip, glanced at him sharply. Something shifted and altered in Ogden's look. "Yes, I'd thought of that, too. But—but— Look, Stevens. You might as well tell me, because I'll only find it out when I go up to the house. There were three people back in that room of yours. I saw three glasses. Who was the third?"

"A Doctor Partington."

"Whe-ew!" said Ogden. His look grew thoughtful, with a far-off pleasure in it. "There's something big coming. The unfrocked one, of course. I thought he was safely in England. If he ever finds out— But I might have known it. I see it all now, said he, said he." (This was another irritating mannerism of speech peculiar to Ogden.) "Of course. Mark wanted him to do the whatisit, poke into the innards, and so on. Come on: you might as well tell me. What did you find?"

"Nothing."

"Eh——?"

"I mean we found literally nothing. The body wasn't in the crypt at all."

Ogden drew his head back, and on his face there was a look of such pale scepticism that it was like a light. Stevens had never disliked his face so much as at that moment. After peering for a moment, Ogden slid his hand into the refrigerator, gravely drew out a small dish of applesauce, and pushed it across the drain-board towards the other.

"What you mean," he said, "is that you staunch friends and allies, rallying round the flag, found that poor old Uncle Miles was full of poison. And you hid the body somewhere so that nobody should learn about it. I know Mark's opinion about the police. Do you mind *my* opinion?"

"No. I'm just telling you what happened, that's all.—Mind holding that door open while I carry these cups in?"

Ogden, evidently startled but now very thoughtful, absent-mindedly complied. Stevens could see that his nimble brain was searching into corners, looking after loopholes; and he fixed on his host a gaze of disconcerting quality.

He said: "By the way, where's Marie?"

"She's—still in bed."

"Odd," remarked the other. Stevens was aware that there was probably nothing behind this; that Ogden merely said it on his usual principle of trying to make some one uncomfortable, even out of a casual word; but, nevertheless, it tightened the strain. Carrying the two cups, Stevens went on ahead to the living room. Ogden, who had apparently come to a decision, strode past him and saluted Miss Corbett with his glass.

"I had intended, my dear, to speak to you before," he began. "But the fact is I needed liquid sustenance first. *À votre santé.*"

Stevens thought: If he keeps on using these *clichés*, I think I'll empty this cup over his head. Miss Corbett, who was sitting with her hands folded calmly in her lap, eyed Ogden, and was not impressed.

"About this matter of the telegrams," Ogden continued; "what does yours say?"

"What makes you think I got a telegram?" inquired the nurse.

"Must I explain it to everybody? All right; here goes again. Because I got one myself. As I told our friend here, I got it last night. But I was barging from house to house in a round of parties, and so——"

"If you were barging from house to house in a round of parties," said Miss Corbett, practically, "how was the telegram delivered to you?"

Ogden's eyes narrowed. He seemed about to say something in a manner of heavy and coy sarcasm, intended either to be

101

crushing or to rouse the other person's indiscreet ire. But he had the shrewdness to see that this would be wasted.

"Like to pin me down?" he enquired. "As it happens, I dropped in at the Caliban Club, and it was waiting for me there. No, seriously: why not be frank with me? You'd better, you know, for I'll find it out when I go up to the house. And you can speak frankly in front of Ted Stevens; he knows all about it. Besides, in a way, it's probably a very good thing you were called here. Your evidence may be important to the police. You can't tell."

"Thank you," said the nurse, gravely. "My evidence about what?"

"About Uncle Miles being poisoned, of course."

"You have absolutely no reason to say that!" she cried, and coffee spilled over the edge of her cup. "If you have anything to say, say it to Doctor Baker. There was no reason whatever to think——" She stopped. "I'll admit I was worried afterwards; not on account of any suspicion like that, but because I was out on the night it happened, and I'd——"

"And," interposed Ogden, pouncing instantly, "you had carefully locked up your own room; and, if he *did* happen to have a seizure, nobody could get in to get any remedies. So possibly, in one way, you killed your own patient. If that isn't culpable negligence, I don't know what is. It won't be altogether good for your reputation when the story comes out."

This was what was worrying her, they all knew, and Ogden deftly led her on.

"Oh, I'll admit you had reason," he conceded. "Uncle Miles was supposed to be practically well again. And, since somebody had just stolen a deadly poison out of your room—well, maybe you were right to try to prevent it happening again. But didn't it make you suspicious at all? I know Baker's an old fogey, and just about at his dotage; but didn't it make even him suspicious? A poison is stolen from you on Saturday. On the following Wednesday night, Uncle Miles dies. Very funny, if you ask me."

Ogden was enjoying himself so much that his purpose, which was trouble-making rather than detection, suddenly became apparent; the nurse realized it, and her face became stolid again.

102

"You seem to know a lot more than anybody else," she told him, wearily. "So you ought to know this. *If* anything was taken, in the first place it couldn't possibly have caused anybody's death; and, in the second place, it couldn't possibly have caused any of the symptoms Mr. Despard had."

"Ah, I thought not. So it wasn't arsenic. What was it?"

She did not reply.

"Besides, you must have some idea who took it——"

Very carefully Miss Corbett put down her empty cup on the table. Stevens, who felt himself that morning abnormally sensitive to atmosphere, knew that a new element had come into the questioning. He felt that for some reason the nurse was looking round the room; looking towards the stairs; waiting or listening; and that she wished very strongly to talk if only Ogden's presence were removed.

"I haven't any idea," she answered, calmly.

Ogden was persuasive. "Come now. You'd better tell me, you know. It'll make things easier for your conscience, and I'll only find out——"

"Haven't you used that dodge often enough?" asked Stevens, curtly. "For God's sake try to act like a human being. You're not the police. Actually, you don't give a curse what happened to your uncle——"

The other turned round, alert and smiling. "Now I wonder what *you* have to hide?" he asked. "I'm certain there's something. You haven't been your old bright jolly self all morning. It may be that bunk you told me about Uncle Miles's body having disappeared. Or it may not. I reserve judgement." He glanced away again as the nurse got to her feet. "Not going? Yes? Let me give you a lift up to the house."

"No, thank you."

The air of tension had grown. Ogden remained watching them, like a fencer keeping two opponents in play; his neck was hunched down into the upturned collar of his camel's hair coat, and on his long face there was the same sceptical smile. He remarked that his company did not seem welcome. He thanked Stevens for the whisky, observing judicially that, all things considered, it was not bad; and he left them. Not until the front door had closed did the nurse follow Stevens out into the hall. Then she put her hand on his arm and spoke rapidly.

103

"The real reason I came here," she said, "was that I wanted to speak to you. I know it's not important, but just the same I thought I'd better warn you that——"

The front door opened abruptly, and Ogden appeared in the aperture.

"Excuse me," he said, grinning like a wolf. "But this does look like an assignation, after all. It's a terrible thing, with your wife sleeping upstairs, too. Or is she? I notice that the car's gone from your garage. Just to preserve the purity of public morals, I really think I'd better tail along with you when you go up to the house."

"Get out," said Stevens, calmly.

"Tut, tut," Ogden urged, pleasantly. "Also, I see that the lights in your bedroom are full on. Does Marie sleep with the lights on?"

"Get OUT," said Stevens.

Though Ogden's manner did not change, something in this appeared to make him think he had better. He had the best of the situation, nevertheless, for he drove his car at the speed of two miles an hour, following them as they went up to the Park. Although the mist had thinned a little, it was still impossible to see more than a dozen feet ahead; hedges, trees, and lamp-posts swam suddenly out of the white murk, and in the Park itself there was an utter deadness of silence. There was an utter deadness of silence until they heard the sharp rapping of the front-door knocker rise insistently, and die away, and rise again. Its effect, in that muffling fog, was not pleasant.

"God!" Ogden said, abruptly. "You don't suppose they're all——?"

What peculiar quirk had struck Ogden at that moment, Stevens could not tell; but the car, slowly as it was going, almost collided with one pillar of the *porte-cochère*. On the front porch, shifting from one leg to another during the intervals in which he pounded at the door, stood a thick-set man with a briefcase in his hand. He turned round at their approach, and looked at them dubiously. He was a neat figure in a dark-blue overcoat and soft grey hat. Under the down-turned brim of the hat he had humorous eyes, a sandy complexion, and a broad jaw; his face looked much younger than his age, for the sides of his hair were slightly grizzled. His manner was genial and almost deprecating.

"Any of you live here?" he asked. "I know I'm early, but it seems like there's nobody at home." He paused. "My name is Brennan. I'm from police headquarters."

Ogden whistled two notes and his manner grew much calmer; yet Stevens had a feeling that he was suddenly on the defensive. "Well, well, well. I imagine they were all up late last night, and that's why they're sleeping in. Never mind; I've got a key here somewhere. I live here. I'm Ogden Despard. And what would you be wanting with us this morning, Inspector?"

"Captain," said Brennan, looking at Ogden. Ogden did not seem to be making himself popular with anyone this morning. "I believe it's your brother I want to see, Mr. Despard. If——"

The front door opened so suddenly that Brennan's hand over the knocker was left in the air. The hall inside looked even bleaker and gloomier than the mist-filled porch, despite a heavy sooty drizzle from the chimneys which filled the mist with grit. Partington, fully dressed and shaven so closely that he looked scrubbed, was surveying them from the doorway.

"Yes?" he said.

The captain cleared his throat. "My name is Brennan," he repeated. "I'm from police headquar——"

At this point Stevens became convinced that the whole world was wrong. Partington's face had turned a muddy color. He put his hand on the post of the door, sliding it down for a better grip; and if he had not held to the door it seemed that his knees might have buckled under him.

XII

66 **A**NYTHING the matter?" asked Brennan, in an ordinary tone. It was so completely matter-of-fact that it helped Partington pull himself together in a second, as though you had jerked the wires of a loose doll.

"Police headquarters," he repeated, in a noncommittal growl. "Yes. Of course. No, nothing's wrong. Or, if I told you what it was, you wouldn't believe me."

"Why not?" asked Brennan practically.

Partington blinked a little. He seemed so puzzled that for a moment Stevens wondered whether he was drunk; but Partington dispelled that idea as a new thought appeared to strike him.

"Brennan!" he said. "I knew that name was—Look here, are you the man who sent those messages to everybody, asking them to come home?"

The captain looked at him. "We seem to have got the wires crossed," he said, patiently. "Can I come in and talk this over before we get 'em more crossed? I didn't send any messages. What I want to know is who sent *me* one. I want to see Mr. Despard, Mr. Mark Despard. The Commissioner sent me to see him."

"I don't think the doctor is quite himself this morning, Captain Brennan," said Ogden, with unction. "In case you've forgotten me, Doctor Partington, I'm Ogden. I was at school when you—left us. Also, in case you've forgotten, this is Ted Stevens, whom you met last night. This is Miss Corbett, who nursed Uncle Miles."

"I see," said Partington. "Mark!"

Yellow light penetrated into the hall as the door to the big front room opened, and Mark stood in the doorway. Behind every move that was made now there was a curiously repressed and muffled significance, like a note of warning. It was like seeing the edge of some crisis whose meaning just eluded the spectator. Mark stood loosely, and yet drawn up, with the light along the side of his face. He wore a heavy grey sweater with a rolled collar, which gave his shoulders a topheavy look.

"Well, well, well, well," said Ogden. "We seem to have run into some trouble, brother. This is Captain Brennan of the Homicide Bureau."

"I'm not from the Homicide Bureau," said Brennan, a faint roar beginning to be distinguishable under his voice. "I'm attached to the staff of the Commissioner of Police. Are you Mr. Mark Despard?"

"Yes. Come in here, please."

He stood to one side. He might have added, "The-doctor-will-see-you-in-a-minute" in the same tone of voice; it was not like Mark, and it was a bad sign.

"We're a little disorganized here this morning," he went on. "My sister has had a rather bad night. (Miss Corbett, will

106

you go up and see her?) Also, the cook and the maid are away, and we've been trying to get breakfast in the best way we can. This way. Ted—Partington—will you come in here, too? No, Ogden, not you."

Ogden could hardly believe his ears. "Oh, tut, tut! What's the matter with you, Mark? Of course I'll come in. Don't try to pull any of that stuff on me. After all——"

"There are times, Ogden," Mark continued, "when I feel for you a true brotherly affection. There are times when you are the life and soul of the party. But there are also times when your presence is definitely an encumbrance. This is one of them. Go on out to the kitchen and get yourself something to eat. Now I warn you."

He closed the door as the other three went into the front room. The shutters were still on the windows as they had been last night, the lamps still burning; there seemed hardly a hiatus in time. At Mark's gesture Brennan sat down in an overstuffed chair, where he put his hat and briefcase on the floor beside him. Without his hat Brennan was revealed as a middle-aged, shrewd-looking man with grizzled hair carefully brushed to hide the bald spot, a pleasant jaw, and a young face. He seemed hesitant about how to get down to business. Then he took a deep breath and unlocked his briefcase.

"I suppose you know why I'm here, Mr. Despard," he said, "and I suppose I can talk in the presence of your friends here. I've got something I want you to read." From the briefcase he took an envelope and a sheet of notepaper neatly typed. "I got that letter just about this time yesterday morning. As you can see, it was addressed to me personally, and mailed from Crispen on Thursday night."

Mark unfolded the letter without haste. At first he seemed to be studying it without reading it. Then, without lifting his eyes, he began to read it aloud.

"Miles Despard, who died at Despard Park, Crispen, on April 12th, did not die a natural death. He was poisoned. This is not a crank letter. If you want proof, go to Joyce & Redfern Analytical Chemists, 218 Walnut Street. The day after the murder, Mark Despard brought them a drinking-glass that had contained milk, and a silver cup that had contained a wine-and-egg mixture. The cup had arsenic in it. This cup is now locked up in Mark Despard's desk at home. He found it somewhere in Miles Despard's room after the murder. The body of a cat formerly belonging to the house is buried in a flower-bed to the east of the house. Mark Despard buried it there. The cat had probably drunk some of the mixture with arsenic in it. Mark did not do the murder, but he is trying to cover up.

"The murder was done by a woman. If you want proof of this, see Mrs. Joe Henderson, who is the cook. She saw the woman in Miles Despard's bedroom on the night of the murder, handing him the same silver cup. You can catch her away from the house and make her tell you. But go easy, as she does not know it is murder, and you will learn a lot. You will find her staying with friends at 92 Lees Street, Frankford. It is to your advantage not to disregard this.

AMOR JUSTITIAE."

Mark put the letter down on the table. "I like that business about Amor Justitiae. It's not much as a model of composition, is it?"

"I don't know about that. The point is, Mr. Despard, it's true.— Now just a minute," Brennan added, more sharply. "I've got to tell you that we had this Mrs. Henderson at City Hall yesterday. And I've been sent here by the Commissioner, because he's a personal friend of yours, to help you."

"You're a damned funny sort of detective," said Mark. And suddenly he began to laugh.

Brennan grinned broadly in reply. Stevens thought he had never seen a more complete puncturing of tension, a more sudden cessation of hostilities. The real reason for it occurred to him at last; and it occurred to Brennan too.

"Yes, I could feel what you were thinking the minute I walked in here," he declared. His startled grin became a chuckle. "Let me ask you something. Did you expect me to come charging in here, pointing my finger in everybody's face, insulting people right and left, and roaring for blood? Listen, Mr. Despard. I can tell you this: the cop who acted like that would get his pants thrown out of the police department so quick you couldn't see 'em for dust. Especially if the party concerned happened to have an ounce of influence, or was a personal friend of the Commissioner's: like you. When people write those stories, there's one thing they seem to forget—and that's politics. But *we* can't forget it. And there's more to it. We have a job to do. We try to do it as well as we can, and I think we do it pretty well. We're not a side-show or a monkey-house. And the ambitious young fellow who tries to turn us into one, and make a splash for himself, is the one who doesn't get on with the department. That's only common sense. As I say, I'm here representing Mr. Cartell, the Commissioner——"

"Cartell," repeated Mark, and sat up. "Of course. He was——"

"So," concluded Brennan, with a broad gesture, "what about telling me the whole truth? I've told you this so that you'll see where I stand; and the Commissioner wants me to help as far as I can within the law. Is it a deal?"

This, Stevens reflected, was probably the one course which would have won over Mark Despard. Captain Brennan was not only a representative of the head of the department; he was a clever man. Mark nodded, and Brennan opened the briefcase again.

"First of all, though," he said, "you'll want to know about my end of the business, to show that this isn't any bluff.

"As I told you, I got that letter early yesterday morning. Now, I know all about you here; I've got a cousin who lives down in Merion. So I took that letter straight to the Commissioner. He didn't think there was anything to it, and neither did I. But I thought I'd better go round and see Joyce and Redfern, the chemists. And," said Brennan, running his finger down a typed sheet, "that part of it was right, anyway. You went to them on Thursday, April 13th. You took a glass and a cup for analysis. You said you thought your cat had been poisoned, and the cat had been lapping some stuff out of one of these two. You asked them not to say anything about it if anybody asked. You came back next day and got the report. Glass O. K., but two grains of arsenic in the cup. Description of cup: about four inches in diameter, three inches high; solid silver; a design like flowers round the top; very old." He raised his eyes. "Correct?"

In the ensuing minutes Brennan demonstrated that, beyond doubt, he had a way with him. Mark always said afterwards that it was like being lured into a purchase by an expert salesman: so painlessly, so imperceptibly, that before you knew what you were doing it suddenly occurred to you that you had promised to buy the article. Brennan—with a bland and catlike pleasantness, his ear inclined, his grizzled head bent over his notes—was as confidential as a Balkan diplomat. He could mention even the weather in terms of one imparting a grave secret. But he received as much information as he gave. Imperceptibly he got Mark to tell the story of Miles's illness, of Miles's death

109

and the events of that night, of the finding of the cup in Miles's room; and he established that, if poison had been drunk at all, it must have been drunk out of that silver cup.

Then Brennan went on to tell how Mrs. Henderson came to give her evidence. This part of it was not clear. But, Stevens guessed, Brennan had probably gone to Frankford in the guise of a friend of Mark's, had seen Mrs. Henderson, and had encouraged her in her natural tendency to gossip. For—Brennan admitted—Mrs. Henderson had no suspicion that anything was wrong until she was invited to come to City Hall and repeat her statement to the Commissioner of Police. Afterwards, Brennan also admitted, she had departed in tears and hysterics, swearing that she had betrayed the family and that she could never bring herself to look on their faces again.

From a typed copy Brennan read the statement made by Mrs. Henderson about the night of April 12th. And, in essentials, it was exactly the same thing she had told Mark. There was only one thing absent from the police record—the intangible quality of atmosphere. This record contained no suggestion of anything supernatural or even supernormal. It contained merely the statement that Mrs. Henderson, at 11:15 p.m., had peeped through a gap in the curtain and seen a woman in Miles's room. At this time Miles had been in perfect health. The visitor was a small woman who wore "queer old-fashioned clothes," or fancy dress. Mrs. Henderson had supposed that it was Mrs. Lucy Despard or Miss Edith Despard. She knew that both had gone to a masquerade that night; but she had just returned from a visit to Cleveland, had not seen either, and did not know what costumes they were wearing. The visitor in "queer old-fashioned clothes" had been carrying a silver cup whose description corresponded with that later found to have contained arsenic, and had given this cup to Miles Despard. Miles was seen to have the cup in his hand, although he was not actually seen to drink from it.

So far, the record had sounded all the more damning since it was shorn of atmosphere and suggestion. All the same, Stevens wondered how Brennan's matter-of-factness would treat the end of the story—the visitor's exit through a door which did not exist.

Then Brennan came to it.

"Now, Mr. Despard," he confided, "the only part of it that

wasn't just straight was right there. Mrs. Henderson says that this woman 'walked through the wall.' It's right here—'walked through the wall.' She couldn't or wouldn't make it clearer than that. She said the wall 'looked like it changed, and then changed back again.' Get me? All right. Well, the Commissioner said to her, 'I think I know what you mean. You mean the door to a secret passage, don't you?' That made sense, naturally. I know myself that this is a very old house."

Mark had been sitting back rather stiffly, his hands in his pockets and his eyes fixed on the detective. His face was as inscrutable as Brennan's. "And what," he asked at this point, "did Mrs. Henderson say to that?"

"She said, 'Yes, I guess that's what it must have been.' And it's the thing I wanted to ask you. I've heard a lot about secret passages, but, to tell you the truth, I never actually SAW one. A friend of mine claimed he had one in his attic, but it was a fake; it was only the place where they kept the fuse-box, and you could see the door if you looked close. So, naturally, I was pretty interested. There's one in that room all right, isn't there?"

"So I've heard."

"Yes, but there *is* one? You could show it to me, couldn't you?"

For the first time Mark seemed to feel that he was fighting on his own ground, with words rather than facts.

"Sorry, Captain. They didn't have fuse-boxes in the seventeenth century. Yes, there was once a door there. It led to another part of the house, which has been burned down since. The trouble is, I've never been able to find the catch or spring that opens it."

"All right," said Brennan, eyeing him. "The only reason I asked was that, if you could have shown Mrs. Henderson was lying beyond any doubt, we wouldn't have needed to be suspicious of anybody but *her*."

After a pause, during which Mark seemed to be cursing inaudibly, the captain went on.

"So that was the situation we had on our hands. If we believed her, we had a cut-and-dried case. And there's no use saying we didn't believe her. I can sort of smell a liar the minute I see one." He gave a slight wave of his hand, looking round the room. "We had the time of the murder fixed at

111

about 11:15. We had the cup containing arsenic, seen in your uncle's hand. We had a description of the dress worn by the woman——"

"You had everything, in short," said Mark, "except any actual evidence that murder had been committed at all."

"That's right!" Brennan agreed, instantly, and tapped the briefcase. He seemed pleased that Mark should have appreciated the point. "So you see how we were situated. First we phoned Doctor Baker and asked privately, what he thought of the idea of Mr. Miles Despard being poisoned. He said we were crazy. He said it was impossible, though he admitted that the symptoms with which Mr. Despard died might have been the symptoms of arsenical poisoning. Of course his attitude was plain. No family doctor wants to start trouble of that kind if he can help it. If there's an exhumation order, and an autopsy, and it turns out that he was wrong—well, it's just too bad for him. Next the Commissioner tried to get in touch with you, to see what you had to say to all this. But he couldn't locate you, at either your office or your home. . . ."

"No," said Mark, who was regarding him with a hard and wary stare. "I was in New York. I went to meet a friend of mine just arriving from England. Mr. Partington over there, as a matter of fact."

Partington, who had been sitting by the fireplace with his clasped hands on his knees, looked up. The shadows showed deep wrinkles in his forehead, but he did not comment.

"Yes. We found that out," Brennan answered, briefly. "Now face the facts," he went on. "A woman in masquerade costume was in the room. We knew from Mrs. Henderson that your wife and your sister, and you as well, were at a masquerade at St. Davids on that night. It looked as though it must have been one of the two: pretty certainly your wife, because Mrs. Henderson—the day afterwards—saw the costume Mrs. Despard had been wearing, and admitted it was like the dress worn by the woman in that room. Easy now! I'm just telling you.

"But yesterday we couldn't get hold of either your wife or your sister because both of 'em were in New York too. So the Commissioner decided to check up on all your movements for the night of the 12th. He could do it without kicking up a rumpus, because he knows the man who gave the party, and knows a lot of the people who were there.—Now, Mr. Despard, I've got a full report on all of you, particularly for those critical times around 11:15. If it's all right with you, I'll give you the gist of it."

There was a sort of bursting pause. It was very hot in the room, where two centuries seemed to wait and listen. Out of the corner of his eye Stevens had seen the door move; somebody must have been listening from the first. He thought it was Ogden. But, as the door opened still farther, he saw that it was Lucy. Lucy Despard came in very softly and stood in the corner by the door, her hands straight down at her sides. She was so pale that the faint freckles stood out on her face; and her hair, parted at one side as though with an angry sweep of the comb, showed dead black against it; but she looked mutinous.

"First of all," Brennan pursued, without looking at her or seeming to notice her presence, "we'll take you, Mr. Despard. Yes, yes; I know nobody would be likely to mistake *you* for a small woman in a low-cut dress. But, to prove the absence of any funny business, we'll just take it in order. You've got a cast-iron alibi for the whole evening, especially as you didn't wear a mask. Two dozen people are willing to swear where you were at any given time. I needn't give you all the dope because it's not important. But it's established that you couldn't have left the house and come here. So that's that."

"Go on," said Mark.

"Next there's Miss Edith Despard." Brennan ran his eye down the sheet. "She got there with your party at about 9:50. She was wearing a white hoopskirt outfit with black trimmings, a white bonnet, and a black domino mask. She was seen dancing between 10 and 10:30. At about 10:30 the hostess met her. Your sister had managed to tear some lace bloomer, or pants, or some damn thing, that she was wearing under the hoopskirts——"

"Yes, that's right," assented Mark. "She was still grousing about it when we came home."

"——and she didn't like it. So the hostess told her there were bridge tables in another room, and asked her if she would like to play bridge. She said she would. She went to this room, and naturally she took off her mask. From about

113

10:30 until 2 A.M., when all of you went home, she was playing bridge. There's a whole crowd of witnesses of this. Result: complete alibi."

Brennan cleared his throat.

"Now we come to your wife, Mr. Despard. She was wearing a silk dress colored blue and red, with wide skirts and things like diamonds in it. She didn't have a hat, but had a gauze scarf over the back of her head. She also wore a blue domino mask with lace on the edges of it. She started dancing right away. At about 10:35 or 10:40 there was a telephone call for her——"

"A telephone call!" said Mark, sharply, and sat up. "A telephone call at somebody else's house? Who was it from?"

"That's the part we can't get," snorted Brennan. "We don't know who answered the phone. The only reason it was noticed at all was because some man dressed like a town-crier (nobody seems to know who he was, including the host and hostess) started going among the dancers imitating a town-crier and saying Mrs. Mark Despard was wanted on the phone. She went out. Next, the butler saw her come into the front hall about 10:45. The butler is sure of this. There was nobody else in the hall. She was going towards the front door, and she didn't have her mask on. The butler noticed her especially because he saw she was going out, and he went to open the door for her; but she hurried out before he could get there. As it happens, the butler stayed in the hall. Well, about five minutes later Mrs. Despard came back again—still not wearing her mask. She went across towards the room where they were dancing, and was asked to dance by a man dressed as Tarzan. She had two successive partners after this: we've got the names of both. At 11:15 she was dancing with some one everybody noticed—a big figure about seven feet tall, thin as a rake, and with a skull for a head——"

"By God, yes!" Mark cried, softly, and struck the arm of the chair. "I remember now. It was old Kenyon—Judge Kenyon, of the Superior Court. I had a drink with him afterwards."

"Yes. We found that out. Anyhow, it was noticed; because the host said to somebody, 'Look, there's Lucy Despard dancing with Death.' They both noticed this because Mrs. Despard leaned back and lifted up her mask to get a better look at Death. The time, as I say, was exactly 11:15. Result——"

Brennan put down the paper.

"Complete alibi," he said.

XIII

A GREAT weight had gone from Mark Despard. He straightened up in the chair; he seemed gradually to commence to see things; and in this shaken condition he acted with what was—for Mark—something like a flourish. He jumped up from his chair and turned towards Lucy.

"Let me," he said, in a rolling voice like an actor's, "present you to the lady who danced with Death. Captain Brennan, this is my wife."

He somewhat marred the effect of this by adding in a peevish tone, "Why the devil couldn't you have told us all this as soon as you got here, instead of fooling around for so long and making us feel like murderers?" But Stevens's attention was concentrated on Lucy and Brennan.

Lucy had come forward immediately, with her free and easy stride, and that manner of hers which put everyone at ease. Though her light-brown eyes had a twinkle of amusement, she was still pale and she did not seem so relieved as a spectator would have expected. Stevens noticed that she glanced quickly at Mark.

"I think you know, Captain," she said, "that I overheard everything you were saying. I'm rather sure you intended me to. But there are a whole lot of things that—that should have been discussed before, and are only just coming out now. I— I—" Her face tightened, and momentarily she was on the edge of tears. "I never knew there was so much behind this. It would have been better if I had. Anyhow, I'm terribly grateful to you."

"Oh, that's all right, Mrs. Despard," said Brennan, surprised. He stood in front of her, shifting from one foot to the other and avoiding her eye. "Just the other way round, I'd say. But I'm telling you it's a good thing you decided to come back after you went out, that night of the party, and the butler saw you come back. You can see for yourself you'd have been in a jam if you hadn't."

"By the way, Lucy," Mark put in, casually, "who was that telephone call from? Where were you going?"

She made a gesture of her wrist towards him without looking at him. "That doesn't matter. I'll tell you about it later. —Mr. Brennan, Mark asked you a minute ago why you didn't tell him all these things flat out as soon as you came in here. I think I know the reason. I've heard of you. In fact, I've been warned against you, in a way." She grinned. "No offence, but tell me, is it true that at City Hall you're known as Foxy Frank?"

Brennan was unabashed. He returned the grin and made a deprecating gesture. "Oh, I wouldn't believe everything I heard, Mrs. Brennan. The boys——"

"They say, to put it vulgarly," Lucy told him, severely, "that you could talk a crook out of his back collar-button, and arrest him afterwards. Is that true? And if it is, have you got anything else up your sleeve?"

"If I have, I'm going to tell you what it is," he replied, and stopped suddenly. "Where did you hear about me?"

"Hear? I don't know. It stuck in my mind, somehow. From the Commissioner, maybe. But why? When we all got those telegrams from you, telling us to come home——"

"Yes, that's what I mean. I didn't send you any telegrams or messages. But somebody sent me one; I mean that letter signed Amor Whateveritis. Whoever wrote that had all the dope, and had it straight. Who did write it?"

"I think I can tell you that," snapped Mark.

He strode across the room to where, in the clutter along the walls, stood a square desk-like box in walnut, covered with a cloth. Pulling the lid up with a bang, he revealed a folding typewriter-desk with a rather dusty Smith Premier machine. After searching in vain for some paper, Mark compromised by whipping an old letter out of his hip pocket and rolling the back of it into the machine.

"Try this," he suggested, "and compare the typing with the typing on that letter."

Brennan gravely fitted on a pair of owlish shell-rimmed glasses, sat down like a maestro at a piano, peered at it for a few moments, and then struck gingerly. *Now is the time,*

116

he wrote, *for all good men*— The typewriter pecked sharply, like a hen after corn; Brennan studied it and sat back.

"I'm not an expert," he admitted, "but it strikes me you don't need to be. There's no fingerprint plainer than this. They're the same. Somebody in the house wrote it, all right. Got any idea who it was?"

"OGDEN wrote it," said Mark, patiently. "Ogden wrote it, of course. I knew that the minute I looked at the letter. Ogden wrote it because he's the only person in the house who could have written it. Look." He turned to Stevens and Partington, fiery with the certainty of a new idea. "That part about me burying the cat was a dead give-away. Do you remember last night, when I was telling you about it? I told you that, while I was just finishing the burying, the lights of Ogden's car came up over the hill and I was afraid he had seen me? Well, he did see me. Only he didn't say anything. He watched."

Lucy's eyes were moving from corner to corner of the room. "And you think he sent the telegrams to us, too? But, Mark, that's horrible! Why should he do a thing like that?"

"I don't know," Mark replied, rather wearily. He sat down in the chair and ruffled the hair at his temples. "There's no real harm in Ogden. I mean that. He wouldn't—that is, *intentionally*—I'm not making myself quite clear, but the point is he probably didn't think there was anything really wrong. He simply did it to make a little trouble and watch, people jump. Ogden is the sort of person who, if he were giving a jolly little dinner party, would invite two notorious enemies and seat them together at the table. He can't help it; he's like that. That quality sometimes makes great scientists, sometimes great sneaks, and sometimes both. But as for thinking there was anything actually——"

"Oh, rubbish, Mark," said Lucy, with asperity. She was in a flouncing, bouncing mood, possibly because she appeared worried. "You simply cannot seem to believe there's ever anything wrong with anyone. There's something wrong with Ogden. He's—changed, somehow. He was never so bad as this before. And he seems positively to hate Marie Stevens. (Sorry, Ted.) Do you mean to say he could write a letter like that, practically accusing a member of his own family of murder, and not think there was anything wrong?"

"How should I know? He's certainly been one first-class

117

spy, the damned young whelp! I wonder he didn't guess we were going to open the cryp——"

Mark stopped dead. There was a palpable silence in the room, broken by a slow, measured tapping. Brennan, at ease in the straight chair by the typewriter, had removed his glasses and was tapping them on the top of the desk. Brennan regarded the company with grim affability.

"Go on," he said. "Go on. Don't stop there, Mr. Despard. You were going to say, 'open the crypt.' I've played square with you, and I've been waiting for you to play square with me."

"Foxy Frank—" said Mark. He opened his mouth and shut it again. "Do you mean to tell me you know about that, too?"

"Yes. That's what's been worrying me. That's what's been on my mind. That's why I don't know what in—" Brennan's almost elephantine delicacy in front of a woman made him break off and roar *thunderation* with some effect of anticlimax—"to make of this nightmare, this foolishness, this jungle of unadulterated bunk! And I've been waiting for you to tell me what you found in the crypt."

"If I told you what we found there, you wouldn't believe me."

"I'd believe you all right. You bet I would. Mr. Despard, I know every move you and your friends made yesterday, from the time you met Doctor Partington at pier 57 in New York. There was a 'tail' on you."

"You know about last night?"

"Listen!" urged Brennan, holding up one finger with an arresting motion and taking another paper out of his briefcase. "You came back from New York with Doctor Partington at 6:25 p.m. You came up to this house. At 8:05 you left it again, and both of you drove down to the little white house on the left-hand side of King's Avenue as you come up it. The house belongs to a Mr. Stevens. . . . I guess that's you," he added, turning to Stevens with matter-of-fact pleasantness. "You stayed there until 8:45. Then you and Doctor Partington returned to this house. You two, with a servant named Henderson, went back and forth from the house to Henderson's house, gathering up tools. At 9:30 Mr. Stevens joined you. At 9:40 you four started to open the crypt, and you got it open at just a quarter to twelve."

"Henderson said there was some one watching us," Mark growled, uneasily. He glanced at Brennan. "But——"

"Three of you went down into it. Doctor Partington went back to the house, but joined you in two minutes. At 12:28 Doctor Partington, Mr. Stevens, and Henderson came pelting out of the crypt so hard that the 'tail' thought something was wrong, and followed. But it was evidently the odor of the place: the first two came up to this house with Doctor Partington, got two step-ladders, and returned at 12:32. Doctor Partington returned at 12:35. At 12:45 there was a devil of a noise of you upsetting some marble urns. At 12:55 you gave it up and went to Henderson's place——"

"You can spare us the details," growled Mark. His voice took on a note of urgency. "There's just one thing, though. Never mind what we did; we know that well enough. But could this 'tail' of yours *hear us?* Could he overhear what we were saying?"

"He could while you were in the crypt or in Henderson's house. In case you don't remember it, the windows of Henderson's living-room were open. So he heard most of your talk."

"Sunk," said Mark, after a pause.

"No, don't let it get you down," advised Brennan, picking up his glasses again. "I'm telling you all this in detail—well, to explain why I showed up on your doorstep so early this morning. The 'tail' stuck to your party until three o'clock this morning. He didn't interfere with you; he had orders not to. But as soon as he left he came chasing out to Chestnut Hill, where I live, and proceeded to wake me up. He said he couldn't have slept last night if his life depended on it: it's the first time I ever saw Burke rattled. He said: 'Captain, they're a bunch of loonies. They're stark, raving nuts. They talk about dead people coming to life. They say maybe the old man got up out of his coffin and walked out of that vault, and that's why it's empty now.' So I thought I'd better get out here as soon as I could."

Mark, who had taken to striding round the room again, stopped and stared at him with dry glee.

"Ah, now we come to it. Now we approach the fount and origin. Do you believe we're a bunch of loonies, Captain?"

119

"Not necessarily," said Brennan, considering the question down the side of his nose. "Not necessarily."

"But you agree that the body disappeared out of the crypt?"

"I've got to. Burke was pretty emphatic about that. He said you thought of everything the police department could think of. My own guess is that he was too plain scared to go down into the crypt himself after you had all left and it began to look a little spooky. Especially as—" He glanced towards his briefcase and checked himself abruptly.

Mark was alert. "Here! Just a moment. 'Especially as—' what? This whole interview has consisted in taking unexpected rabbits out of the hat. I'll ask the same question Lucy did a while ago: have you got any more rabbits in your hat?"

"Yes," said Brennan, calmly. "For instance, I've got a complete check-up on the movements of the other members of this household for that night, April 12th."

After a pause he went on:

"The trouble with you, Mr. Despard, is that you've been hypnotized by Mrs. Despard. I mean," he rumbled, hastily, shutting his eyes as though in apology, "by the possibility of her being guilty. And your sister, too. But there were others in the house. I'll take them in turn, beginning with your brother, Mr. Ogden Despard—the same as I did with your group. All right. Now, I'd understand from what Mrs. Henderson said that he was out of town yesterday; so I couldn't question him, or thought I couldn't. But I put a man to look him up, and, by a piece of good luck, we found out what he was doing on the night of the murder."

Mark reflected. "As far as I remember, he had intended to go to an alumni dinner of his preparatory-school year at the Bellevue-Stratford in town. But we held him up so long here, waiting for Mrs. Henderson to get back from Cleveland, that he must have missed it. I remember he was still here when we left for the masquerade at half-past nine."

"I wonder—" said Lucy, suddenly, and stopped.

"You wonder what, Mrs. Despard?"

"Nothing. Go on."

"Well, that's right, anyhow," said Brennan. "Mrs. Henderson remembered where he was going. He left here about 9:40, driving a blue Buick. He drove to town, and got to the Bellevue-Stratford Hotel at about 10:35, when the dinner was

120

over but the speech-making was going on. He was seen to come in. Afterwards, it seems, some of the alumni had rooms at the hotel, and were doing some celebrating. He joined the party, and his movements can be proved from 10:35 until 2 a.m. Result—another complete alibi. Again I'll admit that nobody would be likely to mistake him for the visitor, any more than they would you. But I'm being thorough.

"Next on our list there's Miss Myra Corbett, trained nurse." Brennan looked up from his notes, grinned, and made a gesture. "Well, now, I didn't think it was very likely that trained nurses run around murdering their patients. But it was another thing that had to be checked. I put a good man on to it, *and,*" said Brennan, significantly, "we got an interview with her as well as checking her movements."

"You mean," Lucy put in, quickly, after a pause, "you got her to talk about—things that happened while she was here?"

"Yes."

Lucy regarded him as though she were searching for a trap.

"You've still got something up your sleeve," she accused him. "Did she—did she say anything about a little bottle of something being stolen from her room?"

"Yes."

"Well?" demanded Mark, exasperated. "Does she know who stole it, whatever it was?"

"She believes it must have been one of two persons," replied Foxy Frank, looking at them with great deliberation. "But we'll go into that in a moment. First, her movements. The night of the 12th was her night off. We traced her back to her—um—sinister lair in the Spring Garden Street Y.W.C.A. She got there about seven o'clock. She had dinner at the Y.W.C.A., went to a picture-show with a girl-friend about 7:30, came back about 10, and went to bed. This is confirmed by another nurse, who shares a room with her. One more complete alibi.

"Next and last we have Margaret Lightner, your maid, now staying with her parents in West Philadelphia. . . ."

"Margaret?" cried Lucy. "Did you even go after her? I remember. I gave her permission to go out on a date that night."

"Yes. We found that out. We also got hold of her boy-friend, and another couple who'd been out on a double-date with them. The four of 'em spent the evening driving (and

121

by this they mean parking) all over the place. Anyway, from about half-past ten to midnight they were stopping somewhere out in the wilds in Fairmount Park. So that gets rid of any idea that the maid—she's Pennsylvania Dutch; did you know it?—might have been the woman in your uncle's room at 11:15."

Mark was staring at him with puckered eyelids.

"I don't see what Margaret's being Pennsylvania Dutch has to do with it," he remarked. "But the implications of this are getting beyond me. Look here. You believe Mrs. Henderson's story, don't you?"

"Yes," said Brennan, thoughtfully. "Yes, I believe it."

"And you don't have any idea that old Joe Henderson, her husband, was mixed up in it, do you?"

"No."

Mark put his fists on his hips. "In that case, my lad, you've eliminated the whole crowd! You've proved an alibi for every single person in the house or associated with the house. There's nobody else who could have done it. If the police are going to believe that this business was supernatural, after all——"

"Man," said Brennan, with a sort of wild petulance, "I wish you'd snap out of this and try to see just what did happen here that night. I've been explaining to you like a kinder-garten-teacher because you're all as jumpy as rabbits, and you wouldn't have answered any questions unless you could get it out of your systems that one of *you* was guilty or that it was some tommyrot about ghosts. What I wanted to show you was plain all along. I knew it the moment I heard about the business. This little stunt was pulled by an outsider."

After a pause he went on, broadly:

"Don't look so flabbergasted. It's good news, isn't it? Now figure it out for yourselves. The poisoner was a woman. On the night of the 12th she knew that most of you would be out. She knew that Mrs. Despard was going to a masquerade, and she knew the kind of costume Mrs. Despard would wear. That's a cinch: she even imitated it down to the extent of a gauze scarf over the head and shoulders. So she came here —probably wearing a mask, too—knowing that if anybody saw her they'd take her for Mrs. Despard. And that's just exactly what happened.

"But it's not all she did. Mrs. Despard was going to this

122

party and wearing a mask. Sure; but there was a chance that everybody in the place would know who she was and be able to give her an alibi afterwards. So the poisoner cooks up some kind of fake telephone call to Mrs. Despard at St. Davids." He glanced over at Lucy with sudden shrewdness. "We don't know who that call was from or what it was about. Mrs. Despard doesn't seem to want to talk about it."

Lucy opened her mouth to speak, flushed, and hesitated.

"But never mind. I'll bet you ten dollars to a plugged nickel that the call was a fake. It was intended to send Mrs. Despard out on some wild-goose chase so that she couldn't prove where she was. Remember what time the call was made? About twenty minutes to eleven. If she went out, and stayed out for three-quarters of an hour, or an hour— See what I mean? But Mrs. Despard changed her mind and didn't go.

"The real murderer (or maybe I ought to say murderess) wasn't much afraid of being seen. And I'll tell you why— because she came by a secret passage. But then up came Mrs. Henderson, to listen to the radio. And there was a hole in that curtain over the window looking on the sun porch. Still, this didn't bother the woman, because she'd still be taken for Mrs. Despard unless somebody saw her face. Mrs. Henderson talked a lot of how still this woman was, and how she didn't seem to move at all. You can bet your bottom dollar she didn't! She didn't move because she'd have had to turn around, and she might have been recognized.

"Now, I've been gassing away here. But you're the people who have got to do the thinking now. You want to find somebody who knows this house inside out and is an intimate friend of yours and knows what was going on that night. Have you got any ideas?"

Lucy and Mark turned to stare at each other.

"But that's impossible!" Lucy protested. "You see, we keep ourselves pretty secluded here. We don't go out much. I like going out, but Mark hates it. That masquerade was something of a treat. And, you see, we have no intimate friends except——"

She stopped.

"Except—" prompted Brennan.

Lucy turned slowly round and looked Stevens full in the face.

XIV

H E HAD seen it coming. Faintly at first, a word here, a phrase there, going off the path, coming back again—Stevens had seen it insistently approaching and growing larger, all the more ugly because its movements were so haphazard. It was a blind thing, flapping its way, but it had come into the room at last. And he was powerless to shut it out.

"Except Ted and Marie, of course," said Lucy. She smiled uncertainly.

Stevens could see the idea come into three minds at once. Mark and Lucy looked at him. Even Partington, who had remained in a brown study throughout the whole interview, raised his head a little. In that almost fey state which comes with a stringing-up of the nerves for battle, Stevens thought that he could see into Mark's brain and follow every thought. Thus the idea sprang into Mark's head. He pictured Marie visually; there was a blank interval; a little twitch of incredulity came to his lips. He pictured her again; the incredulity grew to a broadening smile.

And, as though to prove it, Mark spoke.

"I'll be hanged," he said, in the flat tone of one making a statement. "I never thought of that. You know, Ted, you asked me last night whether I could stand having a case made out against my own wife. It looks as though the tables are turned. It looks as though I'll have to ask you the same question."

"That's fair enough," said Stevens, answering his casual lightness. "As a matter of fact, I hadn't thought of it myself. But I can see the point."

But he was not concerned with Mark. Out of the corner of his eye he was watching Brennan, who had turned round with a courteous mask of a face. He wondered how much Brennan might know. He also had an unreal sensation that this whole scene had been played out somewhere before. But he realized that the next few minutes might be the most critical of his life—for he was about to try a wrestling-fall with Foxy Frank.

"Ted and Marie?" repeated Brennan, inclining his head with just that degree of broad heartiness which Stevens had expected. "I suppose that's you and your wife, Mr. Stevens?"

"Yes, that's right."

"Well, man to man, now. Do you know any reason why either of you should want to poison Miles Despard?"

"No; that's just it. We scarcely knew him, either of us. I don't think I've talked with him a dozen times, and Marie rather less. Any of the family will tell you that."

"You don't seem very surprised."

"At what?"

"At being accused," said Brennan, blinking a little as though he were pulled up short.

"That depends on what you mean by surprised. I'm not going to jump up and yell, 'Damn you, what are you insinuating?' I know what you're getting at, all right, Captain; and I don't blame you. The trouble is, it's not true."

"For the sake of argument," said Brennan. "I've never had the pleasure of meeting your wife, Mr. Stevens. I'd like to know what she looks like. For instance, is she about the size and build of Mrs. Despard? What do you say, Mrs. Despard?"

Lucy's eyes were shining strangely, yet it was with a blank stare which seemed to be turned inward. Stevens had never seen such an expression on the face of the placid, easy-going Lucy he knew, and it disquieted him.

"Yes, she's about my size," she admitted. "But— Oh, this is absurd! You don't *know* her! Besides . . ."

"Thanks, Lucy," Stevens said. "What Mrs. Despard was probably going to say," he went on, easily, "is something that I'm afraid is bad for your theory, Captain. Let me understand this. You think that the woman went there disguised in a mask and a costume exactly like Lucy's, so that, if somebody happened to see her, she would be mistaken for Lucy?"

"Yes, I'm pretty certain of it."

"Good. And it's furthermore agreed that this woman, whatever else she wore, did not wear a hat. Isn't it?"

"Yes, that's what I was telling you; she was imitating Mrs. Despard's costume, and Mrs. Despard didn't have a hat. But both of 'em had a gauze scarf over the shoulders."

"Then," the other said, decisively, "you can get rid of any idea that it was Marie. Lucy, as you can see for yourself, has hair of the color that the poets compare to a raven's wing. Marie is a blonde. Therefore——"

Brennan held up his hand. "Whoa, there! Don't go so fast. We asked Mrs. Henderson about that. She said she didn't notice, or couldn't tell exactly, what color hair the woman had; so you can't prove anything by that. Mrs. Henderson said the light was too dim."

"The light was too dim for her to tell the color of the hair—although she told you every color in the dress. What's more, this woman was standing silhouetted against the light. Gauze scarf or no, that's exactly the position where hair does shine, if it's blonde, with a light on the edges of it. Yet Mrs. Henderson didn't notice. You can see for yourself that what she saw was some woman with black hair like Lucy or dark brown hair like Edith. That's why she thought it must be either Lucy or Edith. Whereas Marie's hair would have been like a brass kettle, and Mrs. H. would have known it wasn't either one of them." He paused. "But that isn't the point. Let's suppose Marie is going to disguise herself as Lucy. Now, if a blonde is masquerading as a brunette—muffled up in heavy clothes, mask, and scarf—let me ask you this: is it reasonable to think she'll wear no hat and thus leave exposed the one part of her which will show, twenty feet away, that she *isn't* the brunette?"

Mark reached up and made a gesture as though he were pulling the cord of a bell.

"End of round one," he said, critically. "He's got you there, Captain. I thought I'd stand by as *amicus curiae*, Ted; but it doesn't seem to be necessary. I warn you, Captain, this fellow is an academic terror. The Jesuits aren't in it when he begins to argue."

Brennan considered. "It's true, in a way. Though I've got a feeling we're being steered away from the main issue, somehow." He frowned. "Let's just get back to straight facts. Where were you and your wife on the night of the 12th?"

"Right here in Crispen. I admit that."

"Why do you say you 'admit it'?" Brennan asked, quickly.

"Because it wasn't usual. As a rule we come down here only on week-ends, and that was a Wednesday. I had business in Philadelphia."

Brennan turned to Lucy. "Did Mrs. Stevens know you were going to that masquerade, and what costume you were wearing?"

"Yes, she knew that. Marie came up here in the afternoon to say they'd come down unexpectedly for the night, and to ask what we were doing that evening. I showed her the dress. I was just finishing it. I made it myself, you know, from the design of one of the pictures in the gallery."

"May I ask you something, Lucy?" interposed Stevens. "Was that Wednesday afternoon the first time Marie had heard anything about the dress?"

"Yes. I only decided to make it on Monday."

"Could somebody have bought a duplicate of that dress at a theatrical costumier's, or dressmaker's, or somewhere?"

"I should certainly think they couldn't!" said Lucy, with some asperity. "It was much too elaborate and much too distinctive. As I say, I copied it from a painting here. I never saw anything like it. That's why I——"

"Between the time you told Marie about the dress on Wednesday afternoon, and the time the mysterious visitor showed up in Miles's room at 11:15, would there have been time for her to make one of them herself?"

Lucy's eyes opened wide, and then narrowed. "Good Lord, no! Of course. I never thought of that. It took me three days as it was. She wouldn't even have had time to get the materials. Besides, now I remember it, she stayed here with me until half-past six. Then she went down to meet you."

Stevens sat back and looked at Brennan. For the first time Brennan was genuinely worried. Though he was holding himself in well, a faint stir of temper began to show under the brisk exterior. He covered it with smiles and a confidential air.

"I can depend on that, can I, Mrs. Despard?" he asked. "I don't know much about these things, but it strikes me that if some one worked fast——"

"It's absolutely impossible," declared Lucy, wagging her head with the air of a schoolmistress. "My dear man! It takes the best part of a day just to put on those paste diamonds. You ask Edith."

Brennan scratched the back of his neck. "But *somebody* copied the dress! If— No, wait; we'll come back to that. We're getting sidetracked again. I'll go back to the questioning." He faced Stevens with sour good-nature. "How did you spend the evening of the 12th?"

"With my wife. We stayed at home, and went to bed early."

127

"What time did you go to bed?"

"At exactly 11:30," said Stevens, advancing the real time by one hour. It was the first tangible lie he had told Brennan; and, as he told it, Foxy Frank's eyeballs seemed to grow larger. Through the effect of his own imagination, his voice suddenly sounded wrong. "Eleven-thirty, Captain. I happened to notice it particularly."

"Why should you notice it?"

"Because it was the first time we had been at Crispen during the week. I had to set the alarm-clock so that we could get up in the morning to drive back to New York."

"Have you got any witness besides yourself? Any kids? Any maid?"

"No. There's a maid, but she only comes in during the day."

Brennan appeared to come to a decision. He thrust his glasses back into the breast pocket of his coat, slapped his knees, and got up. He looked sharper and more dangerous.

"If it's agreeable to you, Mr. Despard," he said, "there's one point in connection with this business that we'll settle now. Is that nurse, Miss Corbett, in the house? I'd like to ask her something about a theft."

"She's with Edith. I'll get her." Mark regarded him shrewdly, but with a curious wariness. "And I'm glad to see you've stopped barking up that tree. The point about the dress pretty well proves it; but we all knew Marie couldn't have had anything to do with this thing——"

"Yet," said Lucy, "you didn't hesitate to believe *I* might have had something to do with it."

It flashed out of her; she could not seem to check herself. The next moment she obviously regretted it. Lucy's square little jaw grew set, and her eyes went roving; but she did not look at Mark. She stood with a heightened color, staring at a picture over the stone mantelpiece.

"What would you have thought, I ask you?" enquired Mark. "I— Oh, damn it, think! The dress. The appearance. The— Besides, I never thought you did have anything to do with it! That's the whole point."

"I don't mind that," said Lucy, still staring at the picture. "What I do mind is that you should have discussed it carefully with other people before you even mentioned it to me."

Mark was stung so badly that he hit back by instinct. "Discussions of such things don't seem to be very popular with anyone hereabouts. I was worried. I'd have had even more reason to be worried if I had known that a telephone call almost took you away from the masquerade as it was. Not having heard about that phone call—"

"*Tais-toi, imbécile,*" said Lucy, changing her mind but not lowering her eyes from the picture: "*les agents ont des oreilles longues. Ce n'était pas un rendezvous, je t'assure.*"

Mark nodded and stumped out of the room, and there was anger in even so small a thing as the ape-like swing of his arms. At the door he gestured to Partington, who rose, nodded gravely to the company, and followed him out. Stevens was startled even to remember the doctor's presence there. Remembering Partington's placid but very talkative mood of the night before, he wondered whether the doctor would need several eye-openers before he became his dignified self. But Stevens was concentrated on Brennan, and on whether Brennan had really left off the attack or whether he was only preparing to return to it.

Lucy lowered her eyes and smiled.

"I'm sorry, Mr. Brennan," she said. "It was the very worst taste to speak in French, the way you spell out words before a child when you don't want it to understand. It was dreadfully banal, too. I have an idea you understood quite well."

Brennan, it was clear, had taken a genuine liking to Lucy. He waved his hand.

"You seem a whole lot bothered about that phone call, Mrs. Despard. I'm not: that's straight. I don't know the exact truth about it, but I won't press you yet. There's more important things we have to do."

"But *what?*" cried Lucy. "That's what I was going to ask you. The thing is so mixed up with—ghosts, and nonsense, and that horrible business of Uncle Miles's body disappearing, that I don't even see where you're going to start."

"Why, I'm going to find that body, of course," said Brennan, opening his eyes wide. "We can't get anywhere without it. The old man was poisoned; there's no doubt about that. And the murderer, learning in advance that Mr. Despard was going to open the crypt, got scared and stole the body out of it. That's easy. We can't prove the man was poisoned until we do find the body. How did somebody swipe it? Don't ask me

129

how! I haven't found the private entrance to the crypt—yet." He turned round and eyed Stevens frowningly. "There's one little bit of information, though, I'll give you free of charge. I know you four people who opened up the crypt weren't up to any funny business last night. If you'd come to me this morning and told that story, I'd have believed you cooked it up among yourselves. But I had a man there watching you, and I know better."

"Yes. That," said Stevens, "is the only piece of luck we've had so far."

Lucy was uneasy. "But where are you going to look for it? I mean, are you going to—dig up the grounds, or something? That's what they always do in the stories. With lanterns and things."

"If it's got to be done, I'll do it. But we may not have to make as much mess as that. It's entirely in the cards"—he spoke with calmness, but with an eye on both of them—"it's entirely in the cards that the body may be in this house."

"In the house?" said Stevens, startled without knowing why.

"Yes. Why not? There must be a private way into the crypt. There's also a private door somewhere in Miles Despard's room. Personally, I've got a hunch that the two are connected, and probably connected with each other."

"But, good God, Captain! You don't suggest that this woman, after she had given Miles a cup of arsenic, went out through the secret door and retired to one of the coffins in the crypt?"

" 'Suggest.' 'Suggest,' " snapped the other. "No; I'm not crazy enough for that. But I say this. I say that last night, while you four were taking two hours to open up that vault, the woman might have got in there and pulled the body out—so that it's somewhere in the passage between the crypt and the house." He raised his hand. "Don't say she wouldn't have had the strength." He considered, and went on with an indulgent light of reminiscence in his eye, "My old dad was a son-of-a-gun."

Lucy blinked at him. "We're not discussing questions of heredity," she said. "Why the change of subject?"

"He was born in Cork," said Brennan, "and he came out

to this country in '81. He was six feet three inches tall. When he sang the 'Shan Van Voght' in Rafferty's saloon, you could hear him from Second Street to Independence Hall. Well, sir, he used to get drunk every Saturday night, and I *mean* drunk. When he came home he was lucky if he got past the hatrack in the hall before he keeled over. He was a dead weight. And yet my mother—who wasn't a big woman, mind you—always got him to bed." Brennan paused, and added in a brisk tone: "That's what I meant. Does it sound wild?"

"Yes," said Stevens, briefly.

"Let's look at the physical side of it. Never mind who was guilty, just at present. Say it was anybody. But, granting there was a way into that crypt, would it have been hard to open the coffin? That is, they don't solder or weld the lid on, do they?"

"No," the other was forced to admit. "This was a wooden coffin, anyhow. There are just two automatic bolts down through the sides. But, though it doesn't take long, it takes a whale of a lot of strength to lift the catch. A female shot-putter or discus-thrower might have managed it."

"I never said the murderer mightn't have had an accomplice. You're pretty husky yourself.—What about the old man? Was he big?"

Lucy shook her head. The puzzled look which had been in her eyes a while ago had returned. "No. He was rather small. Five feet six at the most; rather under that, I should say. He wasn't much taller than I am."

"Heavy?"

"No. He wasn't well, you know. While he was getting better, the doctor used to make him weigh himself on one of those bathroom scales, and it used to make Uncle Miles furious. He was all skin and bones; he weighed 109, if I can remember correctly."

"Then—" said Brennan, and stopped. Miss Corbett had come into the room, with Mark, eager to hear.

The nurse still had her coat on, but she had removed her hat. Stevens was so obsessed with this notion of the color of the hair that he half hoped to see a brunette like Lucy or Edith; but her hair was a pale and somewhat washed-out yellow, in contrast with the strong square face and level brown eyes. Hers would have been a very attractive face if it had

131

not been for an almost complete lack of animation except the animation of duty or annoyance. With some ceremony Brennan installed her in a chair.

"Miss Corbett? Good. Yesterday afternoon a man from our department, Detective Partridge, came round to see you, didn't he? And you gave him a statement."

"I answered his questions."

"Yes, that's what I mean," said Brennan, looking at her quickly. He got after his papers again. "You said that on the evening of Saturday, April 8th, at some time between six and eleven o'clock, a two-ounce bottle of quarter-grain morphia tablets had been taken out of your room."

"So it *was* morphia!—" said Mark.

"Let me handle this, please," snapped Brennan. "When you found the bottle gone, who did you think had taken it?"

"I thought at first that Mr. Despard had taken it. Mr. Miles Despard. He was always wanting morphia, but naturally Doctor Baker wouldn't give it to him. Once I found him in my room, looking for it. That was why I thought it must have been Mr. Despard."

"What did you do when you found the bottle gone?"

"I looked for it," said the nurse, practically, as though she found the dulness of man somewhat excessive. "I spoke to Miss Despard about it, but I didn't say much because I believed Mr. Despard had taken it and I could make him give it back to me. He swore he hadn't, though.—And there wasn't much time to do anything. The bottle was returned on the night afterwards."

"Had anything been taken from it?"

"Yes. Three quarter-grain tablets."

"Speaking from a legal point of view," interposed Mark, "I should call this irrelevant, incompetent, and immaterial. Why the devil are all of you harping so much on that morphine? There's no suggestion that Uncle Miles was poisoned with it, is there? And three quarter-grain tablets wouldn't have hurt even him."

Brennan looked briefly over his shoulder. "I think we'll get down to the point of it, though. Miss Corbett, I'd like you to tell me what you told the sergeant yesterday—about how the bottle was returned and what you saw on that Sunday night, the 9th of April."

She nodded.

"It was about eight o'clock in the evening. I had just gone into the bathroom at the end of the hall upstairs. From the bathroom door you can see straight down the hall past Mr. Despard's door, and the table outside it. There is a light there. I wasn't in the bathroom longer than two minutes. When I opened the bathroom door again I looked down the hall, and there was a person just going away from Mr. Despard's door towards the staircase. I could see that there was something on the table now, although I couldn't tell what it was at that distance. There had been nothing on the table before. When I got there I saw that it was the two-ounce bottle, which had been returned."

"Who was the person you saw coming away from the table?"

"It was Mrs. Stevens," said the nurse.

Hitherto her manner had been as impersonal as that of a constable giving evidence before a magistrate, rattling through to get a duty done. Now she turned to Stevens and spoke with grave intensity.

"I'm sorry. I tried to see you or your wife this morning, but my dear friend, Mr. Ogden Despard, butted in. I wanted to tell you what I actually *had* said to that numbskull of a policeman yesterday. He tried to get me to say I had really seen Mrs. Stevens putting the bottle on the table. And that's one kind of thing I won't stand for."

There was a twinkle in Brennan's eye, but it was not a twinkle of amusement. "Now, now, that's very commendable. But what else could you think? Who else could it have been?"

"I still don't know. It might have been Mr. Despard."

"But what did you do? Didn't you speak to Mrs. Stevens about it?"

"I couldn't. She was already downstairs and out of the house, and they were off to New York. She had come up that night to say good-bye. I thought I would just wait and see."

"Yes; and then?"

"Well, I wasn't going to stand for any more of *that* foolishness," said Miss Corbett, raising her pale eyebrows. "Whoever was doing it. So I simply locked up my room whenever I wasn't in it. I bolted the door communicating with Mr. Despard's room on my side. The door of my room giving on the hall was

133

harder, because it's a common type of lock. But my father happens to be a locksmith, and I know a few things. I simply took the lock apart and altered it. Houdini himself couldn't have got in unless I had shown him how to manipulate the key. I wouldn't have gone to all the trouble, but Mrs. Stevens turned up unexpectedly on the following Wednesday afternoon, and that was to be my evening out——"

"The afternoon of the day Miles Despard was murdered?"

"The afternoon before Mr. Despard died," she said sharply. "And by that time I'd begun to think——"

"Now," interposed Brennan, and turned to Mark, "now we're coming to it. Now you're going to see why I'm plugging away at these questions. Did Mrs. Stevens ever"—he looked at his notes—"did Mrs. Stevens ever say anything to you about poisons in general?"

"Yes."

"What did she say?"

"She asked me where she could buy arsenic."

There was a thick, eerie silence in the room. Stevens was conscious of eyes turned on him, of a ring of eyes. Miss Corbett's forehead showed reddish and rather spotted; but her own eyes faced him levelly and determinedly. He could hear her breathing. Brennan's eyes were catlike and bland as he looked over his shoulder.

"That's a strong accusation," Brennan suggested.

"It's not an accusation! It's not! It's only——"

"And it ought to be supported," Brennan pursued; "that is, if it can be. Did anybody else hear her say that to you?"

The nurse moved her head. "Yes. Mrs. Despard did."

"Is that true, Mrs. Despard?"

Lucy hesitated, opened her mouth, hesitated, and then faced them.

"Yes, it is," replied Lucy.

Stevens, his palms pressed flat against the arms of the chair, was conscious of the great heat in this room and also of the ring of eyes. He noticed in a detached way that the ring of eyes had been increased by another pair. Over in the gloom by the door he saw now the jeering, calm stare and down-pulled mouth of Ogden Despard.

XV

BRENNAN leaned across the top of Miss Corbett's chair, his arm along the back of it, and spoke to Lucy.

"I've been trying to follow the way your mind was working, Mrs. Despard," he said. "Your face showed a whole lot. When I first sprung this on you, you looked surprised. But you began to think about Mrs. Stevens. And the more you thought, the more kept occurring to you. You got mad because it did occur to you, but you couldn't keep it out. Then somebody brought up the point about that masquerade dress, and how nobody could have copied it in such a short time. That seemed to settle things for you. And you thought Mrs. Stevens couldn't have had anything to do with it. But now you're not so sure. Am I right or am I wrong?"

"I—" said Lucy. She took a few quick steps up and down the room; then she folded her arms. "Oh, this is ridiculous! How should I know? You speak to him, Ted."

"Don't worry. I will," said the other. "Am I allowed to cross-examine, Captain?" It was sheer bravado. He had not a thought in his head.

"As soon as you have something to cross-examine about," said Brennan. "Let's get back to it, Miss Corbett. When did Mrs. Stevens ask you where she could buy arsenic?"

"About three weeks ago. On a Sunday afternoon, I think it was."

"Tell us what happened. Let's have the whole story."

"Mrs. Stevens and Mrs. Despard and I were sitting in the dining-room. We were sitting in front of a log fire, because it was the end of March and the weather was blowy. We were eating buttered toast with cinnamon on it. There was a case in the papers just then, some murder case in California, and we were talking about it. Then we started to talk about murders. Mrs. Despard was asking me about poisons——"

"You mean Mrs. Stevens," said Brennan.

"No, I don't," retorted the other, turning on him sharply. "I mean Mrs. Despard there. You ask her. Mrs. Stevens did not say one word the whole time. Oh, except once. I was telling them how one of my first cases as a probationer was when a man was brought into the hospital after he had drunk strychnine, and how he acted; and Mrs. Stevens asked whether I thought he suffered much pain."

"Ah, that's what I wanted to know. What was her manner then? How did she look then?"

"She looked beautiful."

Brennan stared in annoyance, glanced at his notes, and up again. "What kind of an answer is that? You don't seem to see what I'm getting at. Beautiful. What do you mean by that?"

"That's exactly what I do mean. She— May I speak frankly?"

"Sure. Why not?"

"She looked," said the witness, in a cold and steady voice, "like a woman suffering from sexual excitement."

A cold shock of rage went through Stevens and spread inside him like an explosion or like strong liquor. But he continued to look steadily at her.

"Just a minute," he interposed. "That's going a little too far. Miss Corbett, would you mind giving us your impression of a woman suffering from sexual excitement?"

"Here!" snapped Brennan, while a dull color went over the nurse's face and made it appear shiny. "Go easy with that stuff! Try to act like a gentleman. You've got no reason to go and insult her. She was only trying——"

"I didn't mean to insult her. If I did, I'm sorry. All I mean is that a term like that doesn't mean anything; or rather that you can make it mean anything you like. And I'd like to know what this does mean. Accuse all you want to, but don't turn this thing into a damned psychologist's case-book. Let's have short words, Miss Corbett. Do you mean you think my wife is a homicidal maniac?"

"That's the stuff," said Mark Despard, coming to the defence with angry bewilderment. "I don't quite understand what's going on here. Look, Captain: if you think you have a case against Marie Stevens, why are you talking to us? Why don't you see *her*? Ted, why don't you ring up Marie and ask her to come up here and answer all this for herself?"

A new voice spoke.

"Yes," it said. "Oh yes. Ask him. Ask him why he doesn't."

From the doorway Ogden Despard sauntered forward, nodding so deeply that his long chin went down to his collar. He had not removed the camel's hair coat or changed his clothes. He surveyed Stevens with an expression which was too judicial to be called pleasure, but he was obviously enjoying himself so much that his personality dominated this room.

"If you don't mind, Brennan," he remarked, "I'll ask this fellow a few questions. It'll be to your advantage, because I guarantee to tie him up into knots in about a minute.—Well, Stevens, *why* don't you call her up?"

He waited, like one listening for the answer of a child. Stevens had to get a grip on himself in order to conceal his rage. He didn't mind Brennan; Brennan was a good fellow. But Ogden was an altogether different proposition.

"You see he doesn't answer," said Ogden. "So I see I'll have to make him answer. It's because she's not there, isn't it? She ran away, didn't she? She's not there this morning, is she?"

"No, she's not there."

"And yet," pursued Ogden, opening his eyes, "when I dropped in on you at seven-thirty this morning, you told me she was still in bed."

"That's a lie," said Stevens, calmly.

It brought Ogden up short; for about a tenth of a second he did not know what to say. He was used to making certain of his suspicions, and then bringing them up; at which time the victim usually admitted the truth, but immediately began to justify himself, which put Ogden in the position he liked. To have the accusation denied was a new experience.

"Go on," he said, patronizingly. "Don't lie. You know you said it. You were heard, so you might as well admit it. Didn't he say that, Miss Corbett?"

"I really don't know," the nurse returned, with composure. "You two were in the kitchen, and I don't know what he said. So you can't prove it by me."

"All right. But you admit she isn't there. Where is she?"

"She went in to Philadelphia this morning."

"Oh, she went in to Philadelphia this morning, did she? What for?"

"To do some shopping."

"That's what I wanted you to say. She got up before seven-thirty this morning, in order to rush in and do some shopping. Do you expect anybody to believe that?" enquired Ogden, raking his chin round his collar and peering satirically at the others.

"Did Marie Stevens ever before in her life get out of her warm bed at a time like that, to 'go in and do some shopping'?"

"No, she never did. As I think I told you in front of Miss Corbett, both of us had been up all night."

"But she felt she just had to be at the stores bright and early in the morning. Why was that?"

"Because this is Saturday. They close at noon."

Ogden smirked. "Oh, this is Saturday, is it? This is Saturday, and that's why she runs out on you. Why don't you stop lying? You know she ran away last night, didn't she?"

"If I were you," said Stevens, judicially, "I wouldn't try that sort of thing too long or too far." He looked at Brennan. "Is there anything else you'd like to ask me, Captain? It's quite true my wife went into town this morning. But, if she isn't back by the afternoon, I'll confess to the murder. I shouldn't be inclined to put too much stock in what our friend Ogden says. By the way, he's the fellow who writes you anonymous letters and forges your name to telegrams, so you can judge how reliable he is."

Brennan's face was black with doubt. He stared from Ogden to Stevens.

"I'm not going to be side-tracked every time I get down to something important," he growled, "but this at least is a side track worth going into.—Is that true, young fellow? Did you write that letter to me and send all these other people telegrams to come back here?"

Whatever Ogden's other qualities might be, at least he had plenty of courage. He took two steps backwards, and remained coolly looking round him. His nimble brain was obviously debating courses, yet his face remained without expression whatsoever.

"You can't prove anything, you know," he remarked, lifting one shoulder. "I'd be careful, if I were you. You're talking libel. Or is it slander? I never can remember which is which; but at least it's something you'd better be careful about."

Brennan surveyed him keenly. For a short time Brennan remained quiet, a stocky figure jingling coins in his pocket. Then Brennan shook his head.

"It strikes me, young man, that you're trying to play detective in the way your favorite books have taught you. Let me tell you it's a rotten way. It's also the wrong way. If I acted the way you think I ought to, I'd have you in the can before you could say Jack Robinson. As far as proof is concerned, that wouldn't be hard. We could find out who handed those telegrams in."

"Learn your law, Foxy Grandpa," said Ogden, also shaking his head with a pale smile. "Those telegrams aren't forgery. According to the law, forgery is an act in which it can be shown that personal profit is directly gained from it. If I write a note to the president of the Chase National Bank, saying, 'This is to introduce Mr. Ogden Despard, who is my personal messenger, and to whom I wish you to give ten thousand dollars,' and I sign it, 'John D. Rockefeller,' that's forgery. But if I write a note saying, 'This is to introduce Mr. Ogden Despard, to whom I wish you would extend every courtesy,' and sign it with the same name, that's no forgery. It's a fine point. There's not one word in those telegrams for which I could be prosecuted."

"So you did send them, then?"

Ogden lifted one shoulder. "I never admit anything. It's not good policy. I pride myself on being tough, and I *am* tough."

Stevens glanced over at Mark. Mark had been leaning indolently against the bookcase beside the fire-place. Mark's light-blue eyes were very mild, very thoughtful; his fists were dug into the pockets of his grey sweater, which pulled it out of shape.

"Ogden," he said, "it's hard to understand what has come over you. Lucy's right; you never were as bad as this before. Maybe getting a slice of Uncle Miles's money has gone to your head. But it's possible, when I get you alone, that I'll try to find out just how tough you are."

"I wouldn't if I were you," Ogden told him, with an instantaneous turn like a jump. "My value to the world is the number of things I know. I'm just interested in things. I think you were a fool, for instance, to bring Tom Partington over here. He was getting along very well as it was, drinking all the English pubs dry, and considering his past. He never learned. But now he might learn something about Jeannette White. Wasn't once enough for you? Are you going to pick it up all over again?"

"Who," asked Brennan, quickly, "is Jeannette White?"

"Oh, a lady. I don't know her, but I know a lot about her."

"You know a great deal of things," said Brennan, explosively; "but do you know anything that has to do with this case? Anything more? No. Sure of that? All right. If that's true, we'll

139

go on—about arsenic and Mrs. Stevens. You were telling us, Miss Corbett, about the Sunday three weeks ago when you talked about poisons. Go on."

The nurse reflected.

"We talked a little while longer, and then I had to go and get Mr. Miles Despard his beef tea. I had gone out into the hall, where it was a little dark, and Mrs. Stevens followed me out. She came up behind and grabbed my wrist. Her hand was as hot as fire. Then she asked me where she could buy arsenic." Miss Corbett hesitated. "I thought it was queer at the time, because at first I couldn't make sense of what she was saying. At first she didn't call it arsenic. She called it Somebody's 'receipt.' Somebody's receipt—I have forgotten what the name was. I think it was some French name. Then she explained what she meant. Just afterwards Mrs. Despard came out of the dining-room, and I think Mrs. Despard overheard her."

Brennan was puzzled. "Somebody's receipt? Can you help us out, Mrs. Despard?"

Lucy frowned uneasily. She looked at Stevens as though with appeal.

"I can't tell you very much, although I heard her. I don't know what the name was: but I think it began with a 'G.' Something like *glacé*, which doesn't seem to mean anything. Also, she spoke very fast, and I hardly recognized her voice. It seemed different."

It was at this point that Mark Despard turned his head and slowly looked around. He blinked like a man in front of a bright light; then it was as though he tried to accustom his eyes to it. He took his hands out of his pocket, and lifted one of them to rub his forehead.

"Can you, either of you," insisted Brennan, "try to remember exactly what she said? You can see how important it is."

"No," replied the nurse, vaguely troubled and irritated. "It was confused, and she spoke in a queer kind of way, just as Mrs. Despard says. She said something like: 'Who keeps it now? Where I lived it was not difficult, but the old man is dead.'"

Brennan, who was making notes with a pencil, frowned over them. "Makes no sense!" he complained. "I don't see—Here; wait a minute! You mean she was having difficulty with the language? Her name is Marie, you say. And she used a French name. She's French, then?"

140

"No, no, no," said Lucy. "She speaks English just the same as you or I. She's a Canadian; of French descent, of course. I think she told me once her maiden name was Marie D'Aubray."

"Marie D'Aubray——" said Mark.

An almost frightful change had come over his face. He came forward a little and spoke with a lumbering lucidity, making a little movement of his forefinger at each word.

"I want you to think, Lucy, and think hard, because somebody's soul may depend on this. 'Somebody's receipt.' Could that have been 'Glaser's receipt'? Could it?"

"Yes, I believe it was. But why. What on earth is the matter with you?"

"You know Marie," he pursued, with the same fixity of look, "better than most of us here in the house. In all the time you've known her, did you ever notice *anything* strange in her behavior besides that? Anything at all that struck you? No matter how nonsensical it sounds?"

During this time Stevens had a sensation of being on a railway track and seeing a train flying closer towards him, without power to move from the tracks or look away from the hypnotic eye of the locomotive. He could hear the roar of the thing. But he intervened, nevertheless.

"Don't be a fool, Mark," he said. "This seems to be contagious. That's the old principle of 'The whole world is queer except me and thee, and thee is a little queer.' On that principle I'll undertake to prove that everyone in this room is cracked, particularly yourself."

"Answer me, Lucy," said Mark.

"I never did," Lucy answered, promptly. "I certainly never did. Ted's right about one thing; you're the one whose actions could bear investigation. I happen to know that Marie thinks your interest in murder trials and things like that is morbid. No, I never noticed anything in the least odd about her. Except, of course——"

She stopped.

"Except——?"

"It's nothing. She can't stand the sight of a funnel. Mrs. Henderson was putting up preserves in the kitchen, and straining the juice, and . . . well, I never knew Marie had so many lines around her eyes, or that her mouth could go out of shape like that."

There was a silence, a silence of almost physical coldness. Mark remained shading his eyes with his hand. When he took his hand away again, his face had an expression of ordinary earnestness and simplicity.

"Look here, Mr. Brennan. The shortest way out of this will be to show you what's behind it.—I want the rest of you to go out of the room, if you will, all except Ted and the captain. No argument, please. Just go. Ogden, you might make yourself useful. Go down to Henderson's place and rout him out; he doesn't seem to be up yet. Tell him to bring that small scout-axe of his, and a chisel. There's a larger axe here in the kitchen, I think. I'll use that."

It was clear from Brennan's look that the captain half-wondered whether Mark's brain might not have been unhinged. It was a little like a look of alarm, followed by a deprecating air but a settling of the shoulders as though Brennan prepared to deal with it. Nevertheless, the others obeyed Mark's order.

"No, I'm not going to kill anybody with the axe," Mark said. "Now, we might get an architect out here to examine the wall between the windows in Miles's room, and find out whether there's really a secret door there. But it would mean more delay and fooling around. The shortest way will be to knock open that wall and see for ourselves."

Brennan drew a deep breath. "Good. Good! If you don't mind wrecking the room——"

"But let me ask you just one question. So far, your theories about this case are pretty cut and dried. I'm not going to say anything; I want you to deduce it for yourself. But I want to ask you just one question. Suppose we don't find any secret door in that wall, or anywhere in the room. What would you think then?"

"I'd think the Henderson woman was lying," Brennan retorted, promptly.

"Nothing else?"

"No."

"And it would make you think Marie Stevens was innocent?"

"We-el," said Brennan, cautiously, and hunched up his shoulders, "I wouldn't go so far as to say—still, yes, I kind of think it would. It would certainly bust the whole thing wide open. You couldn't very well take a case to court when the defence could prove your star witness was a liar. No human being can walk through a stone wall, I'll tell you that."

Mark turned to Stevens. "That's good news, isn't it, Ted?" he asked. "Let's go."

They went out into the high and dusky hall. Neither Brennan nor Stevens spoke while Mark hurried back to the kitchen, returning with a basket of tools and a short-handled axe.

Upstairs, at the end of the gallery on the right-hand side as you ascended the stairs, was the door of Miles Despard's room. Stevens noticed the portraits on the walls of the gallery, but it was too dim for him to find the one in which he was interested. Mark opened the door of Miles's room, and for a moment they studied it from the threshold.

It was a room about twenty feet square; but, like the other rooms in this house, with a somewhat low ceiling after the fashion of the late seventeenth century. On the floor was a bright-patterned carpet in blue and grey, faded and begrimed. The uneven floorboards showed at its edges. The walls were panelled in dark walnut to a height of about eight feet; and above this was plaster painted white like the ceiling, except where the oak beams showed through. At the junction of the two walls towards their left—as they stood in the doorway —was a gigantic cupboard or wardrobe standing cater-cornered. It was built of patterned oak; and its door, which had a brass handle, stood partly open to show ranks of suits hanging inside, and a great display of shoes in their trees.

In the left-hand wall, which formed the back wall of the house, were the two small-paned windows. In the space between them stood a very high-backed Carolean chair in black oak. Hung on the wall over it was the Greuze head, a circular painting of a curly-haired child in a light frame. A short electric socket, with a bulb in it, depended from the ceiling over the head. By the far window stood a big basket-chair.

The next wall—that which faced them from across the room —contained the bed with its foot towards the hall door. A brass warming-pan and a seventeenth-century woodcut hung on this wall. In the right-hand corner, at the junction of this wall with the one on their right, was the glass door opening on the sun porch, still curtained in brown velvet. The right-hand wall showed first a highly ugly gas-stove (there was no fireplace), and then the door to the nurse's room, with Miles's

143

blue quilted dressing-gown depending from a hanger against it. Finally, completing the tour to the wall of the hall door, there was against this a bureau almost smothered in a vast display of ties.

But what took their attention was the panelling of the wall where the picture and the chair showed so uncompromisingly. Down the panelling, where a door would have been, were very faint bulges in the wood like the outlines of door-posts.

"You see?" said Mark, pointing. "I told you that the door there once led to another part of the house, which was destroyed by fire early in the eighteenth century. They filled it in with brick and panelled it over, but the doorposts were stone and you can still trace them."

Brennan went over to it, studied the wall, and struck it with his fist.

"It seems solid enough," he said, and stared round. "Damn it, Mr. Despard, if *this* won't work—" He strode over to the glass door in the other wall, examining the curtain and taking measurements with his eye. "Is the curtain now just as it was when Mrs. Henderson looked through it?"

"Yes. I've been making experiments."

"The chinks aren't very big," Brennan grunted, dubiously, peering back and forth. "Not much larger than a dime. You don't think she could have seen some other door across the room, do you? Like the door of that wardrobe?"

"It's absolutely impossible," said Mark. "Try it for yourself. The only thing you can see is just what she did see across the room: The Greuze head, the top of the chair, the outlines of the doorposts making a bulge in the walls. There's no other angle for the eye however you twist your neck. Even if it weren't for the picture, the chair, and the doorposts, nobody could ever mistake that whacking big wardrobe door, which sticks way out into the room and has a brass handle, for a secret entrance of any kind. . . . What's the matter, Captain? You're not afraid to get down to it, are you?"

With an air of ferocious pleasantry Mark squared off and cradled the axe across his arm. It was almost as though the wall had done him an injury, and he looked on it as a living thing. You might even have fancied a cry, as though from the house, when he swung up the axe and crashed it into the panelling. From a long way off a voice said:

"Satisfied, Captain?"

In the room was a faint gritty haze, and the acrid smell of chipped mortar. That haze showed like the thinning mist outside the windows, from which you could see down across the sunken gardens, the crazy paving of the path, and the rich-blossoming trees of the park. Panelling and wall were gutted to ruin. After the woodwork was gone, mallet and chisel had pried into the bricks and pulled them out as the searchers burrowed through. In several places, nakedly, you could see daylight through the wall.

There was no secret door.

XVI

FOR a time Brennan did not speak. His exertions had made him red in the face, and even his jowls looked wilted. After staring at the wall, he took out a handkerchief with an air of grave deliberation, and mopped his forehead and neck like one performing a ceremony.

"I wouldn't 'a' believed it," he said. "I wouldn't 'a' believed it. Do you think there might be a door or a trap-door somewhere else along that wall, and the witness was just looking at the wrong place?"

"Oh, we'll have the panelling down all around the place, just to make sure," Mark told him. Mark's grin was so sardonic that he seemed to be showing his teeth. He lounged against the grey light of the window, and spun a chisel round in his hand. "But I rather think, Captain, that you've been taken by the slack of the trousers and pitched into belief. What price are you offering for a material universe now?"

Brennan went over and looked unhappily at the door of the cupboard.

"No," he muttered to himself. Then he craned his neck round again. "By the way, I see there's a light hanging over that panelling we've just torn out. Was that light on when our visitor sneaked out through the door that's not there? No, wait! The old lady said——"

"That's right," agreed Mark. "It wasn't on. There wasn't any light except that little reading one at the head of the bed, which is poor at the best; that's why we have no more information about the visitor, including the color of her hair. Those, you can see, are the only lights in the room. Mrs. Henderson says——"

Stevens found rising in himself a feeling of blind exasperation. Whether the absence of a secret passage was a complete relief he could not be sure; very probably it was. But he was certain of the exasperation.

"May I point out," he said, "that there is not one single blasted point in this case which does not depend on 'Mrs. Henderson says.' To be frank, the repetition of 'Mrs. Henderson says' is giving me a pain in the neck. Who is Mrs. Henderson? What is she? Is she an oracle or an augur or a mouthpiece of Holy Writ? Where is Mrs. Henderson? She seems to be about as elusive as Mrs. Harris; for we certainly haven't seen her here at the house, despite the fact that she knows she's put the police on the track and almost literally tried to raise the devil. You've accused Mark's wife of murder. You've accused my wife of murder. You've checked up on the smallest circumstance in connection with them, despite the fact that Lucy has a cast-iron alibi and it's been proved by independent witnesses that Marie could not possibly have procured or made a dress like the Brinvilliers one. Very well. But when Mrs. Henderson says that blood flows uphill, or that there is a door where we can see for ourselves there isn't a door, you believe her solely on the grounds that her story is so wildly incredible."

Mark shook his head. "That's not as paradoxical as it sounds," he said. "If she had been lying, why all the fancy trimmings? Why didn't she simply say she saw the woman in the room giving Miles a drink, and let it go at that? Why add a statement that we could prove was untrue, and therefore wouldn't believe?"

"You've answered your own question. Because you still do believe it, don't you, or you wouldn't be arguing with me?"

There was a silence.

"But that," Stevens went on, "is aside from the immediate point. You ask me why Mrs. Henderson should swear so positively that a dead woman walked through a brick wall. Let me ask you, why should *Mr.* Henderson swear so positively that a dead man walked through a granite wall? Why should he be so insistent that not one stone was disturbed in a sealed

crypt? We've got two flat impossibilities in this case
only two: first, the disappearance of the woman from
room; second, the disappearance of the body from the
And it's a curious thing that the only two witnesses to both
those happenings are the Hendersons."

Brennan was whistling softly through his teeth. He reached
into his pocket, produced a package of cigarettes, and passed
it round; and each accepted a cigarette, like duelists accepting
swords.

Brennan said, "Go on."

"Let's take the physical circumstances of this murder, if it
was a murder. You, Captain," Stevens went on, "maintain that
the murderer must have been an outsider. I deny that. It seems
to me almost certain that the murderer must have been a
member of this household. For there's just one thing which
seems to have been generally overlooked: the *way* in which
the poison was administered. It was administered in an egg,
milk, and port-wine mixture."

"I begin to see—" said Brennan.

"Yes. To begin with, is it likely that an outsider would come
sneaking in here, get the eggs out of your ice-box, beat them
up, add milk from the ice-box and port from your cellar, to
make up the mixture? Or, conversely, that an outsider would
walk across the fields carrying a bowl of the stuff in order to
fill a silver cup on your sideboard? But it leads up to the biggest difficulty: how could any outsider expect to make Miles
drink the stuff? You know what trouble you had with him
about things that were good for him, particularly on that
night. If an outsider had wanted to poison him, an outsider
would have chosen something he would certainly drink—like
champagne or brandy. No; that homely egg-and-port combina-
tion is something that would have occurred to a member of the
household, who would (1) think of making it, (2) be able
to make Miles drink it. Lucy might have done it, Edith might
have done it, the nurse might have done it, even the maid
might have done it. But Lucy was dancing at St. Davids, Edith
was playing bridge, Miss Corbett was rioting at the Y.W.C.A.,
and Margaret in Fairmount Park. Which brings us to the
question of alibis. There are just two people whose alibis you
haven't checked or even questioned. I don't need to mention
them. But kindly note, with regard to the homely mixture,

that one of them is the cook. And both of them, I think you've said, inherit substantially in your uncle's will."

Mark shrugged his shoulders.

"I can't believe it, and that's flat," he returned. "In the first place, they've been with us too long. In the second place, if they killed Uncle Miles and are cooking up a story to cover it, why should they make the story *supernatural*? What good would that do them? It seems a highly unusual and romantic way to go about it, when ordinary murderers can't get away with plain lies."

"Let me ask you something. Last night you told us her story about the mysterious visitor, and about the qualms she had: the 'funniness' of the figure, even that pleasant little detail about the possibility that the visitor's neck might not have been securely fastened on. . . ."

"WHAT?" said Brennan.

"Now think, Mark. Did you put that idea into her head, as we thought last night—or did she put it into yours?"

"I don't know," Mark said, abruptly. "That's what I've been trying to think."

"But if she hadn't suggested it to you, would it have occurred to you at all?"

"Maybe not. I don't know."

"Here's something we all know, though. Four of us opened that crypt. Who was the only one of the four who definitely did swear he believed in ghosts? Who tried to throw a supernatural atmosphere over it, even to intimating that there were Powers watching us? Who went to fantastic lengths in swearing that nobody had approached that crypt? Wasn't it Joe Henderson?"

"Yes, I suppose so. But there's where it sticks. Do you mean to tell me that a pair of innocent old family retainers would suddenly turn into a couple of demons——"

"Not at all. They're not demons; you're the one who's been importing the demons. I admit that they're very amiable people. But some very amiable people have been known to commit murder. I admit that they're faithful to you. But they had no reason to be faithful to *Miles*, who has been so much abroad that (like you) they hardly knew him. And money was to come from Miles to them only on your father's wish. As for the supernatural story, what was the origin of that?"

148

"Origin?"

Brennan intervened, pointing a cigarette which had burnt crookedly up one side and seemed to express his state of mind.

"All this," he said, "is words and words and words. Just the same, I think I see what Mr. Stevens is driving at. Here's the way I understand it. When the old man died, nobody had any suspicion he'd been poisoned—except you." He nodded towards Mark. "Because you found the silver cup in that cupboard. And right away Mrs. Henderson comes to you with a story of goblins and women walking out of walls— she didn't say anything to me about the woman's head not being fastened on, whatever that is; but all the rest of it's the same—she comes and tells you that story. Because why? Because you'll half-believe it. Because it'll make you *hush the thing up* all the more. The most you'll do is to open the crypt. And then, when you discover that the goblins have apparently stolen the old man's body, you'll hush it up all the more. Doesn't that square with everything that pair have told us?"

Mark contemplated him with sudden amusement.

"Then," Mark asked, "the whole parade of lies and body-snatching was got up just to impress me so that I'd keep it all quiet?"

"It might be."

"But in that case," said Mark, "will you tell me why yesterday, before the crypt was even opened, Mrs. Henderson blurted out exactly the same story to the Commissioner of Police?"

They looked at each other.

"That's true," Stevens admitted.

"Oh, I wouldn't say that, either. Don't forget your brother Ogden, Mr. Despard," said Brennan. "He's a very smart lad, that one is. He suspected, too. And there's no knowing how far he suspected, or the Hendersons thought he did. They'd know *he* wouldn't keep it quiet. So maybe Mrs. Henderson got hysterical and did what many another woman has done: she knew she had committed herself, and she wanted to try out her story."

Again Brennan wandered over to the wardrobe and stared at it, but his air was belligerent now.

"What I'd like to know is how this wardrobe figures in the case. And, friends, I've got a hunch it does—somehow. I

149

don't mean that there's anything mechanically wrong with it. But it was on the floor inside this thing that you found the poison-cup, wasn't it? Now, why did the murderer put it in there? Why were *both* the harmless glass of milk and the not-so-harmless cup of arsenic stuck right in here? Why did the cat follow 'em in, and, it'd seem, drink from the cup?" He poked among the suits hanging inside. "Your uncle certainly had a lot of clothes, Mr. Despard."

"Yes. I was telling the others last night he was supposed to spend a lot of time here changing his clothes for his own edification. But he didn't like any of us to know he was quite so——"

"That," said a new voice, "is not all he did in here."

Edith Despard had come in by the hall door, with such quietness that none of them had heard her. But it was not the quietness of stealth. The underlying expression of her face they did not then understand, and were not to understand until somewhat later. Nevertheless, though her eyes still seemed a trifle sanded from lack of sleep, the thin-boned good looks had a quietness of certainty. To Stevens she appeared for some reason much younger than last night. Under her arm she had two books, on which the fingers of her other hand were tapping gently. In some subtle way she was Fashion; she was handsome and bedecked, though afterwards Stevens realized that he had no notion of what she had been wearing, except that it was black.

Mark was startled. He protested: "Edith, you shouldn't be here! You promised to stay in bed today. Lucy says you didn't sleep at all last night: except once, and that was a nightmare."

"That's right," said Edith. She turned to Brennan with a business-like politeness. "Captain Brennan, isn't it? The others were telling me about you a few minutes ago, when you dismissed them." Her smile had genuine charm. "But I'm sure you won't dismiss me."

Brennan was affable but noncommittal. "Miss Despard? I'm afraid we've been——" he nodded towards the shattered wall, and coughed.

"Oh, that was to be expected. I have the solution of your difficulties here," said Edith, and gently touched the books under her arm. "You see, I overheard you saying you believed the wardrobe there had some connection with this case.

150

It has, very much so. I found these books inside it last night. The second volume turned down easily at one chapter; so I gathered that Uncle Miles, though you could hardly call him a man of books, had found something in it to study. I should like to read you some of it—all of you. You may not find it enthralling. It is academic and even rather dull. But I think you ought to listen. Will you close the door, Ted?"

"Book?" said Mark. "What book?"

"It is Grimaud's *History of Witchcraft*," replied Edith.

Sitting down in the basket-chair by the window, she spoke with no more apology or diffidence than if she were dealing with a laundry-list. Yet, just before she began to read aloud, she lifted her eyes towards Stevens; and he was startled at the interest and curiosity with which she regarded him, as though she wondered. Her voice was clear and fluent, if without great expression.

"The root of the belief in the 'non-dead' *(pas-morts)* appears to have originated in France in the last quarter of the seventeenth century. It is first written of by the Sieur de la Marre in 1737 *(Traité sur la Magie, Sortilège, Possessions, Obsessions, et Maléfices)*; for some years it was seriously discussed even by men of science; and controversy about it was again aroused by a criminal trial so recently as 1861.

"Briefly, the non-dead are those persons—commonly women—who have been condemned to death for the crime of poisoning, and whose bodies have been burnt at the stake, whether alive or dead. It is here that the province of criminology touches the province of witchcraft.

"From the earliest times the use of poison was regarded as a branch of sorcery, nor is the origin of the belief difficult to trace. 'Love-potions' or 'hate-potions,' admittedly a part of magic, have always been the mask under which the poisoner has worked; and to administer even a harmless love-potion was made punishable under Roman law.[1] During the Middle Ages it was identified with heresy. In England, as late as 1615, a trial for murder by poison was, in effect, a trial for sorcery. When Anne Turner was tried before Lord Chief Justice Coke for poisoning Sir Thomas Overbury, there were shown in court her 'inchantments'—figures in lead, parchments, a piece of human skin— and the spectators could feel the wind of the Black Man's passing.

" 'At the shewing of these and inchanted papers and other pictures in court,' writes the recorder, 'there was heard a crack from the scaffolds, which caused great fear, tumult, and confusion among the spectators, every one fearing hurt, as if the Devil had been present, and grown angry to have his workmanship shewed by such as were not his own scholars.'[2]

[1] Paulus, *Sententiae*, v. 21-23.
[2] The Tryal of Anne Turner, Widow, at the King's Bench Bar, 7th Nov., 1615.

"But it was in France, during the latter part of the same century, that the practice of murder-cum-diablerie reached its height. It is stated that in Lisbon there were so many hags practising witchcraft that they had a quarter of their own.[3] Out of Italy (where the ladies of Toffana's secret-society poisoned six hundred people) came Glaser and Exili, who searched for the Philosopher's Stone and sold arsenic. In another chapter we have seen how eagerly the ladies of Louis XIV's court embraced the cult of Satanism, notably the sacrifice of a child on the body of a woman during the Black Mass.[4] Muffled rites took place in muffled rooms. The witch La Voisin evoked ghosts at Saint-Denis. Those enlisted now for Satanism were not, in Gaule's phrase, 'every old woman with a wrinkled face, a furr'd brow, a gobber tooth, a squint eye, a squeaking voice, or a scolding tongue': they were the handsomest women procurable, from seamstress to court lady.[5] And husbands and fathers died.

"Through the confessional, some hint of these underground crafts reached the Grand Penitentiary of Paris. At the Arsenal, near the Bastille, was established the famous 'Burning Court,' whose vengeance was the wheel and the fire. The mysterious death of Madame de Montespan, Louis XIV's favourite, in 1672, gave impetus to the poison-seekers. Between 1672 and 1680 some of the greatest ladies in France were summoned before the Burning Court: among them two nieces of Cardinal Mazarin, the Duchess of Bouillon, and the Countess of Soissons, mother of Prince Eugene. But what opened every secret cabinet to the world was the trial in 1676—a trial lasting three months —of the Marquise de Brinvilliers.

"The activities of the Marquise de Brinvilliers had been revealed through the accidental death of her lover, Captain Sainte-Croix. Among Sainte-Croix's effects was a teakwood box to which was attached a paper of instructions that after his death it 'might be delivered to the Marquise de Brinvilliers, who resides in the rue Neuve St. Paul.' The box was filled with poisons, including corrosive sublimate, antimony, and opium. Madame de Brinvilliers fled; but was ultimately brought back to trial, on a charge of wholesale poisoning, by the efforts of a detective named Desprez. Though she was ably defended by Maître Nivelle, it was Desprez who secured her conviction. He produced in court a written confession which she had privately entrusted to him. It was a hysterical document, containing—among a terrible list of things she had really done—things which apparently she could not have done. She was sentenced to be beheaded and burnt.[6]

" 'After the sentence, in order to make her divulge the names of any accomplices, she was put to the "water-torture." This was a part of the judicial system: the victim was placed on a table, a leather funnel was put into her mouth, and water was poured into it until . . .' "

---

[3] *Encyclopædie des Sciences Occultes.* Paris, 1924.

[4] Montague Summers, *History of Witchcraft.*

[5] John Gaule, Vicar of Great Staughton, the exposer of Matthew Hopkins.

[6] *Procès de la Marquise de Brinvilliers,* 1676. Alexandre Dumas, *Crimes Célèbres.* Madame de Sévigné, *Lettres.* Philip Lefroy Barry, *Twelve Monstrous Criminals.* Lord Birkenhead, *Famous Trials.*

152

Briefly, Edith Despard raised her eyes from the book. The grey light of the window lay flat on her hair; and Edith's expression was only one of great curiosity and interest. None of the men moved. Stevens was staring at the pattern in the carpet. He remembered now the address of the house in Paris to which Dr. Welden had told him to go if he were interested in famous crimes. It was Number 16, rue Neuve St. Paul.

"Madame de Sévigné saw her going to execution afterwards, and laughed and gossiped. A great multitude saw her do penance before Nôtre Dame, in a white shift, barefoot, with a lighted candle in her hand. She was now forty-two years old, and much of her doll's beauty was gone. But she was a model of penitence and devotion, which satisfied the noble Abbé Pirot. She does not appear, however, to have forgiven Desprez: and, on mounting the scaffold, she uttered some words which were imperfectly understood. Her body was burnt in the Place de Grève.

"Due to the revelations at the trial, the authorities were ultimately able to penetrate the net of diablerie beneath the court of the Grand Monarque. La Chausée, a servant of Sainte-Croix, had already been broken to death on the wheel. The witch and poisoner La Voisin, taken with all her accomplices, was burnt alive in 1680. The dancers before Satan were gone; their ashes were scattered; and the great devil grinned alone on Nôtre Dame.

"But all persons do not seem to have accepted this. Although there is no apparent reason of their belief, Maître Nivelle is said to have told the Grand Penitentiary: 'There is something beyond this. I saw them die. They were not ordinary women. They will be restless.'

"Now, what is behind this? It is noted that even today there are outbreaks of Satanism in Europe, as instanced by the investigation of MM. Marcel Nadaud and Maurice Pelletier so recently as 1925.[7] It needs no documentation to show that there have been outbreaks of poisoning, mass-murders—usually by women, and usually without any apparent motive. For instance (argues Perrot), there was Anna Maria Schonleben in Bavaria in 1811, and Marie Jeanneret in Switzerland in 1868;[8] there was Frau Van de Leyden, who poisoned twenty-seven people; there are even men, like Palmer and Cream in England.[9] What motive actuated them? In the case of the women, there was seldom any gain to be derived from the death of their victims, no hope of profit, no wrong to right. They were not mad: even though they seem puzzled to explain their own motives.

"It has been argued that theirs was a simple lust, and that they

[7] *Le Petit Journal*, May, 1925. See also Elliott O'Donnell, *Strange Cults and Secret Societies of Modern London.*

[8] Henry T. F. Rhodes, *Genius and Criminal.*

[9] F. Tennyson Jesse, *Murder and its Motives.* H. M. Walbrook, *Murders and Murder Trials, 1812-1912.* See also the trials of William Palmer and Dr. Pritchard in the *Notable British Trial* series. It seems that the victims of both must have known they were being poisoned.

loved the little white powder of arsenic because it gave them the power of queens and the workers of destinies. But this does not explain all. If the women possessed a desire to kill, it cannot be thought that their victims possessed a desire to be killed. The most curious feature in all of these cases is the ease, the sense of fatality, the complete willingness of these victims to undergo it—even when they must have known they were being poisoned. Frau Van de Leyden said openly to a victim: 'It will be your turn in a month.' Jedago said: 'Wherever I go, people die.' Yet they remained undenounced. It is as though there were some diabolic bond uniting murderer and victim, something not unlike a spell or a hypnosis.

"This theory was first vaguely stated by the Sieur de la Marre in 1737, due to a case which agitated Paris in that year. A girl of nineteen—Thérèse La Voisin, the same surname as the alleged sorceress who was burnt in 1680—had been arrested for a series of murders. Her parents were charcoal-burners in the Forest of Chantilly. She could not read or write. She had been born in the ordinary way; and until the age of sixteen seemed quite normal. But even the ponderous detective wits of the time were aroused by eight deaths in that neighbourhood. A curious circumstance was that under the pillow or blanket of each person was found a cord—usually of hair, but sometimes of string or plaited hair—tied into nine small knots.

"They understood this. Nine, as we have seen, is the mystic number, the multiple of three, and it occurs over and over again in connection with magical ceremonies everywhere. The tying of nine knots in a string is believed to put on the victim a spell which places him entirely in the power of the sorceress.

"When the authorities descended on her house, they found the girl La Voisin in the wood near by, under a thicket, without clothes and with what one of them describes as 'the eyes of a wolf.' Taken to Paris and questioned, she made a statement. She screamed at the sight of fire. Though her parents said she could not read or write, she could do both; and spoke like a court lady. She admitted committing the murders. Asked the meaning of the spell put on them, she said:

" 'They are now one of us. There are so few of us, and we have need of others. They are not truly dead; they are alive again now. If you do not believe me, open their coffins and you will see. They are not in the coffins. One was at the Grand Sabbath last night.'

"It seems to have been true that the coffins were empty, at least. Another strange feature of the affair was that, at her trial, the girl's parents came near proving something like an alibi for one of the crimes: resting on the fact that she must have walked two kilometers in a remarkably short time, and in some fashion penetrated a locked house. La Voisin is said to have replied:

" 'That is of no consequence. I went into the bushes, and I put the ointment on myself, and I put on the dress I had before. Then I had no trouble.' Asked what she meant by the 'dress she had before,' she said: 'I had many dresses. This was a beautiful dress, but I did not wear it when I went to the fire.' At mention of the fire she seemed suddenly to recollect herself, and fell into a fit of screaming. . . ."

"I've had about enough of this," interrupted Brennan, heavily. He passed a hand over his face, as though to make sure it was still there. "Excuse me, Miss Despard, but I've got work to do. This is April, not Halloween. Women on broomsticks are a little out of my line. If you tell me that a woman put a spell on Mr. Miles Despard, and rubbed herself with ointment, and got into a dress several hundred odd years old, and consequently walked through that wall—well, all I've got to say is, I want a case that'll at least get past the grand jury."

Edith, though a trifle supercilious, was not put out.

"You do?" she said. "Then here is one. The part I wanted you to read, really, comes next. But if you can't derive profit from it, I won't bother to read it. It's about a woman named Marie D'Aubray (the same maiden name, I can tell you, as the Marquise de Brinvilliers) who was guillotined in 1861. Whatever you think of the seventeenth or eighteenth centuries, I presume you don't think they were quite so unenlightened in the eighteen-sixties."

"You don't mean she was executed for witchcraft?"

"No. She was executed for murder. The details aren't pleasant, and I don't want to go over them. But I should just like to read you the description of her, written by a contemporary reporter, as she stepped into the dock. It says: 'The case attracted wide attention, not only because of the good looks and comparative wealth of the accused woman, but by the modesty of her bearing; a modesty so great that when, on one occasion, the procurer-general put certain blunt words to her, she colored like a schoolgirl.' And here we are: 'She stepped into the dock bowing timidly to the President of the Tribunal. . . . She wore a boat-shaped hat of brown velvet, with a drooping plume, and a gown of brown silk. In one hand she carried a silver-topped smelling bottle, and on the other wrist she wore a curious antique gold bracelet, with a clasp like a cat's head, and a ruby in the mouth of the clasp. When witnesses began to testify as to the details of the Black Mass in the upper room of the villa at Versailles, and the poisoning of Louis Dinard, several over-excited spectators shouted, "No, no!" It was observed that her only sign of agitation was to finger this bracelet on her wrist.' " Edith closed the book with a snap. "Truth will out, Ted. *You* know who's got a bracelet just like that."

155

Stevens did know it. He remembered seeing that bracelet in the photograph of the Marie D'Aubray of 1861, which had disappeared that night. But by this time he was in such a state of black befuddlement that he could say nothing.

"Yes," Mark interposed, in a dull voice. "That's what I thought, too. But," said Mark, "now it's out, I can't face it."

"*I* can," snapped Brennan. "I see what you've been getting at, and the one I sympathize with is Mr. Stevens. I wouldn't let it worry you, my friend, if that's what you're looking so queer about. It's a funny thing. Mr. Despard strongly defended her until he heard or thought of this guff. I strongly attacked her until I heard of it."

Edith's voice grew sharp. "Do you deny that witchcraft has been practised in the past?"

"Of course I don't," said Brennan unexpectedly. "It's being practised right here in modern America. I know all about that nine-knots-in-a-piece-of-string curse. It's called the witch's ladder."

Mark stared. "But, good God, man! You said——"

"Have you forgotten where you are?" inquired Brennan. "Don't you read the newspapers, even? You're right on the edge of the territory of the Pennsylvania Dutch, where the local witch still makes wax images and puts spells on a cow. Why, there was that *hex* murder up there not very long ago. One of our boys went up to advise 'em about it. You remember, a while ago I put some emphasis on the fact that your maid here, Margaret, was originally Pennsylvania Dutch; and you asked me what that had to do with it. It may have a whole lot to do with it, though I don't think the maid has. As soon as I heard of that piece of string with the knots, I thought some yokel rainmaker was trying to hex, or pretending he was trying to hex, your uncle. And—when I think over Mr. Stevens's theory about the Hendersons—I think I see who it might have been. That's why I wanted to ask you: where are the Hendersons from?"

"Reading, I think," said Mark, "originally. Part of the family moved to Cleveland."

"Well, Reading's a nice town," said Brennan, mildly, "and it's far from being full of yokels. But still it's Pennsylvania Dutch."

"I'm hanged if I understand this, Captain. You're full of

surprises," growled Mark. "Then you do believe witchcraft can be practised? For, if you do——"

Brennan folded his arms and contemplated Mark with his head a little on one side. The reminiscent light was back in his eye.

"When I was a kid," he said, "I wanted a revolver. Wow! how I wanted a revolver!—a big Ivor-Johnson six-shooter with an ivory handle. I wanted that revolver more than anything else in the world. They told me at Sunday school that, if you wanted anything bad enough, all you had to do was pray for it and you'd get it. Well, I prayed. I prayed and prayed for that revolver. I bet nobody ever did pray as much as I did for that revolver. In those days my old dad used to tell me a lot about the devil, specially when he was recovering from the horrors and was resolving never to touch another drop. My dad was very religious, and once he said the devil stuck his head round the corner of the sitting-room door, and pointed at him, and said, 'Shamus Brennan, if you take just one more little drink of whisky, I'm coming for you.' He said the devil was all in red and had curved horns a foot long. But, all the same, I thought if the devil would appear and offer to swap me my soul for the big ivory-handled six-shooter in Clancy's window, I'd do it. And yet, no matter how much I wanted it and how much I prayed, I didn't get that revolver.

"It's the same thing here. Practise magic? Sure I can practise magic, as much as I want to. I can make wax images of all the people I don't like—which is the Republican Party, mostly—but that doesn't say they'll die if I stick pins in the images. So, when you tell me your uncle was murdered and bewitched so that he's joined a gang of ghouls . . . that he walked out of his coffin in the crypt, and might walk into this room at any minute . . . I must take leave to——"

The door of the room banged open with a crash which made them all jump, and brought Mark round with a ringing oath. Ogden Despard, looking somewhat greenish and sweaty, leaned against the door-post. At his very appearance, and for no tangible reason, Stevens experienced a feeling of horror worse than any that had yet crept on him. Ogden drew the back of his overcoat sleeves across his forehead.

"Henderson——" he said.

"What about Henderson?" demanded Mark.

"You sent me out there," said Ogden, "out to his house, to get Henderson and have him bring some tools up here. I've been trying to bring him round. No wonder he didn't show up here early this morning. He's had a fit, or something. He can't, or won't, talk straight. I wish the rest of you would go down to him. He says he's seen Uncle Miles."

"You mean," said Brennan, back to crisp matter-of-factness again—"you mean he's found the body?"

"No, I don't mean that," Ogden said, pettishly. "I mean—he says he's seen Uncle Miles."

IV

SUMMING-UP

" 'And where is your nose?' quoth Sancho,
seeing him now without disguise. 'Here in my
pocket,' and so saying, he pulled out the nose of
a varnished pasteboard vizard, such as it has
been described. . . . 'Blessed Virgin!' quoth
Sancho. 'Who is this? Thomas Cecial, my friend
and neighbor?' 'The same, friend Sancho,' quoth
the squire; 'I will tell you anon by what tricks
and wheedles he was inveigled to come hither.' "
—Life and Achievements of the Renowned
Don Quixote de la Mancha

XVII

THE little stone house under the elm trees, near which ran the broad walk of crazy paving, had its door wide open. All mist had now lifted into a clear, cool day with a freshening breeze that stirred the new leaves of the elms, like green lace. At the end of the pavement the ruined chapel stood up against a pale sky, the door of the chapel boarded over. And, some distance out among a litter of gravel and smashed stones, a tennis-court tarpaulin was spread over the entrance to the crypt, with stones at each corner to hold it firm.

Inside Henderson's house, in the little living-room where they had sat last night, Henderson lay on a leather couch and looked with half-open eyes at the ceiling. His expression was one of sullen defiance mixed with genuine physical illness. There was a bad bruise on his hollowed left temple; his scanty hair looked more than ever like a disarranged cobweb. He was fully dressed, just as he had been last night, and he did not seem to have washed. A blanket was drawn up to his breast, and his hands lay on it snake-veined—and shook. When he heard footsteps outside, he twitched up his head suddenly, without seeming to move the body at all; but he lay back again.

Mark, Brennan, and Stevens stood in the doorway, surveying him.

"Good morning, Joe," Mark said, sardonically.

Some twitch passed over the man's face, some change which might have been humiliation; yet his expression seemed to say that his particular sufferings were more than a human being ought to bear, and it kept his eyes squeezed up with sullen fixity on the ceiling.

"Easy, old boy," Mark told him, not without sympathy. Mark went over and put his hand on Henderson's shoulder. "You've been overdoing it. You're an old man, and you've

161

been working like a dog.—What's this nonsense about your seeing Uncle Miles?"

"Look here, Mr. Despard," said Brennan, quietly: "what's the idea in having it both ways? Why do you say it's nonsense? Not five minutes ago you were all for ghosts and non-deads. And then, when this turns up, you turn around the other way."

"I don't know," said Mark, struck with this. He stared. "Except . . . that is, I know what *you're* going to think about this. You were too much impressed with Ted's theory. And, directly on top of that, here's another member of the Henderson family who's seen a ghost. I know how it will sound to you: it'll sound a little too fortuitous." He turned back to the old man and spoke sharply. "Buck up, Joe! No matter how you feel, try to pull yourself together. The police are here."

Henderson's eyes flashed open; the expression of his face seemed to say that this was too much, that this was a final bedevilment. After looking as though he were going to cry, he pushed himself up to a half-sitting position and looked at them with rheumy eyes.

"The perlice," he said. "Who sent for 'em?"

"Your wife," said Brennan, briefly.

"She never did! You can't fool me. I don't believe it."

"Let's not fight about it," said Brennan. "What I want to know is what you told Mr. Ogden Despard about seeing his uncle's ghost. . . ."

"It wasn't any ghost," protested Henderson, with a wrench in his throat. Stevens, with a twinge of uneasiness, saw that the man was almost literally frightened out of his wits. "Leastways, it wasn't like any ghost I ever heard tell of. If it had been, I wouldn't have been a-skeered of it. It was—it was——"

"Alive?"

"I dunno," said Henderson miserably.

"Whatever you saw," Mark told him, "just tell us about it. Take it easy, Joe. Where did you see it?"

"In the bedroom there." He pointed to a door. "It was this way. I got to think before I forget. Last night, you remember, Miss Edith and Lucy came here while we were—you know. And all of you went up to the house. Miss Edith, she told me to stoke up a big fire in the furnace. So I did. Then you were all talking in the front room, but you broke up before three o'clock. You remember?"

"Yes."

"I got to get this straight," said Henderson, nodding. "You and I was going to get the tarpaulin from the shed by the tennis court, and put it over the opening to that place. But then I thought you looked mighty tired, and it wasn't anything of a job; so I told you to go to bed, and I'd do it. And you said thanks, and gave me a drink. It wasn't till I went out the back door, and heard you locking it . . . it sort of came to me that I'd have to go all down that walk, and sleep here alone. What's more, that tennis court is way over in the south field, and to get there I'd have to go through that little bit of woods I've never liked.

"But I hadn't no more than got started for the south field when I remembered I wouldn't have to go there, after all. Because I'd been mending that tarpaulin for this year, and it was right here in my house—under the sewing-machine over there. So I come back, and in here. Then I saw the lights were out in this room, and I tried 'em, and the bulb wouldn't work. I didn't like that, but I had my lantern. So I grabbed up that tarpaulin from under the sewing-machine, and ran out again, and started to lay it over the opening. I was working faster all the time, holding it down with stones at the edges. Because I thought: Suppose something should sort of push up that tarpaulin from underneath, like somebody coming up the steps and trying to get out?

"I got it done, and I was mighty glad. I told you before, I've never been a-skeered of things like that. It's like what I told you, that Mr. Ballinger told me years ago. 'Joe,' he says, 'don't you be a-skeered of any dead people; it's these *livin'* sons-of-bitches you want to watch out for.' But I didn't like putting down that tarpaulin.

"So when I was through I come in here, and I locked that door. I tried the lights again, but they still wouldn't work. Then I thought my lantern wasn't giving enough light, and I tried to turn up the wick. But I must 'a' got mixed up, or my hand wasn't right, because I turned it the wrong way, and the light started to go out. I didn't have time to monkey with it. I knew there was lights in that bedroom there, and I wanted to get inside with the door locked.

"So I went over to the bedroom. The first thing I heard when I got in there was the rocking-chair creaking. It has a kind of

163

squeak you can always tell. It's over by the window. Then I looked, and I seen something sitting in the chair, rocking back and forth.

"There was enough light for me to see it was your uncle. He was sitting there rocking just like your uncle did when he used to come to see me. I could see his face plain. I could see his hands, too. They was whitish, but they didn't shine much, and they looked soft. I knew it because he reached out his hand and tried to shake hands with me.

"I run out of there. Or leastways I run somewhere, and I slammed the door. Only the key was on the other side. Then I could hear him get up and walk across to the door after me.

"I fell over something in here, and hit my head. After that I don't remember much, except that I fell against the edge of this couch here, and there was a blanket or something on it. I think I had an idea of rolling over the couch, down to the other side, so it would hide me. But that's all I can tell you, until your brother Ogden—he climbed through the winder over there, and he was shaking me."

For a few more sentences, which were incomprehensible, Henderson remained propped on his elbow, his forehead sweated and snake-veined. Then he lay down and closed his eyes.

The others looked at one another, while Mark patted Henderson's shoulder. Brennan was irresolute. After a hesitation, he walked across the room and snapped the catch of the light-switch: the light came on. He clicked it a few times, looking from it to Henderson. Stevens walked past him and out into the fresh air under the trees. As he did so he saw Brennan going towards the bedroom. After a minute or two Brennan also came out of the house.

"If you have no more immediate use for me," Stevens said, "I'm going down home to get some breakfast."

"Go ahead," Brennan said. "But I want to see both you and Mrs. Stevens today; so I'd rather you stuck pretty close to home. She'd better get back from this shopping-trip before evening. In the meantime, I've got a lot to do. A whole hell of a lot," he added, drawing out the words slowly and heavily, "to do."

After turning away, Stevens swung back. "What do you think of—?" he nodded towards the house.

164

"Why, I'll tell you. If that fellow's a liar, he's the slickest liar I've met in thirty years."

"I see. Well—until this afternoon."

"Until this afternoon. You'd better see your wife's back by that time, Mr. Stevens."

In his walk through the Park and down the hill he did not hurry. He did not hurry until he glanced at his watch and saw that it was past eleven o'clock. By this time she might have returned. But she had not returned, as he discovered when he reached his cottage. Ellen had come in and gone again; the whole house was tidy, and a note (another note) in Ellen's Alpine handwriting informed him that his breakfast was in the oven.

He ate hard fried eggs and bacon on the kitchen table, eating slowly. In the midst of it he got up and went out into the front hall. On the telephone table in the hall, Cross's manuscript still lay half out of its container and the briefcase, as he had left it. He drew it out so that he could see the title page. *A Study of Motives for Poisoning throughout the Ages. Gaudan Cross, Fielding Hall, Riverdale, N. Y.* He straightened the sheets carefully, sat down at the table, and picked up the telephone receiver.

"Operator. Operator? Can you tell me whether any long-distance call was put through from this number last night?"

Evidently they could.

"To where?"

"Yes, sir. Riverdale thhr-rr-ee six one," replied the brisk voice.

Replacing the receiver, he wandered into the living-room and took down a copy of *Gentlemen of the Jury* from a shelf. On the back of the jacket the picture of Cross looked out at him, a thin, intelligent, rather sombre face, with hooded eyes and dark hair having only a touch of grey. He recalled the statement of the learned judge, quoted as a blurb, that the man who wrote Cross's account of Neill Cream must have been in the courtroom; he recalled the newspaper comment, during the controversy, on the fact that Cross's age was given as forty. He put the book back, patted it into place among the others, and went upstairs. In the bedroom he opened the door of Marie's wardrobe, looking at each of the dresses that hung there. Since most of her clothes were at the New York apartment, there was not much to be seen.

Upstairs, downstairs, the clocks went on ticking; the usual tap drizzled in the bathroom; a creak or crack sported on the stairway: there rose up in loneliness the fifty noises of an empty house. He tried to read. He turned on the radio. He wondered whether he ought to have a drink; and, in his present mood, decided against it. At four o'clock it was a relief to find that he was out of tobacco, and that he must go down the road to the drug store for it. For he was on edge lest he should hear Brennan's step coming up the walk; it was too quiet; some rolling deviltry must have gathered again round Despard Park.

A few drops of rain struck him in the face when he went out of the house. He walked across King's Avenue and up the short road to the railway station. The tops of the big trees nodded and danced; all things seemed dusky here. He had almost reached the druggist's, where already lights glowed behind glass vats of red and green, when he heard what he thought he had heard the night before—his name called in the street. The door between the two windows labelled *J. Atkinson, Funeral Director,* was open. In the doorway some one was beckoning to him.

He crossed the street. The person who hailed him was a brisk, business-like, middle-aged man, growing somewhat portly, and very well dressed in a severely formal way. He had thin black hair, parted in the middle and brushed in strands across his head like the skeleton of a fish. His face was cherubic and genial, his manner pleasant.

"Mr. Stevens?" he said. "We haven't met, but I know you by sight. I'm Mr. Atkinson—Jonah Atkinson, junior. My father has retired. Would you mind coming inside for a moment? I think I have something for you."

Those discreet dark curtains beyond the windows were deceptive from the outside; they were higher then Stevens had expected. They shadowed the little waiting-room, a muffled soft-carpeted room with a curiously dream-like quality. It had an air of peace, as perhaps it was meant to have, and there was nothing to suggest its purpose except an immense marble urn, rather like the urns in the crypt, on either side of a rear door. Jonah Atkinson, whose every movement was unobtrusive, went to a table at one side of the room. If a certain curiosity was apparent in his manner, he seemed to be doing his best to repress it.

He came back, and held out to Stevens the photograph of Marie D'Aubray, who had been guillotined for murder in 1861.

"I was asked to return this to you," he said. . . . "Good Lord! is there anything wrong?" he added.

How to explain a feeling of nightmare? Even Jonah Atkinson's comfortable personality, even the black fishbone hair across his inclined forehead, partook of it. It was not merely caused by the picture. But Stevens, looking at the table from which he had taken the photograph, saw that on this table were unobtrusive magazines; and that, projecting from one of the magazines, a piece of string lay crookedly, and that the string was tied irregularly with knots.

"No. Oh no. No. Nothing," Stevens told him, remembering the detective-story fantasy he had once had about this place. "Where did you get this?"

Atkinson smiled. "I don't know whether you remember, but you got to Crispen last night by the 7:35 train. I was in the waiting-room here, after something or other, and I happened to look out of the window and see you——"

"Yes, yes, I noticed somebody!"

The other seemed puzzled. "There was a car waiting for you outside here. Just as the car turned round, I heard some one shouting out in the street. I thought I saw some one waving and shouting from the direction of the steps up to the railway platform. I opened the door there to see what was going on. The man who does part-time duty at the ticket office came down the steps when you drove away. It seems you dropped this photograph out of some manuscript, or something, in the train. The conductor noticed it, and tossed it out of the vestibule just before the train started again, to the man at the ticket office—he was just going off duty."

Stevens's thoughts flashed back to the train. In order to examine the photograph better, he had detached it from its clip to the paper. Then, when accosted by Welden, he had hurriedly shoved it out of sight under the manuscript. . . .

"The man," Atkinson said, with a touch of irritation, "came across here after you'd gone, when I was still standing in the door. He said he was going off duty, and would I mind giving this to you if I saw you. He thought it was very funny, that fellow did: he showed the photograph to me and said it was more in my line than his." Atkinson pointed to the inscription along the foot of the photograph, "guil—" "Anyhow, there it is. I thought you might want it."

"I don't think I could tell you," Stevens said, slowly, "how glad I am to get this back. I wish all the questions were as easily solved. Look here. I want to ask you something, but I don't want you to think I'm altogether crazy. It's very important." He pointed to the table. "How did that piece of string get there; the one with the knots in it?"

Atkinson, whose curiosity had clearly been about the picture, roused himself and peered round. Grunting he swept up the piece of string and put it into his pocket.

"That? Oh, that's my father's work. It's a habit of his; he leaves 'em all over the place. He's getting a little—well, you know. But he's always done that. He takes a piece of string and ties knots in it, the way some people smoke and others twist buttons or rattle keys, to keep his hands busy. They used to call him The Old Man in the Corner. Read detective stories? Remember those Baroness Orczy stories where the old man sits in his corner, in the 'blameless teashop,' and eternally ties knots and designs in a piece of string?" Atkinson looked at him sharply. "He's always done it, but he didn't use to be so careless. Why do you ask that?"

The last few minutes had seemed to Stevens a vista of memory. He recalled Partington's words last night, in speaking of Jonah Atkinson, senior, when he had thought Partington was drunk: "Old Jonah was a great favorite of Mark's father; Mark's father, with some sort of private joke, used to ask him whether he was still in his 'blameless teashop' or his 'corner'; I don't know what he meant."

"I'd like to ask a favor in return," Atkinson persisted. "Why do you ask that? It might be important to me. Has there been any—" He stopped. "I know you're a great friend of the Despards. We officiated at Mr. Despard's funeral. Has there been any——?"

"Trouble? Oh no." He wondered what, if anything, he was allowed to tell. "But could one of those pieces of string have—well, could it have got into Miles Despard's coffin?"

"I suppose it could. My father is still officially in charge," Atkinson replied. He added, with a somewhat unprofessional note in his voice: "Hell's bells! That's inexcusable! I hope——"

Yes, but was it to be supposed that Atkinson the elder, with such convenience, invariably made nine knots in a string? And how did that explain the fact that a string tied in nine knots was found under Miles Despard's pillow on the night he died, before the services of J. Atkinson were required? To Stevens, who was absently agreeing with everything Atkinson the younger said, this clarified very little with certainty.

It was both clarified and muddied; it explained the photograph; last night it might have explained everything. But now . . . At least he might make certain that Miles's body had actually been in the coffin when it was carried down into the crypt. Telling the undertaker as much as he dared, he asked his questions. And Atkinson was emphatic.

"I knew," he said, striking the table softly with his hand— "I know there was something queer going on at the Park! I've heard it everywhere. Oh yes; it's between ourselves, of course. But I can certainly tell you what you want to know. There's no doubt whatever that Mr. Despard's body was put into the coffin. I helped do it myself. The pallbearers took over directly afterwards. My assistants will confirm all this. And the pall-bearers, as you know, carried it directly to the crypt."

Quietly the front door of the waiting-room opened and a man came in from the street.

In the street there was a dull grey light, with streaks and slurs of rain on the windows. The newcomer was silhouetted against it. He was a very small man, and much shrivelled, despite the fact that he wore a big fur coat. Some dandyism about the fur coat, or about the rakish brown soft hat drawn down in front, gave an unpleasant suggestion of Miles Despard. Yet dead men do not have limousines, like the Mercedes which was drawn up at the curb outside, with a chauffeur at the wheel. Above all the newcomer had only to take two steps forward, and it became clear that this was not Miles.

The fur coat was not extravagant dandyism; it had the antiquity of what conservative men wore thirty years ago. This man was over seventy. He had a face of remarkable ugliness; a wizened face, an almost simian face despite a good beak of a nose: yet it was not unattractive. Stevens had an impression that the face was familiar and that he had seen it many times, though he could not place it—it was blurred like a drawing. The newcomer's monkey-bright eyes, cynical and rather savage, darted round the room. They rested on Stevens.

"Pray excuse this intrusion," he said. "May I have a word with you, sir? I followed you in. I have come a long way in order to see you. My name is Cross—Gaudan Cross."

XVIII

"YES, it is quite true," the newcomer said, composedly. He reached into the furs and extracted a card. Then he regarded Stevens with a sort of quizzical impatience. "You were thinking that this face of mine," he pointed to it, "is a somewhat older and less attractive one than I insist on having published on the jackets of my books. Obviously. Otherwise I should not have it published there. If you look closely, however, you will see some resemblance to me as I was some thirty years ago. That picture was taken before I was sent to prison."

Again he lifted a gloved hand.

"You were further thinking," he went on, "that my royalties, while tolerable enough, are hardly sufficient to pay for—" He pointed to the car outside. "You are quite right. When I went to prison I had a passable sum of money. A beneficent rate of interest, while I was unable to spend any of the money, brought it up to something like a fortune; and I contrived to add to it by literary work while I was in prison. That is the difference between financiers and authors. Financiers make money and then go to prison. Authors go to prison and then make money. Mr. Atkinson, I hope you will excuse us. Mr. Stevens, please come with me."

He held open the door; and Stevens, in dumb astonishment, followed him out. The chauffeur opened the door of the car.

"Get in," said Cross.

"Where are we going?"

"I have not the slightest idea," said Cross. "Drive anywhere, Henry."

The car hummed softly. It was warm in the grey-upholstered back of the limousine. Cross sat in one corner, regarding his guest intently. Over his face had come the same expression of savagery and cynicism, tempered with something Stevens could

170

not read. He gravely took out a cigar-case and tendered it. Stevens, whose nerves needed tobacco badly, accepted one.

"Well?" said Cross.

With the same air of gravity or cynicism he removed his hat and held it above his head. Though his hair was thick enough at the sides, this revealed a shrunken bald head with one hair standing up and waving above it. Oddly enough, the effect was not ludicrous; it may have been because the monkey-bright eyes were grim.

"Well what?"

"Are you still aflame with jealousy?" inquired Cross. "I refer to the fact that your wife, whom I never saw before in my life, drove innumerable miles last night in order to wake me up at a damned hour and ask me questions. Your wife slept in my house. But you should perceive now that it was no assignation. Altogether aside from the fact that I sleep with Mrs. Murgenroyd, my housekeeper, my age should be a good enough guarantee of that. I hope, sir, you guessed that your wife had gone to me. You will have done so if you have any intelligence, which I am inclined to doubt."

"You have," said the other, "aside from Ogden Despard, probably more unadulterated nerve than any person I know. And, since plain speaking seems to be in order, I'll admit that you're not exactly my idea of a dangerous co-respondent."

"Ah, that's better," chuckled Cross. He added, sharply: "And yet why not? You have youth—yes. Health—I dare say. But I have intelligence. Did your editorial head—what's-his-name, Morley?—tell you anything about me?"

Stevens thought back. "No. He asked me if I'd met you, that's all. Where is Marie now?"

"At your house. No, wait!" He shot his arm across towards the door of the car. "Don't get out—not yet. Plenty of time." Then Cross sat back, smoking his cigar thoughtfully, and his face grew less wizened. "Young man, I am seventy-five. I have studied more criminal cases than a man of a hundred and seventy-five ought to have studied. That was partly because I had a first-hand opportunity: I spent twenty years in prison. As a favor to your wife, I am here to advise you."

"I thank you," said his guest, in the same grave tone. "I shouldn't have spoken as I did a minute ago. But in that case"

171

—he took the photograph of Marie D'Aubray out of his pocket—"will you in the name of sanity tell me what this means? And why she went to you? And the origin of your name, or ancestry, if your name is really Gaudan Cross?"

Again the dry chuckle convulsed Cross before he became grave.

"Ah, so you have been attempting deduction. Your wife was afraid you had. Yes, my name is really Gaudan Cross, in the sense that I have a right to it. I changed it to that by deed-poll when I was twenty-one years old. I was born with the name of Alfred Mossbaum. Do not misunderstand me. I am a Jew, and, like all the great men of my race, I am proud to be one. If it were not for us you would live without foundations and I think your tidy world would go to hell. But I am also," Cross said, rather superfluously, "an egotist. The name of Alfred Mossbaum was not euphonious enough to describe me. You agree?

"You had better know something about me. Crime was my hobby; it has always been my hobby since I was a young man. Of course I was in England when Cream was caught and tried. Of course I was in France when Pranzini was caught and tried. Of course I know the Borden case as few others know it. In my late thirties, in order to show that crime was a matter of simplicity, I committed a crime. You immediately retort: As a matter of demonstrating how simple it is to escape punishment for crime, you spent twenty years in prison. That is true. But I was detected in the only conceivable way I could have been detected—by detecting myself. I got drunk and I boasted."

He blew out a cloud of smoke and brushed it away. Then he turned his monkey-bright eyes round again.

"But what an opportunity! In prison I became the warden's right-hand man. Do you realize what that means? It means that I had direct access to the full records of every criminal case; not only of that place, but of every other place to which the warden chose to send for particulars. In some cases I knew the men themselves, better than the judges who tried them or the juries which condemned them. I knew the man-hunters who caught them. Consequently, I made no application for parole or shortening of sentence. Where could I live better? I lived at some one else's expense while my money was being saved for me. When I came out I should be a rich man."

172

"That," said Stevens, "is undoubtedly one way of looking at it."

"There was one drawback. It was, I think you will admit, a social hindrance afterwards, especially when I began to write. I had served my sentence under the—you acknowledge—unusual name of Gaudan Cross. I flew my own banner. I did not become Alfred Mossbaum again when it became necessary to hide my head. But the name was easily remembered. I did not wish too many people to connect Gaudan Cross, the new and brilliant literary figure, with the Gaudan Cross who had gone to prison for murder in the year 1895. That is why my age is firmly given as forty, and a photograph so early as to be indistinguishable is on every book."

"It was murder, was it?"

"Naturally," answered Cross, with a simplicity of evil which startled his guest. Cross's gloved hand brushed ash off his coat. "But I wished you to understand why I wrote with authority. You ask me why your wife came to me? I will tell you. Because, as she was aware from a glance at the first chapter of my new book—there is not one paragraph which is not annotated with documentation—*I* knew the facts. And she did not."

"The facts about what?"

"About Marie D'Aubray in 1676. About Marie D'Aubray in 1861. About her ancestry; or, more properly, what she thinks is her ancestry."

"You seem to know, or to follow," Stevens began, slowly, "a good deal of what I'm thinking. I am thinking something now . . . not only about the present, but about the past and the long past . . . about the dead and the non-dead. Is there any truth in it?"

"There is not—I regret to say," snapped Cross. "At least, in her own case."

Stevens's thoughts were something like this: I am sitting in a comfortable limousine, smoking a very good cigar, with a self-confessed murderer whom I both trust and distrust. Yet the very presence of this engaging little mummy has done more to lift a weight off my mind, and make me see things in decent perspective, than all those explanations in the undertaker's parlor. He looked out of the window of the car, where grey rain was beginning to shroud the Lancaster Highway.

"You have been married three years, I understand," said Cross, blinking. "Do you know anything about her? No, you do not. Why don't you? All women chatter. If you mention an uncle of yours, she mentions an uncle of hers. If you tell how a respected great-aunt of yours once threw a tomato at a cat and hit a policeman instead, she will reply with a family anecdote of a similarly improving nature. Why didn't you hear any family anecdotes? Because she had something locked up inside. Why was she always condemning certain things as morbid? Because she was afraid of them herself. Bah! I got the whole story out of her in ten minutes. And I was naturally in a position either to confirm or dispel her notions.

"Listen to me. At a place called Guibourg, which is a dismal hole in north-western Canada, there really is a family of D'Aubrays which is remotely descended from the D'Aubrays who hatched the Marquise de Brinvilliers. They also hatched the Marie D'Aubray whose picture you have there. So far, so true. I know this because, in preparation for the essay in my new book, I underwent the martyrdom of spending two weeks in Guibourg, tracing the family records. I wished to see whether there were any more examples of this 'non-dead' legend. I do not listen to legends: I examine birth certificates and parish registers. Your esteemed wife is not even connected with the family, although she thinks she is. She was adopted, at the age of three, by Miss Adrienne D'Aubray, the sole remaining branch of a rotten tree. Her name is no more D'Aubray than mine is Cross. Her mother was a French Canadian and her father a Scotch laborer."

"I don't know," muttered Stevens, "whether we're now in the province governed by the laws of witchcraft or the laws of sense. But look at that picture. There's an amazing resemblance, even to——"

"Why," said Cross, "do you think she was adopted at all?"

"Adopted at all?"

"Yes. Because of that resemblance. No other reason. Because Miss Adrienne D'Aubray, figuratively speaking, is an old witch herself. If I lived all the year round in Guibourg, I should begin to believe she was a real one. Listen. In Guibourg the sky is dark, and it snows a good part of the year. Do you know where even the name Guibourg comes from? In the seventeenth century the Black Mass was known as *La messe de Guibourg*. The

amily lives in a long low house against a hill with fir trees on
t. They own timber, and they are well-off, but they do not go
out much even if there were anywhere to go. The weather shuts
them in to look at pictures in the fire. Miss Adrienne D'Aubray
adopted the child of a Scotch laborer for the sole purpose of
bringing her up to think she had the blood of the non-dead, and
that one day *the* non-dead would creep into her skin. She
showed her pictures. She told her stories, and pointed out
things among the fir trees. When the girl was punished, she was
punished as her alleged ancestress was, with a funnel and
water. She was burnt, to show what it would be like. Do I
need to elaborate?"

"No," said Stevens, and put his face in his hands.

Cross had an extraordinary animation, as though he admired
all this as a work of art. Then he sat back and puffed his cigar
complacently. The cigar was too big for him; it destroyed any
effect at the Mephistophelian on his part.

"That, young man, is the girl you have been living with,"
he said, more gently. "She kept the secret well. The trouble
was . . . I gather it was this. Her marriage to you, it appears,
almost succeeded in getting the past out of her system. Then,
through your association with this Despard family, it seems
that a few accidents began to bring it back again. Mrs. Mark
Despard, one Sunday afternoon, started a conversation about
poisons in the presence of a nurse who was taking care of a
sick uncle—" Cross looked at him sharply.

"I know."

"Oho! You know? Well, your spouse had been repressing
the goblins too long, putting them in a box and shutting the
lid on them; and all of a sudden they got out. The talk about
poisons did it. In her own hardly descriptive phrase, 'she felt
queer all over.' 'The curse is come upon me, cried the Lady
of Shalott,' " said Cross, disgustedly, and spat smoke at the
glass partition. "Good God! She was even foolish enough to
run out of the room after the nurse and gabble something
about poison. She informs me that she can't think why she did
it. A brain specialist could tell her. Actually, there is nothing
in the least the matter with her. She is too fundamentally normal and sound. If she had not been, I dare say Aunt Adrienne's
teaching might have produced a weird graduate. However, it
appears that—not three weeks after this conversation about

175

poisons—the old uncle of the family died. On top of that, you walked in with my manuscript and uttered sinister sound On top of *that*, this Mark Despard entered with a tame docto and informed you (while she was listening at the door), first that he had positive proof his uncle was poisoned; second, tha a woman in a Marquise de Brinvilliers dress had been seer in the uncle's room. He didn't do much explaining, but h hinted at many extra-normal things. If you are unable to im agine her state of mind at this point in the business, you ar even duller than I think you are. She had to know the fact about her own ancestry."

Stevens remained with his head between his hands, starin, at the grey carpeting on the floor of the car.

"Tell the chauffeur to turn back, will you?" he requested after a pause. "I want to get back to her. So help me God, I'l see that she never has the hobgoblins again as long as I live.'

Cross gave an order into the mouthpiece. "This is a mos interesting study," he observed, with monkey-like lordliness "The role of soother of the waters is new to me; and one, may inform you, which pains my neck insufferably. However, —a complete stranger—have been delegated to tell you all thi before she faces you, because she does not seem to like the task. It seems, for some reason wholly inexplicable to me, tha she loves you. Is there anything else you would like to ask?"

"Well, yes, if she said anything about it . . . did she sa anything about morphia tablets?"

Cross was irritable. "Yes. I forgot that. Yes, she stole mor phia. Do you know why? No, don't answer; you do not know why. But carry your mind back. You and she were at this famou (and to me painful) Despard Park on a certain night. Do yo remember the date?"

"Without any trouble. It was the night of Saturday, Apri 8th."

"Yes. Do you remember what all of you were doing a Despard Park?"

"Why, we went up to play bridge, but—" He stopped. "Bu we didn't. The evening was devoted to telling ghost stories.''

"That's true. You were telling ghost stories, and I gathe some highly unpleasant ones, in the dark, before a womar already half insane with a fear she could not reveal to anyone

---

[1] For corroboration of this, it is suggested that the reader consult pages 82-83

There was only one thing she wanted. She wanted sleep. She wanted sleep beyond the remote possibility of remaining awake an instant after she had gone to bed; she wanted to blot out dreams and hags as you turn out a light. I am not surprised *you* didn't notice, but how it escaped the attention of the Despard family is beyond me. The Despards as an influence seem to be bad for both of you. They are great invokers of witches. . . ."

Outside a faint growl of thunder followed the smooth humming of the car. Rain began to tick more steadily on the windows. Cross, letting down one window to throw away his cigar, swore as the rain blew in. But Stevens felt that his mind had been cleaned and swept—of all except one thing. There remained the problem.

"Invokers of witches," he repeated. "Yes, that's just exactly true. Things seem in different focus now, somehow. But still there's the round, flat, immovable fact of impossibility. A man's body disappears from a crypt——"

"Oh, it does, does it?" demanded Cross, jumping like a monkey on a stick. He leaned forward. "That's what I was coming to. I said I was here to advise you, as a favor to your wife, and I insist on knowing what happened. It will take ten minutes before we get back to your house. Tell me about it."

"Glad to. I was only wondering how much I'm supposed to tell. Of course, the police are there now, so it will have to come out, anyway. Captain Brennan——"

"Brennan?" demanded Cross, and put his hands on his knees with an air of alertness. "Not Francis Xavier Brennan? Foxy Frank? Fellow who's always telling anecdotes about his father?"

"That's the man. Do you know him?"

"I have known Frank Brennan," said Cross, cocking a meditative eye, "since he was a sergeant. I get a Christmas card from him every year. He plays an admirable hand of poker; but he is limited. In any case, they all listen to me. Now go on with the story."

As he listened, by some illusion Cross's face seemed to grow alternately younger and older as some point pleased or displeased him. Occasionally he said, "Beautiful!" or gave a fillip to the brim of his rakish hat; but he only interrupted once, which was to tell the chauffeur to go slower.

"And you believed all this?" he asked.

"I don't know what I believed or still believe. When they brought in that witchcraft business——"

"Witchcraft be blanked," observed Cross, using a pungent term. "I trust that you will not insult the nobility of the black arts by comparing them to this piece of charlatanism. It's murder, man! It's *murder:* rather well stage-managed, and perhaps with a fine aesthetic conception behind it; but the contriver was of hesitant and bungling mind, and the best part of it was pure accident."

"Are you going to tell me you have an idea how it was worked and who worked it?"

"Of course I have," said Cross.

An enormous crash of thunder struck low and rolled in split echoes down the sky; it was followed almost instantly by the lightning, and then the windows grew even darker with driving rain.

"In that case, who is the murderer?"

"A member of that household, obviously."

"I've got to warn you that they all have cast-iron alibis. Except, of course, the Hendersons——"

"I think I may assure you that the Hendersons had nothing to do with this. Besides, this was some one rather more intimately concerned with the death of Miles Despard, and affected by it, than the Hendersons could have been. As for your alibis, do not be impressed. When I murdered Royce (who, I may add, quite deserved death) I had a complete alibi: twenty people, including the waiter, were willing to testify that I was having dinner at Delmonico's. It was an ingenious and amusing device, which I shall be happy to explain to you when there is more time. The same thing occurred when I committed the robbery by which I obtained my original means of livelihood. In *this* case there is scarcely an original feature. Even the means by which the body was stolen from the crypt, while executed with some degree of finesse, was improved on by my friend Bastion. Bastion finished his sentence in '06; unfortunately, when he left us and returned to England, they were compelled to hang him; but in the meantime he did certain things which were, from an artistic standpoint, commendable. However, I see that we are slowing down."

Stevens was out on the sidewalk almost before the car had

stopped at the familiar gate. No lights showed in the house. But at the beginning of the walk leading up to the door stood a familiar bulky figure under an umbrella. The figure stared, so that the umbrella wobbled and rain splashed inside upon the neat overcoat of Captain Brennan.

"Frank," said Cross, "come here. Get into the car."

"So it's you—" said Brennan. "Sorry, Mr. Cross, I can't stop now. I've got business here. Afterwards——"

"You foxy-faced bandit," said Cross, "I have learned more about this case in fifteen minutes than you have learned in a day. I'll smarten things up. *I'll* make the fur fly and take the watch-springs out of the miracles! Get into this car. I have somewhat to say unto you."

Brennan, the umbrella flapping inside out, was in some fashion impelled into the car. Stevens, with the rain beating gratefully on his face, watched them drive away. He could not have spoken. His throat was thick, and relief left him almost physically dizzy. But he turned round and went up the walk to the front door, and Marie was waiting for him there.

XIX

THEY stood presently by a rear window of the living-room, looking out into the garden. He had his arm round her, and upon both of them was peace. It might have been six o'clock. The rain had almost ceased to stir and scamper on the eaves; though it was not yet twilight, there was a white mist in the garden. Dimly through it they could see the sodden grass, the shape of the elm tree, the flower-beds which had lost form and color. Their separate stories had been told.

"I don't know why I couldn't tell you," she said, and her hand tightened round his waist. "Sometimes because it seemed too ridiculous, and sometimes because it seemed too awful. And then you were so—so *easy*. About everything. But people don't easily get away from things like Aunt Adrienne. I broke away from her, of course, when I came of age."

"It's all over, Marie. There's no reason to talk about it now."

"But there is!" Marie said, and lifted her head up a little. Yet she did not tremble; the grey eyes were smiling. "That's

179

what's caused all the trouble, not talking about it. I've always been trying to find out about it. You remember the first day we ever met each other, in Paris?"

"Yes. Number 16, rue Neuve St. Paul."

"The house of—" She stopped. "I went there, and sat in the courtyard, and wondered whether I should feel anything. It sounds so completely absurd, now I do talk about it, that Aunt Adrienne must have had horrible powers. You never saw my home, Ted. I don't want you ever to see it. There was a hill behind. . . ." She put her head back, so that he could see the full line of her throat, and it quivered, but not with fear. She was laughing. "Now, I've a sure cure for all this. If I should ever happen to get the blue devils again, or flinch, or have a nightmare sleeping or waking, I want you to do just one thing. You whisper, 'Maggie MacTavish' to me and I'll be all right."

"Why Maggie MacTavish?"

"That's my real name, darling. It's a lovely name. It's a magic name. You can't turn it into anything else, no matter how hard you try. But I wish the Despards weren't so . . . so . . . I don't know what I mean. That house up there is so much like the one I used to live in that it brought the whole thing back to me when I thought you'd chased it out of my system. It's funny; I couldn't keep away from that house. It haunted me, or I haunted it. And listen, Ted, I really *did* ask about buying arsenic! That was the horrible part. I don't know what——"

"Maggie," he said, "MacTavish."

"Oh, that's all right. But I think the climax was that Saturday night when they were telling those ghost stories, and Mark told that foul one about . . . Any minute I thought I was going to start screaming. I felt I had to forget it for a little while or I would go out of my mind. And I did steal those drug tablets, though I put the bottle back next day. Ted, I don't wonder at what you were thinking! Now the evidence against me is all piled up, it would have convinced myself if I'd thought of all of it. People have been burned at the stake on less."

He drew her round to face him, and touched one of her eyelids.

"As a matter of academic interest," he asked, "you didn't

happen to dose both yourself and me on the following Wednesday night, did you? That was the thing that stuck in my head most. I was dog tired that night, and I went to sleep at ten-thirty."

"No, I honestly didn't," she told him. "That's true, Ted. And, anyway, I couldn't have, because I only took one tablet, after all, and I cut that in half when I——"

"One tablet! But there were supposed to be three missing."

She was puzzled. "Then somebody else must have been at the bottle," she said, with positiveness and obvious truth. "I was afraid of the things, really; I didn't know but what I might kill myself, or something. Ted, I wonder what on earth the whole mess is about? Somebody did kill poor Miles. I know *I* didn't, not even in a dream, because I couldn't get to sleep until half-past eleven on that night. I wasn't drugged and I wasn't drunk, and I was lying right beside you and I remember it. You don't know how much it's helped to remember that. But I think that somebody up in the Park guessed what was worrying me. You say Edith . . ."

She broke off, brushing the subject away.

"But, oh my God! Ted, as much as I talk about being free now, it's nothing to how I'll feel if it's shown there's a natural explanation for all this! I mean—the murder. *Is* there? *Can* there be? You say Mr. Cross . . . What do you think of him, by the way?"

Stevens considered. "Well, he's an old brigand, of course. By his own story he's a murderer and a thief and I don't know what else: that is, unless it's all hot air. If I had something he wanted, I should keep my eye open in case he cut my throat to get it. He seems completely without moral sense; if there were really any hang-over from the seventeenth century in human form, my guess is that it would take the form of Cross . . ."

"Don't say that."

"One moment, Maggie. I was going to add that, even when you say all this, the man is immensely likable—he seems to have taken a great fancy to you—and he is about as shrewd as they make 'em. Furthermore, if he manages to solve this mystery I'm going to boost his royalty rate up to twenty-five per cent on the first three thousand."

She shivered. Leaning forward, she started to open the window, and he opened it for her, so that they could both smell the clean air.

"It's misty, though," she said. "I thought I smelt smoke. When this is all over, couldn't you get leave of absence so we could take a trip somewhere? Or maybe I ought to have Aunt Adrienne down here, to see how she looks away from her setting at Guibourg, and prove that she's only an ugly old woman, after all. Do you know, I really can recite the ritual of the Black Mass? I saw it— It's a foul thing; I'll tell you about it sometime. And that reminds me. Just a minute."

She broke away from him and ran out into the hall; he heard her going upstairs. When she returned she was holding out, as though it might burn her, the gold bracelet with the cat's head. Even in the gloom by the window he could see that her face was flushed and her breast was heaving.

"There it is. That's the only thing of *hers* I have now," she said. She lifted her eyes, and he could see the pin-point black pupil in the grey iris. "I kept it because it was rather pretty and because it was supposed to bring good luck. But now I've seen it in the photograph of your eighteen-sixties lady, I want to have it melted down or—" She looked out of the window.

"That's right. Fire it out the window."

"It—it cost a lot of money, though," Marie said, doubtfully.

"Be damned to that. I'll buy you a better one. Here, give it to me."

All his own rage at himself seemed to have become centred in that bracelet as a symbol. With a long, low whip, like a catcher to second base, he sent it flying out of the window; and relief welled up in him with the very swing of his arm. It curved past the elm tree, flicking a branch, and was lost in the mist; and at the same time there rose out of the mist the sudden squall and snarl of a cat.

"Ted, don't—" cried Marie. Then she said, "You heard that."

"I heard it," he said, grimly. "That's a good heavy bracelet, and there was steam behind it. If it caught that cat in the ribs, there was good reason for the cat to yowl."

"But there's somebody coming," she told him, after a pause. First they heard footsteps in wet grass, then on the gravel path. A figure began to loom up out of the mist, hurrying and taking stumping steps.

"Agreed," he replied. "But did you think you were calling spirits out of the vasty deep? That's only Lucy Despard."

"Lucy?" said Marie, in a queer tone. "Lucy? But why is she coming the back way?"

They both went out to the back door before Lucy had knocked. Lucy came into the kitchen, pulling off a sodden hat, and rather fiercely smoothing down her dark hair. Her coat had been put on in such a hurry that her dress was disarranged, and the lids of her eyes were red, though she was not crying now. She sat down in a white chair.

"I'm sorry, but I've really got to inflict myself on you for a while," she said. She looked at Marie as though in appraisal and wonder, but new worries seemed to come into her head and she dismissed the first thought. Her voice was husky. "I couldn't stand it up there any longer. Yes—I will have a drink, if you've got one. There have been awful things happening up there. Ted . . . Marie . . . Mark's run away."

"Run away? Why?"

She remained silent for a moment, looking at the floor. Marie put a hand on her shoulder.

"Because I sent him, in a way; and other things," answered Lucy. "It—it was all right until lunch. We wanted that rather nice police officer—Foxy Frank, you know—to have lunch with us. But he wouldn't; he insisted on going out to a lunch-wagon. Up to then Mark had been very quiet. He still was quiet. He didn't say anything or even show any temper, but that's why I knew something was up. We all went into the dining-room, and just as we were going to sit down at the table, Mark walked up to Ogden and hit him in the face. Then he beat him. How he beat him! I couldn't stand watching it, and nobody could pull him off. You know what Mark is. He beat him until . . . well, afterwards Mark just walked out of the room without saying anything, and went to the library and smoked a cigarette."

She drew a shuddering breath and looked up. Marie, puzzled and uneasy, glanced from Stevens back to Lucy.

"I wouldn't have wanted to see it," Marie said, with a higher color; "but, honestly, Lucy, I can't see anything to make much

183

fuss about. There, if you want the truth! Why somebody hasn't done that to Ogden before I've never been able to understand. He's been asking for it for a long time."

"He has," agreed Stevens. "It was for writing that letter and sending those telegrams, I suppose? Good for Mark."

"Yes, Ogden admitted he did that. But that wasn't all. The person who antagonizes Ogden," said Lucy, in a colorless voice, "is a fool."

"I'm not so sure of that," observed Marie. "*I'm* willing to antagonize him. He—well, he tried to make up to me, once, in a more or less subtle way; and he seemed completely staggered that I wasn't in the least impressed."

"Just a minute," said Lucy. "That's not all. Edith and I washed his face and brought him round; he was beaten clear insensible, you see. As soon as Ogden could get on his feet he called us all together and said he had something to tell us. He took the room next to the one Mark was in, so Mark could hear. . . . I—I don't know how much you've heard about Tom Partington's case. Doctor Partington. He used to be engaged to Edith. But it was discovered that he performed an abortion, and he only escaped criminal prosecution by getting out of the country. Edith always believed, or said she believed, that the girl was his mistress. As a matter of fact, I don't think Edith ever really cared for him. Edith's a grand person, but she's cold, cold as ice; and I believe she was only getting married for the show of the thing. So she broke it off because of this girl—Jeannette White. . . . But Ogden told the truth today. The girl wasn't Tom Partington's mistress. She was *Mark's*."

After a pause Lucy added, in the same colorless voice: "Tom was Mark's best friend, and yet Mark never told him, never told anybody else. He let Edith go on thinking what she did think. Tom Partington never knew who the man was, for the girl wouldn't tell. So Mark kept quiet in spite of how much Tom cared for Edith. You see, Mark was engaged to me at the time, and he was afraid to speak."

Stevens paced up and down the kitchen. He thought: Affairs are too much tangled and incomprehensible in this world. If Mark Despard did that, he did a meaner thing than Ogden has ever done; and yet it does not particularly lower Mark in my opinion; for to me Mark will always remain likable, and Ogden, to put it civilly, something else altogether. He found, with some surprise, that Marie felt the same way.

"So Ogden," said Marie, with contempt, "played tattle-tale."

"That's not the point," interposed Stevens. "How did Partington take it? Was he there?"

"Oh yes," Lucy replied, nodding with a dry, bright glaze in her eyes. "And that wasn't so bad. It didn't seem to bother him greatly. He just shrugged his shoulders—and spoke pretty sensibly. He said ten years was too long a time to bother over anything much, particularly a love-affair. He said that by this time he was more in love with liquor than he could be with any woman. No, it wasn't Tom that made the trouble. It was I. I said some pretty awful things. I also told Mark I never wanted to see him again, and in that quiet, solemn way of his he took me at my word."

"But what on earth for?" cried Marie, opening her eyes. It surprised her husband that this Dresden-china doll, now wearing her spiritual expression again, could go so practically to the point. "I mean, why did you have to say that? After all, it can't be because he—did things to this girl ten years ago. Lucy dear, you find me a man who hasn't done that, and he'll be rather awful, won't he? And it was ten years ago. What's more, it can't be because he let this Mr. Partington down so badly. That's very wrong and terrible, no doubt; agreed; but, after all, it only showed Mark loved you, didn't it? And that's all *I'd* care about."

Stevens had prepared a drink for Lucy, who took it with eagerness. She hesitated over it, put it down, and the color in her face grew higher.

"Because I'm afraid," she said, "he's been seeing the girl again since."

"The same girl? Jeannette White?"

"The same girl."

"And is Ogden," asked Stevens, bitterly—"is Ogden, as usual, the source of information? Personally, I think Ogden must be unhinged. He's had to conceal his malice for so long, under a sort of good-fellowly and pleasant unpleasantness, that now he's come into his uncle's money, it's gone to his head."

Lucy fixed her eyes steadily on him. "You remember, Ted, the mysterious phone call which almost took me away from

185

the dance at St. Davids, so that except for a freak of luck I shouldn't have had an alibi? That call was anonymous——"

"Ogden's touch is discernible again."

"Yes, I think it was Ogden." She took up the glass. "That's why I almost obeyed it. Whatever else Ogden is, he's invariably *accurate*. That call said that Mark was tied up again with his 'old flame, Jeannette White.' You see, at that time I hadn't heard—or at least I couldn't remember—the name of the girl in the Partington scandal; I never connected the two. But it was a woman. And Mark . . . doesn't seem to care much about me any longer."

She got the words out with difficulty. Then she emptied her glass very quickly, and remained staring at the opposite wall.

"The call said that on that very night, using the convenience of masks so that I shouldn't know where he was, Mark was going back to our house and see this girl. In our own *house*. The call said that, if I would take fifteen minutes out and drive to Crispen, I could see for myself. At first I didn't believe it. Then I looked all over the house where the masquerade was being held, and I didn't see Mark. (As a matter of fact, he was playing billiards in a room at the back of the house with two friends of ours; I found that out later.) I started to go out; then I thought the whole thing was ridiculous, and I came back. But then, this afternoon, when Ogden came out with the name of Jeannette White as being the girl in the Partington scandal, I—I——"

"But are you sure it's true?" demanded Stevens. "If Ogden's phone call was wrong that night, why shouldn't this accusation be wrong?"

"Because Mark admitted it. And now he's gone. Ted, you've got to find him! It isn't for me; it's for his own sake. When Captain Brennan learns Mark's gone, he's likely to think all sorts of things that haven't anything to do with this case."

"Doesn't Brennan know it yet?"

"No. He went out a while ago, and came back with an odd little man in an awful fur coat, who's most amusing, but I'm not in the mood for being amused. Captain Brennan asked me whether I'd mind having the man around, because he says this man—Croft or Cross I think his name is—knows criminals' minds as he knows the palm of his hand. They went down into

186

the crypt, and when they came up again Captain Brennan was red in the face and this little man was laughing fit to burst. All I could gather was that they didn't find a secret passage there. I asked Joe Henderson what they were doing, and . . . You know that old wooden door at the foot of the stairs into the crypt, that won't quite close?"

"Yes. Well?"

"Cross was moving that back and forth, Joe says, and laughing again. I don't know what's up, but it scares me. Then they went up to the sun porch—you know, with the glass door looking into Uncle Miles's room. They fiddled with the curtain, and sighted through it, and had a fine time of one sort or another. Have you any idea what they meant?"

"No. But," said Stevens, "there's something else on your mind, Lucy. This isn't all. What else is worrying you?"

Lucy's jaw became set.

"It doesn't worry me, exactly," she responded, with such rapidity as to be almost incoherent. "That is, it might be in any house. Captain Brennan admitted that himself, when he found it; it doesn't necessarily mean anything. All the same, it would worry us horribly if we hadn't known we all had perfectly good alibis for Wednesday night. The fact is, not very long after you left, Ted, Captain Brennan found arsenic in the house."

"Arsenic! Good God! Where?"

"In the kitchen. I could have told him myself it was there, if I'd remembered it. But I had no reason or occasion to think of it, had I? Nobody so much as mentioned arsenic until to-day. . . ."

"Who bought it, Lucy?"

"Edith bought it. For the rats. But she'd forgotten all about it."

There was a silence. Lucy again tried to drain an empty glass. With a little shiver, Marie went over and opened the back door.

"The wind has changed," she said; "there's going to be another storm tonight."

XX

THERE was another storm that night, while Stevens end-lessly drove round Philadelphia in search of Mark. Mark might not necessarily have gone into town, of course; but he had not taken a car or packed a bag. He might have gone any-where. Stevens's first belief, that he had merely reached a point of bedevilment beyond his nerves' capacity and had, therefore, gone on a spree, changed to uneasiness when there was no trace of him at his clubs, at his office, or any usual haunt.

Wet and dispirited, Stevens returned late to Crispen. It had been arranged that Cross should spend the night at his cottage; but he did not see Cross until nearly midnight. He went first to Despard Park, giving Lucy false reassurances about Mark. The house was very quiet, and Lucy seemed the only one still up. When Stevens went back to his own house, he found Cross and Brennan in the former's limousine, just outside.

"Have you—?" he asked.

Brennan seemed rather gloomy than otherwise. "Yes, I think we know the murderer," Brennan answered. "There's one more thing I've got to verify; I'm going in to town to do it now. And then . . . yes, I'm afraid it'll be all up."

"Although in general," said Cross, sticking his neck out of the car, "I deplore these humanitarian notions, which have nothing whatsoever to do with the study of crime, this time I cannot agree with my foxy friend. This, sir, is an ugly busi-ness, a damned ugly and unpleasant business, and I shall not be sorry to see the guilty person electrocuted. Mr. Stevens, I regret to say that I shall be unable to avail myself of your hos-pitality tonight, much as I am obliged for the invitation to spend it under your roof. I must continue with Brennan and prove my case. However, I promise you a solution. If you and your good lady would care to call at Despard Park tomorrow afternoon at two o'clock precisely, I shall introduce you to the murderer.—Henry, forward. Step on her tail."

Marie, she confessed, was not sorry Cross could not remain there for the night. "He's been very nice, and I'm terribly grateful to him," she said, "but there's something creepy about him. He seems to know exactly what you're thinking about."

Though they went to bed at midnight, and though he had had no sleep the night before, Stevens could not close his eyes; he was too strung-up and over-tired. The clock in the bedroom ticked loudly. Thunder was incessant for the first part of the night, and there seemed to be an unusual noise and disturbance of cats round the house. Marie fell into an uneasy doze; towards two o'clock she was stirring and muttering in her sleep, and he turned on the bedside lamp, intending to wake her if she wandered into a nightmare. She was pale, her dark-gold hair spread out on the pillow. Whether at the light, or the rain, or the congested weather, the noise of cats seemed to have come in close round the house. He looked round for something to throw, but he could find nothing except an empty jar of cold cream or something like it in the drawer of Marie's dressing-table. When he opened the window and threw a missile for the second time that day, he was rewarded by a squall of such almost human savagery that he closed the window. He fell into a troubled doze himself about three o'clock, and did not awake until he heard church bells on the following Sunday morning.

When they set out for Despard Park just before two o'clock, they dressed as carefully as though for church. It was a rather heavy spring day, with the sun behind clouds, yet of warmth and kindliness. A Sunday hush was on Crispen and on the Park when they walked up through it.

The front door was opened by Mrs. Henderson.

Stevens examined her with a refreshed air of interest, as though he had never seen her before. She was stout and very plain, with a hard but kindly face, buns of greyish hair over her ears, an ample bust, and a petulant chin. You would diagnose her as a woman who might nag, but who would not see ghosts. Her Sunday-best clothes sat on her with an air of creaking. In the last fifteen minutes she had evidently been weeping.

"I saw you come up the path," she told them, with dignity. "They're all upstairs. All but Mrs. Despard. Why *she*—" Mrs. Henderson broke off plaintively, as at some grievance she thought better to repress in deference to Sunday. She turned round, her shoes squeaking, and began to lead the way. "But *I* say," she added, darkly, over her shoulder, "this is no day for games."

Apparently she referred to the fact that a hoarse voice, of

189

inhuman loudness, was talking somewhere upstairs. It was evidently the radio in the sun porch, for she was leading them towards the sun porch. As they passed along the upstairs hall in the west wing, Stevens saw a figure dodge back into one of the doors. It was Ogden, for he also caught sight of a discolored face; Ogden was evidently not going to attend the conference in the sun porch, but Ogden was going to listen. Ogden's shadow followed them round the turning, seeming very long-necked.

The sun porch was a long and wide room, built chiefly of glass towards the west. Its dark-rose curtains were pulled back before a watery sun. On the side opposite were the French windows opening into the nurse's room, from which that room received its light. At the far end of the oblong was the glass door to Miles's room. Though this was muffled now with the brown curtain, Stevens thought he saw two chinks of yellow light shining through.

The furniture of the porch was wicker painted white, with bright coverings, and there were some unfortunate potted plants. A stiff, formal, brushed air pervaded the company. At one corner, standing sheepishly, was Henderson. Edith sat with some primness in a large chair, and near her Partington (quite sober, and rather Mephistophelian today) lounged on a sofa. Captain Brennan leaned uneasily against the frame of one window. Miss Corbett, with the same formal air, was handing out sherry and biscuits. There was no sign of Lucy, or of Ogden, though they could all sense Ogden's presence in the background. What was most notable was the absence of Mark —a sort of vast absence, as though with a gap in the normal, which you could feel.

Nevertheless, it was Cross who dominated that room, if only by showmanship. At one end of the porch, Cross leaned on the radio as he might have leaned on a lectern or a reading-desk. His bald head, with the one long fluttering hair, was inclined; his simian features showed great suavity. Miss Corbett handed him a glass of sherry, and he placed it on top of the radio as though he could not be interrupted in listening. Out of the radio the hoarse voice was still talking. It was preaching a sermon.

"They're here," said Mrs. Henderson, rather superfluously, pointing to the two newcomers. Edith's eyes went quickly to

Marie; something indecipherable changed behind them; but nobody spoke. "Even on the Sabbath," Mrs. Henderson bawled, in a state of nerves, "do you need to have that radio so loud as——"

Cross touched the switch. The voice was cut off so abruptly that stillness was a clang. If he had meant to play on their nerves, he had succeeded.

"My good lady," said Cross, drawing himself up, "how many times must it be necessary for me to inform the illiterate that Sunday is *not* the Sabbath? Sabbat is a Hebrew word meaning Saturday. The Witches' Sabbath, for example, is a Saturday. But the choice of words is fortuitous; for we are about to discuss witchcraft and sham witchcraft. You, Mrs. Henderson, have been the enigmatic witness throughout this investigation. You can settle our difficulties. You have told at least a tangible, if not altogether coherent, story concerning what you saw through that door . . ."

"I don't believe it," said Mrs. Henderson. "Our minister calls it the Sabbath, and it's Sabbath in the Bible, so don't you talk silly. As for what I saw, never you mind what I saw. I know what I saw all right, without anybody telling me. . . ."

"Althea," said Edith, calmly.

The woman checked in mid-flight. They were all, it was clear, afraid of Edith, who remained sitting bolt upright, with one finger beginning to tap the arm of the chair. Partington sipped sherry without relish.

"I ask you that," pursued Cross, unruffled, "because I should like to make sure you know what you did see. Look down at the door now. You will see that I have adjusted the curtain as I am led to believe it was adjusted on the night of Wednesday, April 12th. Kindly inform me if there are any points of difference. You will also note that a light is burning in that room. It is the light over the head of Mr. Miles Despard's bed. The curtains are drawn in that room, and we have a passable darkness there. Now will you go down, look through the left-hand chink in the curtain, and tell me what you see?"

Mrs. Henderson hesitated. Her husband made a gesture as though to lift his hand. And, behind, Stevens heard footsteps as Ogden Despard approached; but nobody looked round. Mrs. Henderson, a trifle pale, glanced at Edith.

"Do as he says, Althea," said Edith.

191

"And, in order to reproduce the conditions more or less as they were on that night," Cross went on, "I must turn on the radio again. However, I think it was music then? Music? Good. Therefore——"

As Mrs. Henderson went down to the other end of the porch, Cross spun the radio dial. A hollow and broken confusion came tumbling and spinning out of the loud-speaker; followed, with silver clearness, by the tinkle of a banjo and a sugary voice. *"Oh, I went down south,"* sang the voice, *"for to see my Sal, singing polly-wolly-doodle all the day. My Sal she an a lovely gal, singing polly-wolly—"* and then they heard it no longer, for Mrs. Henderson screamed.

Cross clicked the switch, and there was silence. Mrs. Henderson, her eyes looking dull and hungry, had whipped away from the window to face them.

"What did you see?" inquired Cross. "Keep your seats, the rest of you! Don't get up. What did you see? The same woman?"

She nodded.

"The same door?"

"I—yes."

"Once again," said Cross, inexorably. "Take another look. Don't flinch, or I'll have your hide. Once again."

"—for I'm off t'Louisiana for to see my Susie-anna, singing——"

"That's all," said Cross, switching off the radio again. "I must repeat, I should not like anyone to get up yet. Frank, you had better stop that young man; he is too precipitate," Ogden had come round the turning of the sun porch, and, though his face was not pleasant to look at, he had evidently forgotten all about it. Ogden was making for the glass door when Brennan easily put out a hand and restrained him. "With your permission," said Cross, "I will deal first with the smallest, most obvious, and accidental part of this case. It was not intended to be a part of the case at all. On the contrary, it was a chance (or mischance) which almost wrecked the plans of the murderer. It was a matter of *un spectre malgré lui*.

"Throughout this case you have been pelted constantly with two facts concerning Mr. Miles Despard and his room. The first fact is that he spent so much time locked up in his room, having little to do but change his clothes through varying hues

192

and styles; although he was sensitive on this point of vanity. The second fact is the extreme meagreness of lighting arrangements there. There are, in fact, only two lights—neither one of great power. The first is over the bed; the second is high up on a cord between the windows. Finally, most of the time Miles Despard spent in his room was during the evening.

"If you will endeavor, by a concentration of intellect which you all no doubt find fatiguing, to focus your minds on these points, you will at least dimly perceive the significance of this. What are the two necessities of a man who is constantly admiring his own appearance by changing his clothes? Aside from the clothes themselves, he needs two things: he needs a light to see himself by, and a looking-glass to see himself in.

"There is, it is true, a bureau and a glass in that room. But the bureau is placed in an impossible position, where it would get very little light from the windows in daytime, and none at all from the two electric bulbs by night. But there is one curious point. Between the windows, where it does not illuminate anything except a chair and a picture, is a high-hung lamp serving no apparent purpose on a perfectly blank wall. What *sort* of lamp is it? It is the sort which hangs over a bureau. Now if, for the purpose of better illumination, the bureau were rolled between the windows at night . . .

"If this were done, it would be necessary to hang the picture (a very valuable one) somewhere else: as a temporary measure, until the bureau was rolled back again. Where could it be hung? There are no other hooks or nails, unoccupied, in the room—except one. This is the nail in the door to the nurse's room, where this afternoon I saw a blue dressing-gown hanging up at about picture height on the door. Similarly, the chair must be placed somewhere. To avoid anyone coming in unexpectedly (which we are informed Mr. Despard hated) it must be placed with its back propped, as a wedge, under the knob of the nurse's door.

"We have the following conditions. We have the light now turned out over the bureau, so that there is no illumination except a glow over the bed so dim that a witness cannot tell the color of a woman's hair. We have a tiny chink in the curtain, which gives a view *only high up*, for the mysterious woman was seen only above the waist. We have—across from the mirror of the bureau—a door set into the panelling which

193

goes round the room. This is the door to the nurse's room, which would be dimly reflected in the glass, and which is panelled like the wall. On the door to the nurse's room we have the Greuze picture hung up, and the chair beneath. The whole scene takes place almost in darkness. Any noise of footsteps, the click of a lock or the closing of a door, is masked by music on the radio. It is therefore certain that what the witness saw was the reflection of the door to the nurse's room in the mirror over the bureau.

"I think, Mrs. Despard," Cross added, "you may come in now . . ."

The glass door at the end of the sun porch opened; there was a swishing of skirts, and Lucy, in a sombrely brilliant gown of satin and velvet, came out into the porch. The dark red and blue colors were kindled by a glitter of sham diamonds. Lucy, throwing back a gauze scarf off her head, looked slowly round the group.

"Mrs. Despard," Cross went on, "kindly assisted me in a little experiment. She simply walked in and out of that room in almost complete darkness, reflected in the mirror of a bureau now placed between the windows.

"But here again, if we accept this," he continued, enjoying himself so hugely that his monkey-bright eyes opened wide, "we have another apparent impossibility. However the mysterious woman got into the room, it is absolutely certain that she must have *left* it—in a quite ordinary way—by means of the communicating door to Miss Corbett's room. It is now clear that Mrs. Henderson saw her reflection when she went out. But, on that particular night, Miss Corbett had done certain things. In the first place, Miss Corbett had bolted that door *on her side*. Next, on the door of her own room giving on the hall, she had taken apart and so altered the lock that it could not be opened except by manipulation of the key in her hand.

"We have, then, two impregnable doors. The mysterious woman, leaving the room after having poisoned Miles Despard, could not have walked through a bolted door. Even had she done so, she could not afterwards have escaped through still another trick-locked door into the hallway, and, though there are windows in the room, she could not have gone out into the sun porch here, leaving the windows locked on the inside

194

—especially since Mrs. Henderson was actually in the sun porch. Therefore it is certain that one person in this whole case, and only one, could have committed this murder. The only person who could have committed it was one who returned to the house near eleven o'clock; who opened the hall door of the nurse's room by means of a key she alone knew how to use; who passed through her own room; who unbolted the door to Miles's room; who went in with a poison-cup disguised as medicine; who forced him to take it in her own role; who afterwards went back through her own room, bolting the door again on her side and relocking the hall door after she had gone . . ."

Cross brought his hand down softly on the top of the radio, so softly that the glass barely shook. He bowed a little. He said:

"Myra Corbett, it gives me great pleasure to inform you that you are under arrest. The warrant is, I think, made out in your real name rather than the one you have assumed—Jeannette White."

XXI

SHE had backed away very slightly, towards the French windows opening into the room she had formerly occupied. She was not wearing a uniform now, but a neat blue dress which became her. In spite of a none-too-good complexion, the sudden color in her face gave it animation and showed that she had good looks. Her corn-colored hair showed flat and lifeless, plastered in waves against her head. But again, as a sign of animation, her eyes were terrified—and unpleasant.

Myra Corbett moistened her lips.

"You're crazy," she said. "You crazy little man! You can't prove that."

"Just a moment," interrupted Brennan, moving forward heavily. "You can say what you like; this doesn't have to be a formal arrest; but I can warn you to be careful. Do you deny that your real name is Jeannette White? Don't answer; there's somebody here who ought to know. What do you say, Dr. Partington?"

After a pause Partington, who had been staring at the floor, lifted a dark, heavy, ugly face. "Yes, she is Jeannette White," he answered. "As you say, I ought to know. I promised her yesterday I wouldn't say anything, but if she's done this——"

"Yesterday, Doctor," Brennan said, smoothly—"yesterday, the first time I met you, you were jolted up so much I thought you were going to faint. I knocked on the door of this house; I said I came from police headquarters; and right away, over my shoulder, you saw the girl who used to work in your office, on whom you performed an illegal operation. I've heard that you only escaped criminal prosecution by getting out of the country. You risked it again by coming back when Mr. Mark Despard sent for you. Isn't it true that the reason why you were knocked endways was because you saw me and this girl together?"

"Yes, it's true," said Partington. He put his head in his hands.

Brennan turned back to Myra Corbett. "I'll ask you something else. Do you deny that, a year or so ago, you met Mr. Mark Despard again and picked up this same affair?"

"No, why should I deny it?" she cried. They heard the noise of her finger-nails scratching on the sides of her dress. "I don't deny it. I'm proud of it. He's fond of me. I was a better—— than any of his women, present company included. But that's a different thing from murder!"

Brennan looked savage and tired. "I can further tell you," he went on, "that your alibi for the night of Wednesday, April 12th, is blown higher than a kite. It's a funny thing. Yesterday the first person I pounced on was Mrs. Stevens, there," he nodded towards Marie, who was looking curiously at the nurse; "and the reason for it, among others, was that her alibi for that night depended on the word of only one person—her husband, who was sleeping in the same room. It didn't seem to occur to anybody that *there was only one other person in the whole shebang whose alibi also depended on a single person's testimony—yours*, Jeannette White. That testimony was the girl's who occupied the same room with you at the Y.W.C.A. You got her to swear you were there from ten o'clock on. All the others had half a dozen witnesses; even the maid was out on a double-date. . . . Actually, you were here, weren't you?"

At this point the woman almost lost her nerve.

"I came here to meet Mark, yes," she said, breathlessly. "But I didn't see the old man; I didn't want to see him; I didn't even go upstairs. And Mark stood me up. Mark never came here,

196

after all. He must have tumbled to it that *she* was wise, and so— Where's Mark? Mark will tell you! He'll tell you! He'll prove it. But he isn't here, and . . ."

"No, by God! he isn't," Brennan said, softly but grimly. "I think it's going to take a whale of a time to find him, too, even with the drag-net out. The trouble was, he saw it coming. The trouble is, you and Mark Despard planned this murder together. You were to do the actual dirty work, and he was to cover up."

For the space of about twenty seconds nobody spoke. Stevens glanced covertly round the group. Ogden Despard was standing in shadow, the better to hide the condition of his face; but on the puffy lips there was satisfaction.

"I don't believe that," said Lucy, calmly. "Whatever I may think of *her*, naturally I don't believe that. What do you say, Mr. Cross?"

Cross, savoring the situation, remained poised over the radio.

"I was wondering," he said, "when the obviously distracted state of this company would allow it to turn for assistance to a cooler mind and a more developed intelligence. Mrs. Despard, I do not think you had better appeal to me. Appealing to me seems to have become a general habit. The unfortunate truth, Mrs. Despard, is that your husband did plan the murder with Miss Corbett, and that he did cover it up afterwards. He is accessory before and after the fact; but there is one thing to be said in his favor. He had nothing to do with the attempt to throw suspicion on *you*. He never knew of it—until it was done. That was why he tried to shift suspicion off you again, and in doing so he confused, complicated, and made nonsensical a perfectly ordinary murder case.

"Let us consider the matter esthetically. If you are unable to consider it esthetically, pray try to consider it less like howling asses. The most significant point in this case—the point which betrays it—is the curious way in which two murderers, two intelligences, seemed to be pulling against each other.

"As originally planned, it had no flourishes. Mark Despard and his lady of the blunt speech had determined to kill Miles Despard because Mark Despard needed the money. But the victim was to die, apparently, from natural causes. Who could question it? Why should it be anything else? Miles was dying of gastro-enteritis in any case; the family doctor was of little

197

curiosity and moss-grown wits; there could be small chance of any suspicion whatever. There was to be no revealing silver cup, containing arsenic, left so conveniently in a cupboard along with a dead cat and—later—a book on witchcraft.

"That was the simple plan conceived by Mark Despard—a death from natural causes. But it did not satisfy Miss Myra Corbett. No. She not only wanted Miles Despard out of the way; she particularly wanted Mrs. Lucy Despard out of the way as well. It is not unknown, I believe, for a paramour to cherish such sentiments towards her lover's wife. If Miles died, it is obvious that it must be murder and that Lucy Despard must be convicted of that murder.

"To execute such a plan, without the knowledge of Mark, was not difficult. From the beginning of this case it was apparent that the mysterious woman in the Brinvilliers dress came from this house. I have declared to my friend Stevens that I place no particular reliance on alibis. But, in order to believe in the guilt of Mrs. Despard or Miss Edith Despard, we should have been compelled to discredit corporate alibis of such gigantic dimensions that even my suspicions turned pale. The masquerader in the Brinvilliers dress, was not, then, either of them. But who? As some one has shrewdly pointed out, *somebody* had to make a duplicate of that dress. It could not have been an outsider. In the first place, it was not known outside the house that Mrs. Despard planned to make a dress on the model of the picture in the gallery; in the second place, it was impossible that an outsider should have been able to study that same picture in order *also* to make a copy good enough for the purpose of deceiving Mrs. Henderson. But if a painstaking second copy were in the process of being made, and made in absolute secrecy, there is one thing that the maker most certainly had to do . . ."

"Well?" Stevens heard himself demanding.

"She had to keep her room locked up," replied Cross.

"It is true," he continued affably, "that—with miraculous good fortune—an excuse was supplied to her for doing this. An excuse was supplied when Mrs. Stevens stole a bottle of morphia tablets from her room on Saturday night, and returned it on Sunday. It was not (I think we have heard) until Monday that Lucy Despard decided to make a Brinvilliers costume and wear it to the masquerade. Henceforward Myra

Corbett had her excuse for a locked room. For the rest, it was easy. She wears a dress like that of Mrs. Despard; she wears a mask; she even, I suspect, wears a wig. Not only is it of small consequence whether she is seen, but she wants to be seen.

"One precaution, however, must be taken. She must put through a phone call to the house where the masquerade is being held, intending to lure Mrs. Despard away—not only to lure her away, but to lure her to this house. Thereby will be achieved complete damnation beyond alibi.

"Our murderess comes to this house and puts on her disguise. She knows that Mrs. Henderson will be in this sun porch at eleven o'clock to listen to the Soothing Hour. She can, at her leisure, make that wine-and-egg mixture in the kitchen, because there is nobody there to see her: Mrs. Henderson is in the stone house beside the crypt. It is the sort of drink, medicinally, which she can force him to accept. She can get to his room before eleven. Her costume will not surprise Miles; he knows there is a masquerade that night, even if he had not been aware she was invited. Even the wig will rouse no curiosity, because it is a masquerade.

"Nevertheless, she wishes to be observed—hence the chink in the curtain. I call your attention to one point which, from the first, should have resolved any doubts. Kindly examine this sun porch. Mrs. Henderson was sitting here by the radio, where I am, at one end of the room. Completely at the other end, behind a closed door with a muffling curtain, is Miles's room. Finally, a radio is playing. Yet our witness distinctly heard a woman's voice speaking in that room. It is conceivable that a murderess would speak in a low tone. It is even conceivable that she might speak in an ordinary tone. But it is not conceivable that she would speak with such shattering and obvious loudness—while handing a poison-cup to her victim—unless she deliberately wished to call attention to her presence. I leave you to imagine why she wished to call attention to it.

"The one flaw in the calculation, of course, was that extra chink by which she was seen in a mirror. But her work was over by that time. She had given her victim the drink, of which he did not take all. She fed the dregs to a convenient cat. She placed the cup conspicuously on the floor of a wardrobe—all the actions of a woman wishing deliberately to call attention to murder, to underline it in the heaviest pencilling. I also call

199

your attention to the point that no person, wishing it to be believed that a man had died of natural causes, would have given so enormous a dose of arsenic—a dose of which two grains remained in the very dregs of the cup.

"Very well. Miles Despard has no suspicion that he is poisoned. He pushes the bureau back to its original position on the other wall; he hangs up the picture again and replaces the chair. It is this exertion which brings on so quickly the shattering cramps and renders him helpless in so short a time. He was cut off in the house; he could reach nobody.

"At past two o'clock Mark Despard returns—to find his uncle dying, as he had expected. But also to find (with, I should suspect, no small degree of horror) plain evidences of murder blazoned round the room like bloodstains. I here wish to point out that all the evidence of Miles's weird and supernatural actions that night—his babbling sinister words to Mark, his request that he be buried in a wooden coffin, even the finding of the string tied with nine knots under his pillow—rest on the testimony of one person—Mark Despard. Did anybody else hear him ask for a wooden coffin? Did anybody else, at that point, see the string with nine knots? No; those things were afterthoughts. Thus:

"Mark Despard had good reason to feel sweat and panic. He had good reason to hide the glass and the cup, and to bury the cat's body deep. But there was worse. On the following morning he learned from Mrs. Henderson that a woman—in a dress like the one his wife had been wearing—was seen giving the poison-cup to Miles. He knew now that his lady-friend and ally had deliberately planned to throw the blame on his wife. And he did not know what to do. First he swore Mrs. Henderson to secrecy, with, I venture to say, complicated and frightful oaths. . . ."

Cross paused, and glanced at Mrs. Henderson. The woman, who was oily white, nodded.

"I can't be saved," she answered. "But him"—she stabbed her finger at Brennan—"him, with his soft soap, he got me to tell it."

"First, however," Cross continued, "he had to make sure that these really were murder intimations, and that either the silver cup or the glass actually contained poison. When he received the chemist's report, he was sure. But there was still

200

worse. It has been constantly reported how, from the very beginning of the case, a formless but insistent report has everywhere been circulated that this was murder—a report dating from the day of Miles Despard's death. Mark could not stop this rumour. Sooner or later (he realized this on Thursday, the day after the death) such a rumour must culminate in exhumation. I think we know who started the rumour.

"That must be prevented. The body must disappear with the tell-tale arsenic in the stomach. The funeral was to be on Saturday. But, up to and including the time of the funeral, he had no opportunity for disposing of it without suspicion; first, because officialdom was in charge; second and more important, because his ever-watchful ally was on guard, and would have prevented it. If he moved, he had to move secretly.

"The course pursued by Myra Corbett, I concede, had been extremely ingenious. She might, it is true, have announced immediately after the death of her patient that she believed he had been poisoned; she might have told the doctor to order a post-mortem immediately. But this was far, far too dangerous. She could not afford to be in the limelight in any way whatever. It was possible and even probable that her past connection with Mark might have been dug up. It was even possible that some one might inquire how she came to figure in the business. From her safe position as X, as a nurse, as an automaton, publicity might turn her into something else. The safest course was to let Miles be buried, while she declared to everyone how he died a natural death . . . and then let secret channels, let the evidence she had planted, do its work in the course of a month or so. She would be safe, because by that time she would be inconspicuous.

"And now it becomes pull-baker, pull-devil, pull-murderer. Mark turned over plans of his own. It is probable that the idea was first put into his head by the story, which he heard on Thursday morning, about a woman 'walking through a wall.' What he actually thought of this we shall not know until he is caught. But it gave him his idea, along with the remembrance of a book on witchcraft which Miles had once read, and which seems to have impressed Miles enormously—especially the chapter concerning the Non-Dead. So Mark, at this moment bent on befogging the issue as much as possible, first told his story about finding under Miles's pillow a string tied with

201

nine knots, and also tried out tentatively the 'walking through the wall' story on a friend of his, Edward Stevens. *He threw all this dust to cover up the one really vital and essential part of his scheme, his unsupported statement that Miles had asked to be buried in a wooden coffin.*

"An unusual request, surely. One that must arouse suspicion on merely human grounds; but we have the word of King James the First that, 'such convicted of the horreid cryme of witchcraft are thought to be commonlie fond of wood or stone, but steele they cannot abide'; and this afforded excellent camouflage——"

Partington got up out of his chair.

"Camouflage for what?" he demanded, stung out of his stolidity. "If Mark stole that body out of the crypt, how did he do it? What difference did it make whether the coffin was steel or wood?"

"Because it could be more easily moved," said Cross, impatiently. "Even for a man of Mark Despard's enormous physical strength, a steel coffin would have been too much."

"Moved?" said Partington.

"Let me now enumerate a few facts concerning the body and the crypt. These are (1) the coffin, although its two bolts require strength, can be opened instantly; (2) Miles Despard was a very tiny and light man who weighed only one hundred and nine pounds; (3) at the foot of the steps leading down into the crypt, blocking any view inside, is a rotted wooden door which you on your Friday night investigation found closed; (4) in the crypt are two enormous marble urns, stuffed with flowers——"

Stevens interrupted, with a vivid picture of the place in his mind.

"Look here," he protested, "if you're going to say the body was doubled up in one of those urns, it won't work. We looked in them."

"If those who have asked my assistance," Cross said, testily, drawn out of his relish at telling the story, "would kindly refrain from interrupting until I have explained, I think I can make clear what I do mean.

"And the last point, which points irrefutably to the truth, is (5) that, when you penetrated into the crypt on Friday night, you noticed a great many scattered flowers lying on the floor

202

nder the urns. Why were those flowers on the floor? They
ame, obviously, from the urns. But funerals are usually char-
cterized by neatness, and it is not reasonable to suppose that
hey were flung there during any rioting at the funeral itself.

"Now let us examine what happened at the funeral, on the
fternoon of Saturday, April 15th. Mark Despard told you
bout it, and he gave (substantially) quite a correct account.
Ie had to do so, since it could be confirmed by disinterested
vitnesses. But kindly recall what happened.

"By his own admission, he was the last to leave the crypt.
All the others had gone—except the parson, whom Mark had
detained. But was the parson actually in the crypt? No; again
by Mark's own confession; for no human being cares to stand
he air of that crypt longer than necessary. The parson was
waiting up the stairs, near the top where he could get air.
Between him and the crypt was a wooden door shutting off
his view. Meanwhile, Mark had remained behind on the pre-
ext of gathering of some *iron* candle-brackets. He states that
e remained behind not much longer than a minute; and I
ee no reason to doubt him. Sixty seconds would suffice for
what he had to do. If you will take the trouble to consult your
watch, and execute in pantomime the following movements,
ou will see that the time is sufficient. Thus:

"He went through the following movements. He slid out
he coffin; he drew the bolts; he picked up the body and walked
across the crypt with it; he thrust the body, doubled up, into
one of the urns; he relocked the coffin and returned it to the
niche. Any noises he might have made—a bump, a metallic
rasp of a bolt—would have been easily disguised to the ear
of the parson under the guise of handling iron brackets. The
body was now covered by a vast mass of flowers. The only
race he left to anyone looking into the crypt was (necessarily)
some spilled flowers on the floor.

"All these things were only preliminaries. For the stage was
now set; he was ready to perform his 'miracle.'

"This miracle had a double purpose. If—after all the atmosphere of mystery and secrecy he had created—his dupes
thought that the theft of the body was supernatural, he had
no objection. His purpose was to throw a veil over things, in
order that an arsenic-filled body could be removed. But, until
the body actually was out of the crypt, until the miracle had

203

been performed, he must not press the supernatural elem
too far, or his dupes might think he had gone mad and men
refuse to help him. And they had to help him. It was essen
that the crypt should be opened in complete secrecy. No li
of day, no interfering policemen, nothing that would mitig
against the cloud of suggestion with which he had surroun
it. . . .

"I will first deal briefly with the mechanics of how he foo
you. It is the one part of the business on which I am dispo
to praise him, for it was undeniably excellent acting. He w
bargaining on the psychological effect of your finding no b
in the coffin, and he had calculated to a nicety how it wo
make you feel.

"You descended into the crypt. Mark was the only one w
had a light—a flashlight. He refused to let *you* take lante
down there, saying that it would use up too much air. Y
opened the coffin . . . and found nothing. You were, I d
say naturally, stunned. After a first impulse not to believe y
eyes, what suggestion was immediately put into your head
Mark had anticipated, and, if I am correct, is a suggestion
actually made himself? What were the first words spoken af
you discovered the body was missing? Does anyone remember

"Yes," replied Stevens, blankly, "I remember. Mark look
up at the tiers, and flashed his light on them, and said, 'Y
don't suppose we've got the wrong coffin, do you?"

Cross bowed gravely.

"It served," he said, "to fix your attention firmly on the i
that, since the crypt was bare, the body *must* be somewh
there. All this time, of course, the body was actually in
urn covered by flowers. But Mark had one enormous advanta,
he had the light. He could direct it just as he could dir
proceedings, and all of you believed the body must be in c
of the other coffins. Well, what happened? First, you search
the lower tier: with no result. Then it was suggested that
body might have been put higher up; and so we come to
simplest part of the whole affair. *Mark Despard's entire p
pose was to create some excuse whereby all those present exc
himself would leave the crypt for just a few minutes, a
would return to the house; while he was left alone there.*
got his excuse, as you know. Henderson and Stevens were
patched back to the house to procure step-ladders. Parting

as dispatched back to the house (not a difficult matter) to
et a drink. We have the word of a police officer who was
atching you that, at 12:28, Stevens, Partington, and Hender-
on left the crypt and came up to the house. Stevens and Hen-
erson did not return until 12:32, the doctor not until 12:35.
f that police officer had only remained watching at the crypt
uring those crucial times, the whole plan would have crashed.
ut he did not remain; he followed the three to the house.
Ience from 12:28 to 12:32 Mark Despard had four minutes
ntirely alone and unobserved.[1]

"Do I need to tell you what he did? He simply picked the
ody up out of the urn, went upstairs with it, crossed over to
Ienderson's house, and hid the body there—probably in the
edroom. *Then,* when the others came back to the crypt, he
vas ready to suggest: 'As a last resort, let's turn out the urns.'
Vhich you did: with, of course, no result."

At this point Joe Henderson came forward shakily. He had
ot spoken heretofore. The bruise on his temple was an ugly
lue.

"Are you telling me, sir," he said, "that when I saw old Mr.
Miles sitting in my bedroom that night—by the winder, in the
ocking-chair——"

Cross lifted his glass of sherry from the radio, but he set it
lown again.

"Ah yes. The entrance of the supernatural folly, the first ap-
earance of a manipulated ghost, had better be dealt with here.
That was another completely unintentional business, which
Mark Despard had forced on him. You did not see Miles's
ghost, my friend. But you really did see Miles.

"As is evident from even a short consideration of the course
f events, once Mark had removed the body from the crypt, his
lan was now on its way to a conclusion. Now he could tell his
tory of the phantom woman walking through the wall. Now he
ould plant his book on witchcraft in Miles's room—where Miss
Despard later found it. I shall also always wonder whether the
iece of string found in the coffin was not, as a matter of fact,
eft there by that Old Man in the Corner, Mr. Jonah Atkinson,
enior. If so, it must have given Mark a turn. I also think that,
vhen he suddenly discovered yesterday what a case could ap-

[1] Should there be any doubt of this, it is suggested that the reader examine
ages 58 and 118-19; on the first of which is given the course of events, and on the
econd an actual time-schedule for those events.

205

parently be made out against Mrs. Stevens, he must hav
wondered whether his brain had not given way and whethe
the dark world had not pressed through. It appears to me th
one thing which caused him genuine surprise.

"As for disposing of the body, his intentions had been sim
ple. Once the body was out of the crypt, he intended—as soo
as he could—to get rid of Stevens and Partington. The first h
would send home, the second he would send to the house, drunk
Henderson alone remained, and the body was at the time con
cealed in Henderson's bedroom. But that was not difficult. W
have heard at great length about the theft of some morphia tab
lets. Mrs. Stevens took them—but, as a matter of fact, she too
only one tablet. Two more had been abstracted by Mark him
self, with or without his accomplice's knowledge.

"As soon as he had got rid of Messrs. Stevens and Parting
ton, Mark intended to give Henderson a strong drug in a drin
of liquor. When the old man slid out of sight and tension, Mar
could then take the body up out of the bedroom and destro
it——"

"Destroy it?" Edith spoke out suddenly.

"By fire, appropriately enough," said Cross. "In the roarin
blaze which has been going so hard for the last two days in tha
furnace downstairs; you have all, I think, noticed the pall o
smoke over this house outside, and the extreme heat inside. . . .
But there was a hitch in the plan. For Mrs. Despard and Mis
Despard, summoned by telegrams, unexpectedly appeared o
the scene. That threw the scheme out of gear; the body was stil
hidden in that bedroom; but the scheme, after all, was only de
ferred. When everyone had retired for the night, and the visitor
were gone, Mark prevailed on Henderson to go down *alon*
and cover the crypt with a tarpaulin. . . . But, in order to get tha
tarpaulin (as both of them thought) Henderson would have t
walk several hundred yards through a wood to a field on th
other side of the estate. This would be time enough for Mar
to get the body out of Henderson's house and ready for the fur
nace.

"Unfortunately, Henderson remembered that the tarpauli
was not near the tennis court, but in his house. When Hender
son returned, Mark was actually in that little stone house
Fortunately, however, he had taken one precaution—he ha
given Henderson a drink drugged with morphine, and its effect

206

were already being felt. A light unscrewed in its socket . . . a corpse propped up in a chair, used as a doll or dummy for a ghost scare . . . a man behind, rocking that chair and even lifting the hand of the corpse . . . it all had its effect on a man already frightened half out of his wits; and the morphia took care of the rest. Mark was then free to carry the body to the fire."

Cross paused, and turned on them a broad smile of urbanity and charm.

"I may add something which you have doubtless already noticed: the house is unusually cold this afternoon. That is why I thought we should remain upstairs. Captain Brennan's men are now engaged in dragging out that furnace. They may not find anything, but——"

Myra Corbett took two steps forward, and it was apparent that her knees were shaking. She was clearly so horrified that it produced in her a drawn ugliness.

"I don't believe that! I don't believe it," she said. "Mark never did that. If he did, he'd have told me. . . . "

"Ah," said Cross. "Then you do admit that you poisoned Miles Despard. By the way, my good friends, there is just one point remaining in connection with our friend Jeannette. It is true that she told a story yesterday which appeared to incriminate Mrs. Stevens. To the surprise of everyone (including herself), Mrs. Stevens really did ask where arsenic could be bought; just as Miss Edith Despard actually bought some. But don't you see the significance of the story, the part our nurse was trying to stress? Who actually began that conversation, who asked ten thousand questions about poisons and their effects? *She* said it was Lucy Despard; she corrected you sharply and insisted on that. She was still being consistent. And her accusations were only shifted when it became apparent that Mrs. Despard had an unmistakable alibi. So, if she admits that she poisoned . . . "

Though she marred the gesture with something very like a snarl, Myra Corbett put out her hands as though she were praying.

"I didn't kill him. I did not. I never thought of it. I didn't want any money. All I wanted was Mark. He didn't run away because he did anything like that. He ran away because of that ——that's his wife. You can't prove I killed the old man. You can't find the body, and you can't prove it. I don't care what you do to me. You can beat me till I die, but you won't get anything

207

out of me. You know that. I can stand pain like an India
You'll never——"

She broke off, choking. She added, with sudden rather te
rifying misery: "Doesn't anybody believe me?"

Ogden Despard, smashed and ugly, put out his hand. "I'
beginning to think *I* do," he said. He looked at them. "Whateve
I've done in the past," he added, coolly, "I've had a perfect rig
to do, and I advise none of you to question it. But there's on
thing I must correct you on. This woman at least never ma
any telephone call to St. Davids, on the night of the masquerac
party. *I* did that. It struck me that it would be amusing to se
Lucy's reactions when she heard Mark had picked up his ol
affair again. You can't do anything to me, you know, so yo
might as well take it calmly."

Brennan stirred and stared. Cross, with an air of simian cou
tesy, lifted his glass of sherry, saluted Ogden, and drank.

"I drink your health," he said, "on the pretext of what I a
compelled to recognize as the one time in your doubtless usele
life when you have attempted to do anyone a service. Thoug
I am never wrong in my diagnoses, I can assure you that I pr
serve a mind sufficiently open to acknowledge an error. If it we
the last word I ever——"

He stopped, making a slight gesture with his glass. They ha
looked at the nurse, who was coming forward, when they hea
a small bumping sound. Cross had gone forward across th
radio, and seemed to be trying to writhe over on his back. The
saw his eyeballs; he seemed to be trying to draw air through li
too thick for him. He succeeded at last in writhing over, b
resistance was gone, for he fell on his back. It seemed to St
vens's stupefied wits a long time before anyone moved. Cross l
convulsed in a fawn-colored suit, spilled beside the radio, wi
the glass in his hand; but he had stopped moving by the tin
Partington reached him.

"This man is dead," Partington said.

Stevens thought afterwards that if the doctor had made an
other statement in the world, however incredible, any horror
fantasy or reality, then he might have believed it. But he cou
not believe this.

"You're crazy!" shouted Brennan in the midst of a pause. "H
slipped. He fainted, or something. He couldn't just—like th
——"

208

"He's dead," said Partington. "Come and see for yourself. By the smell of him I'd say it was cyanide. It's as nearly instantaneous as anything in the codex. You had better preserve that glass."

Brennan put down his briefcase very carefully, and came over. "Yes," Brennan said—"yes, he's dead." Then he looked at Myra Corbett. "He took that glass from you. You were the only one who touched either the decanter or the glasses. He took that glass from you, and walked over there to the radio by himself. Nobody was near him, nobody could have put cyanide there except you. But he didn't drink immediately, as you hoped. He was too much of an actor. He waited until he could get a good excuse for a toast.—You devil, there wasn't enough jury-evidence against you before. But there is now. You know what'll happen to you? You'll fry in the electric chair."

The woman was smiling, weakly and foolishly and almost incredulously. But her former self-control had almost gone, and when Brennan's men came upstairs they had to give her a supporting hand while she walked down.

V

VERDICT

"The tendency has gone so far that one is led to ask oneself, not without the gravest apprehension, 'Is there, then, no evidence of extreme depravity?' For the wholesale elimination of the utter villain from history could hardly be regarded save in the light of an aesthetic calamity."
—THOMAS SECCOMBE, *Twelve Bad Men*

EPILOGUE

THE brittle, bright autumn weather had faded from dusk into night. A few leaves, shaded like the colors of a vase, still clung to the trees when the wind rose; the bowl of the valley was brown. A desk calendar in the neat, snug room showed in red figures that it was the 30th of October, which is the night before All-Hallow's Eve.

It was a room with fat-bowled lamps on the tables, and chairs covered with bright reddish-orange material, and a good copy of a Rembrandt—*The Lovers*—above the fireplace. On the divan lay an open newspaper, whose headlines showed along with a part of the story:

DEMON NURSE ESCAPES CHAIR
Innocent, Says Myra, as Life Term Begins

Still declaring her innocence, Myra Corbett, the "demon nurse," who was sentenced to death on October 9th for the murder of Gaudan Cross, author, heard today that the pardon board had commuted the sentence to life imprisonment. G. L. Shapiro, her attorney, admitted that no trace had yet been found of the "phantom accomplice," Mark Despard; but said that——

The firelight flickered on black headlines, for the fire was the only light in the room. It distorted and made unfamiliar common objects. By the rear window a woman stood looking out into the garden. Her face was reflected in the dark glass. It was a plump, pretty face, with ringlets of dark-yellow hair. The reflection, slightly blurred, showed heavy-lidded grey eyes set in an expression which might be called spiritual, and a very faint smile. She was thinking:

Upon the whole, I am sorry she is not to die, after all. She deserved to die, if only for telling tales about me. I was incautious that day when I asked after the old man's receipt; but then I had not used it for a long time. Also, it is a pity she was not really guilty; she should

213

have been, for she would have made an addition to our number. We must be very numerous now.

Outside, in the dark garden, the October woodsmoke drifted lightly. The sky was dark also, except for three bright stars; and, in the fields beyond, a mist was on the wigwams of the corn. One fine hand of the woman's moved out and touched a small desk between the windows, although she did not turn her head.

It is well that I am beginning to remember. At first I could remember only faintly, as I see my reflection in this glass now. Once, when the smoke lifted in the Mass at Guibourg, I thought I remembered— an eye there, a tip of a nose there, or ribs with a knife through them. I wonder, now, when I shall see Gaudin again. His was a crooked reflection; perhaps the headgear was different, but I knew him at once. At least I knew quite clearly that I must go to him for help. It is true that, this time, I was in no danger from their lawyers. But I did not wish my husband to guess, not yet. I love him, I love him; he will be one of us presently, if I can transform him without pain. Or too much pain.

The hand moved across the writing-desk, and there was a key in the hand. It began to unlock some curious compartments, one beyond the other; although still her head did not turn. The hand seemed to move with a life and volition of its own. Inside the last compartment there was a teakwood box, and a little jar.

Yes, I knew Gaudin. He had been seeking me, too, it seems. Nor have I denied his cleverness. It was clever of him to pluck a physical explanation, a thing of sizes and dimensions and stone walls, out of all those things which had no explanation I was prepared to give them. I wondered that he could do it so cunningly, for I am not clever. I am sorry, too, he must accuse Mark Despard, for I liked Mark. If I am not clever, as they say, still I think I had the better of Gaudin, after all. Gaudin asked Gaudin's price for what he did, and it was unfortunate that he wished to return to me. He would have been impossible as a lover. And Gaudin was flesh and bone, until the ointment was used. He will return to flesh and bone presently, but I have the better of him now.

The white hand, moving fluent and snakelike, touched first the box and then the jar; still the plump face was reflected without motion in the glass, though it smiled curiously. . . .

There was the noise of a key in the outer door of the cottage, the opening of a door, and the sound of footsteps in the hall. Whatever luminousness, or even transparency, seemed to move round wall or window—this was now gone when she ceased to touch the jar. Her face became the face of a pretty wife, and she ran out to meet her husband.

As she passed, her skirt brushed to the floor the newspaper on the divan, turning it over and exposing the continuation of a news item:

. . . that no trace had yet been found of the "phantom accomplice," Mark Despard; but said that no effort would be spared to trace him. It is understood that Attorney Shapiro has produced new evidence. High-lights in the trial of the "demon nurse" will be recalled in Attorney Shapiro's attempt to prove that Author Cross—determined to convict the nurse of a poisoning-charge he could not prove—might himself have dropped cyanide into his own glass.

"If the defence," said District Attorney Shields, "seriously means that any man will drop four grains of potassium cyanide into his own glass in order to prove a theory, the state is content to rest at this moment."

"The defence means," retorted Shapiro, "that Cross may have had a confederate who supplied him with this poison, telling him that it was only a little arsenic which would make him sick, but really intending to kill him. In capsule form——"

At this point there was some commotion, and Judge David R. Anderson said that if any more laughter were heard in a court of justice, he would order the court to be cleared.

JOHN DICKSON CARR

The man many readers think of as the most British of detective story writers was born in Uniontown, Pennsylvania in 1906. After attending Haverford College, Carr went to Paris where, his parents hoped, he would continue his education at the Sorbonne. Instead he became a writer. His first novel, *It Walks By Night*, was published in 1929. Shortly thereafter, Carr married and settled in his wife's native country, England.

The Thirties were a highly prolific period for Carr, who was turning out three to five novels a year. Some of these were published under what became his most famous *nom de plume*, Carter Dickson. (Because the Dickson novels contain a great deal of a certain type of comedy, many of their earlier readers attributed them to P.G. Wodehouse. Could an American write like this? Never!)

In 1965 Carr left England and moved to Greenville, South Carolina, where he remained until his death in 1977.

In his lifetime, Carr received the Mystery Writers of America's highest honor, the Grand Master Award, and was one of only two Americans (the other was Patricia Highsmith) ever admitted into the prestigious—but almost exclusively British—Detection Club. In his famous essay "The Grandest Game in the World", Carr listed the qualities always present in the detective novel at its best: fair play, sound plot construction, and ingenuity. (He added, "Though this quality of ingenuity is not necessary to the detective story as such, you will never find the great masterpiece without it.") That these qualities are prevalent in Carr's work is obvious to his legions of readers. In the words of the great detective novelist-critic Edmund Crispin, "For subtlety, ingenuity, and atmosphere, he was one of the three or four best detective-story writers since Poe that the English language has known."